A Highly Improbable Fake Dating Trope

Haley Klinge
A Highly Improbable Fake Dating Trope

All rights reserved
Copyright © 2024 by Haley Klinge

—

Published by - Spines
ISBN: 979-8-89569-593-7

A Highly Improbable Fake Dating Trope

Haley Klinge

Trigger Warning

This book contains mentions of:

Cheating, depression, falling short of parental expectations, sex, and bondage. If you are not in the mental space to be able to handle any of these topics, please do not read.

Put yourself first, always, and know that you are loved.

If none of these topics are a trigger for you, please enjoy!

To my very own Josie, thank you for pinching me in the arm in sixth grade while we waited in line for picture day so my headache would go away.
I love you.

Highly Improbable

Vinyl Edition

Side B:
1. You're so vain By: Carly Simon
2. Shots By: LMFAO, Lil John
3. Swing, Swing By: The All-American Rejects
4. American Honey By: Lady Antebellum
5. All-American Bitch By: Olivia Rodrigo
6. Animals By: Nickelback
7. Stupid Love By: Lady Gaga
8. Million Reasons By: Lady Gaga
9. We are Never Ever Getting Back Together By: Taylor Swift
10. Vindicated By: Dashboard Confessional

CHAPTER 1

JOSIE

Have you ever just wanted to just kick a guy in the balls? You know, just a swift little tap. Well, at this exact moment, the temptation is all too real, because Maximiliano Rossi is so fucking annoying, I'd do just about anything to get him to shut up for five minutes. If I didn't think he'd use the pain as an excuse to get out of helping me, I would've already done it by now.

However, I'd do just about anything to make my best friend, Ella, happy. Including suffering through the next hour with Max, Ella's boyfriend Liam's best friend, and getting the backyard ready for their housewarming party tonight.

After a year of ups and downs, Liam and Ella (mostly Ella), finally pulled their heads out of their asses and figured out they were meant for each other. Honestly, the whole will they, won't they, thing was getting out of control.

As a woman who frequently enjoys a good romance novel, it was very much giving shut up and just fuck each other already. Being caught in the middle, and the only person at work that even knew they were together, was exhausting. Trying to cover the asses of two people that are God awful at lying was basically a full-time job on its own.

It may sound like I'm not happy for them, believe me I am, but healing from my own heart break while trying to fix my friend's love life has just been a lot. I'd never admit it out loud but being there for Ella made it easier to forget about my own shit. Now that she and Liam are virtually flying off into the sunset in an old Ford convertible like Sandy and Danny in *Grease*, I've been forced to reevaluate.

At the behest of my mother, I may or may not have unblocked a certain douche bag's number. A certain douche bag that may or may not have ruined our engagement and seven-year relationship by bending his receptionist over his desk while I brought him lunch. The irony is that if Trevor's receptionist was doing her job instead of him, she would've been there to stop me from walking right in and catching them.

Irony can go fuck itself.

My phone vibrates in the back pocket of my jean shorts and I pull it out, reading the notification with the name "Satchel of Richards" on my home screen. I can't even read the text, I'm not ready yet.

The summer sun beats down my back as I swipe away the notification and put the phone back in my pocket. Max and I finally finish hanging the patio lights, and if he wasn't so busy needling and flirting with me, I would've been done twenty minutes ago.

I take my lucky orange scrunchie off my wrist and tie up my curls in a messy bun on top of my head before surveying my so-called partner I've been assigned to. I'm saying the term partner loosely because I feel like I could've done this faster myself. The entire time we've been out here it's just been me fixing all of the stuff he's messed up.

"Those corn hole boards aren't nearly far enough apart!" I comment while trudging through the grass in my neon green high tops. I grab the edges of the wooden corn hole board and pull it back to its appropriate distance.

"And you're not nearly controlling enough!" He yells back sarcastically.

I grab a bean bag off the corn hole board and lob it at him, missing his head by a mile. Damn it. "I swear you get off on pissing me off," I seethe.

He gives me a lazy smile, showing his perfect teeth, "So, you admit you think about getting me off?"

I grit my teeth and flip him off before wiping the sweat off my brow with the bottom of my 'Virginia is for lovers' t-shirt. Don't fall for it Josie. Don't do it. He's just trying to get a rise out of you.

"Go fuck yourself Max," I yell. *Yep, I feel right into that.*

While heading into the little suburban bungalow that is now the home of both Liam and Ella, I hear him call from behind and chuckle, "I'm obviously trying not to fuck myself! Is it not working?"

I scoff and slam the sliding glass door to the kitchen shut. I see Ella, her blonde hair piled on top of her head while cutting up veggies with a smirk on her face, "Max trying to seduce you again?"

I snort, "If you call doing the opposite of everything I ask him to do, and spending more time on a 'carefully crafted' Spotify playlist than actually helping me as seduction, then yes."

Ella chuckles while wiping her hands off on an apron that says, 'Shut up and eat my meat' before turning around to face me, "He does seem to like getting a rise out of you."

I grin at her apron and see her gray eyes are full of mirth, she's enjoying this. "Too much. He actually had the audacity to tell me that he should do the playlist because he knows not to put anything on it that was made after 2012. As if I don't know what kind of music my best-friend likes!"

Her smile grows wide, "Aw that is so sweet!"

I narrow my eyes at her, "Annoying is more like it."

She unties her apron and goes to hang it on the hook with the rest of her collection, "He's really not bad Jos, if you'd just give him a chance..."

"Absolutely not! I already know where this is going, and I told you I don't want to be set up," I groan defensively while leaning over the kitchen island.

Ella folds her arms across her chest, covering Prince's face on her *Purple Rain* t-shirt, "Jos, it's been almost a year since 'He Who Shall Not Be Named.' Don't you want to get back out there? I know you said you were ready to move on, but you haven't really tried."

I cut her off, "El, I am ready. I just haven't found the right guy yet, and trust me when I tell you that Max is definitely not the guy I want to 'get back on the horse' with if you catch my drift."

She smirks, "I don't know, he might be the perfect guy to ride." She says in a singsong voice. "After all, it's not like you have to be together. He's not the dating kind of guy anyway... unless he's not your type?"

I snort at the thought; physically how could he not be? He's tall with broad shoulders and muscled arms coated in tattooed olive skin. His hazel eyes are ringed in green with golden flecks, and his hair is so dark it's almost black. With pouty lips that always pull into a cocky smile, whose type wouldn't he be? That's the problem. He's everyone's type, and he knows it. I've been burned before, and after everything that happened last year the last thing I want is a guy who wouldn't know the meaning of the word commitment if it was tattooed on his eyelids.

"His personality isn't my type. I dated one cocky asshole and that was enough for a lifetime. Plus, what am I going to do? Hook up with him and then be forced to see him at every event you and Liam have for the rest of our days?" *And if the thought of getting hurt again makes my heart start to palpitate? Well, I'll never admit it.*

"Fair enough," she muses. Ella walks over and pulls me in an embrace, squeezing tight. "I just want you to be happy Jos," she mumbles against where my shoulder meets my armpit. She's always been so much shorter than me, I used to call her pocket sized. Seeing her and Liam together makes me laugh because she always refers to hooking up with him as climbing a tree, and I don't think I'll ever be able to unsee that visual.

I pat her head lovingly before pulling away, "I am happy, El. Don't worry about me so much. You're doing that thing that couples do when they're stupid happy and want to set everyone around them up, so they're stupid happy too. It's brainwashing and I won't have it," I say haughtily.

She chuckles, "Oh God, I am doing that aren't I? How cringe."

"Trying to set me up with Max? Definitely cringe. You must want me to kill him," I smirk.

Speak of the devil and he shall appear. No sooner do I say his name he waltzes through the sliding glass door dripping wet, his white t-shirt all but pasted to every single muscle on his chest. "Ladies," he says in a mock bow. "El, do you have a towel I can dry off with? I got hot so I sprayed myself off with the hose."

"Yeah, sure thing!" she chirps before walking to the laundry room and grabbing a towel, leaving me momentarily alone with Little Italy's version of a wet t-shirt contest. I feel like I swallowed a burlap sack full of cotton balls.

God damn this man is so fine...

As he walks into the kitchen and slides the door shut, I try not to stare, I really do, but he's impossible to miss when his flimsy white t-shirt is clinging to him in the *sluttiest* way possible. His broad shoulders were already pulling that t-shirt impossibly tight, but soaked through it might as well not be on at all. Swirling colors of ink curl over pecs, shoulders, arms, and hands. My traitorous hormones must short circuit my brain because I start thinking about using my tongue to trace the inked lines all over his body.

What the fuck is wrong with me? I must be ovulating or something. Yeah, that's it. I'd find a damn garden gnome sexy if I looked at it for too long. When my ovaries start dropping eggs like a middle school physics assignment I start getting feral.

My face feels insanely hot, and I know I must be obvious because even without making eye contact I can feel his smirk. "See something you like *gattina*?" his voice rumbles as I watch him run his hands through his dripping hair from the corner of my eye.

Before I can try and piece together the scrabble tiles that my brain has turned into, Ella walks back in with a fluffy white towel in her hand. His hazel eyes crinkle as they look directly at me with a lethal amount of self-confidence. I watch his muscles contract in his arms while he slowly works the towel through his hair. "You want to help me dry off?"

I scoff, "And on that note, I'm going to your room to change." I say to Ella before I turn on my heels and walk down the hallway to their bedroom. I vigorously try to get the image of Max in a white shirt that's basically see-through clinging to what are very obviously rippling ab muscles out of my brain.

Think of the personality attached to the body. Think of the personality attached to the body, I chant to myself as I walk into the adjoined bathroom and turn the shower on cold.

———

After I've tried and failed to calm myself down with a cold shower I change into my outfit for the party: a simple black dress cut low to expose just a hint of cleavage paired with my *Star Wars* converse and a silver necklace with a tiny J hanging from it.

I put my coconut scented body spray on my neck and wrists before lightly swiping my lashes with mascara and adding a bold red lip to stand out against my black dress. I open my bottle of curl cream and run a dollop of it through my hands before putting it in my hair. After I finish, I look into the mirror and make sure my dress hugs all my curves in the right places before I leave the bathroom.

I walk into the kitchen to see Ella in a flurry, trying to set the rest of the food out on the back patio table before guests arrive. "El, you still aren't dressed!" Her eyes look half-crazed as they meet mine, the *Purple Rain* t-shirt she's wearing contains a mysterious stain while her hair falls out of the knot on her head.

"Go get ready, I'll finish up. People are supposed to start showing in twenty minutes." I reply before shooing her away.

"Oh shit! Thanks, Jos!" She yells before booking it back into the house to change.

I finish setting the array of snacks on the table when I see Max walking towards me. He's changed too, and although I'm pretty partial to the soaking wet t-shirt, the white button-down slightly undone at the top to expose the olive skin of his chest is a marvel of its own. I try to think of something clever to say, but my mouth seems incapable of forming words.

"Wow, Josie... you look incredible," he says while his gaze rakes up my body, leaving behind a trail of invisible fire in its wake.

"Th-thank you," I stutter. Honestly, I'm shocked any sound came out at all. You would think I'd never spoken to another human being before. It's like I ogled him so much earlier my brain turned into scrambled eggs exposed to some form of gamma radiation, and now I don't know how to talk to Max without thinking about him dripping wet.

Because somewhere out there is a merciful God hell bent on putting me out of my misery, the doorbell rings and I hightail it so quickly towards the front door you'd think the Wiley Coyote was chasing me.

Relief washes over me as I open the door to find Shoshanna and Hank, Ella's parents, on the other side. Shoshanna's bangle-covered arms wrap me in a tight embrace, her patchouli scent is like a weighted blanket, heavy and all encompassing. In high school I spent almost as much time at Ella's house as I did my own. She and I were inseparable, and considering to this day I receive more warmth from Shoshanna than I do from my own mother, I'm all the more grateful for it.

"Hello, my sweet, Josie," she says while pulling away from our hug with a smile. Her wild blonde waves are held back with a paisley scarf, and a giant turquoise pendant hangs from her neck. Her gauzy purple shawl is wrapped tightly around her small frame despite the summer heat. True to form as per usual.

She leads Hank in through the door dragging him behind her as she mumbles something about looking for the Tibetan sound bowls she left at the house last time she was here. "Hello, Josie!" He smiles fondly before being tugged along by his wife.

My phone buzzes and I pull it from the pocket of my dress (dress pockets the girls that get it get it) and feel the acid in my stomach begin to boil. A notification with the name "Satchel of Richards," again. It's been like this since I got opey-doped into unblocking him. I haven't even responded to him. I have no idea how he knows I'm getting them with my read receipts off, but I swear he's been lying in wait for me to give in. Like a snake in a basket waiting for the first note of a pungi to be played, he was there trying to contact me.

Texting.

Constantly.

Internally I know I should've never done this, given him an opportunity to slither back into my life. In a weak moment of my parent's constant barrage of Trevor propaganda, I did it. Their words leaked through the dam I've built around him in my head like water coming out of the cracks.

"Jojo Bean, you can't just give him another chance?"

"Seven years? Just like that? From one little mistake you're going to throw away your entire financial future?"

"Jojo, don't let your pride ruin everything we've all worked so hard for. This is our legacy sweetheart, the future of the firm, and since you won't be taking it..."

That's all it ever is with them. The firm and their appearances. They weren't always this consumed with money and success, but somewhere along the way what everyone else thought became more important to them than their own daughters and their happiness. My sister Makenzie drinks the Jones parent's Kool-Aid, but I've sworn off the stuff. I used to drink it, but now it just tastes fucking bitter. I'd rather do it all myself than have them help me. It's not that I hate them or anything, they're my parents and I love them, but If I ask for anything from them it'll just prove them right. To them that just proves that I need Trevor and his generational wealth to be happy. Jokes on them though, I'd rather live in a refrigerator box under the overpass than go back to that dumb idiot.

I quickly swipe away the notification, only glimpsing the words *Come on baby...* before tucking it back into my pocket. I hear a loud squeal as I turn around to see Ella and her mom embracing. "I'm so happy for you, my sweet girl!" she murmurs into Ella's long strawberry blonde hair that matches her own.

A wisp of green-envy smoke curls in my gut before I brush it away. I've always wanted what they have. I love my parents, don't get me wrong, but the moment I came out of my mom I've felt nothing but expectations from them. Ella could shit on the hood of a car and Shoshanna would cheer her on.

It can't be helped I suppose, my parents had to overcome a lot to get to where they are, so in some ways, I do understand it.

My father, Cecil, was the only black man at the first firm he ever worked at when he met my mom, who was also a lawyer. My mom came from money, but you wouldn't know it with how hard she worked, like she had something to prove. It was only exacerbated when my parents fell in love and wanted to get married, but my grandfather didn't approve of his only daughter marrying a black man. My mom became the outcast of the family, and my grandmother did nothing to intervene.

I've never even met them, but it's a sore spot for my mom, so we don't talk about her parents much.

The way she explains it, her anger towards her parents just fueled her to work her ass off even more. My parents raised my sister and me while building their own law firm that specializes in civil rights cases. They're incredible and I admire them so much, but it's made them very protective of everything they've created. They're so protective that when I told them I didn't want to pursue a law degree of my own they were less than thrilled. Apparently, having a daughter that's a middle school guidance counselor doesn't look nearly as good as one that's a lawyer.

Because he's also a lawyer, my marriage to Trevor would've meant that when both of our parents retired, we would be able to join his family's firm with mine. His father is just one of the many men in the Smith family to run the company, and Trevor is expected to take over once his dad passes it down to him. The perfect merger of a law empire, until he stuck his dick in his receptionist and somehow now it's my fault for not forgiving him, but I digress.

Before I can drown in a pool of my own thoughts, the doorbell rings and I go to answer it. I must be getting good at summoning people with my mind, because on the other side of the door are Cecil and Laura, otherwise known as my parents.

Completely overdressed in a suit with a bald head so polished he reflects the porch light; my dad is the first to speak. "Jojo Bean," he says with a smile before bending down to plant a kiss on top of my head. He walks through the doorway revealing my mother behind him.

"Hi dad, hi mom, come in!" I say as my mom wraps her arms around me and the smell of her Chanel number five perfume floods my nose. She never leaves home without it. My mom is so short she practically has to crane her neck to look at me, but she gives me a tight smile, frown lines that would be there if not for the Botox she got recently seem to be preventing her from showing more affection. I think Jennifer Coolidge in *A Cinderella Story* moved her face more than this.

"Hi Jojo," she says as a perfectly manicured hand cups my cheek and walks past me into the living room.

"Hi Cecil! Hi Laura!" Ella smiles widely, and my parents embrace her wholeheartedly. They regard her with more warmth than they do their own daughter, but then again, I guess you don't have to worry about a constant stream of disappointment when the person isn't actually related to you.

Conditional affection is reserved for blood relatives only.

"Ella! So good to see you," my father's deep baritone greets her, his smile so wide you can see the small gap in his front teeth.

"Ella, love we're so happy for you! Thank you for inviting us," my mother smiles widely. *Oh, so the Botox isn't actually preventing her from smiling...*

I need a fucking drink.

The doorbell rings and Ella excuses herself to go answer it, her hot pink wrap dress and white Toms she's wearing are the complete epitome of her style. The only thing that would make it even more so is if she somehow incorporated a shirt with a band on it that broke up before she was even born.

I'm so proud of her, she's really come into herself this year.

*Now if only you could do the same...*the voice in my head says before I cram it behind the dam in my brain where I try and keep the bad thoughts. I wave manically as I see Sergio, Stella, Lola, Jack, and Nadia walk in together, our closest co-workers at Valley Creek Middle School where we both work. They must've carpooled.

Liam pokes his head out from the kitchen, brushing a curl out of his face that's obstructing his glasses, "Hey guys! Party's out back!"

Everyone follows, except my parents and I, standing awkwardly in the living room. I really should've told Ella not to invite them. There's no way I'm going to be able to relax with them here.

My mother flings her stick straight brown hair behind her shoulder, a clear sign she's about to say something that is sure to piss me off. "So, I spoke with the Smith's the other day..."

Fuck.

"Mom..." I try to interrupt, but get shut down quickly when her sharp blue eyes meet mine.

"It seems Trevor has been trying to reach out to you to apologize, but you refuse to respond to him."

Yep. Definitely something that is sure to piss me off.

"For good reason," I mutter. He's lucky I even unblocked his number at all.

"Jojo Bean, how long can this go on? You can't punish him forever," my father supplies.

"How is this my fault?" I say weakly. Why do they bring this part out of me? The cowering part I try so hard to keep under wraps comes through around them without fail every time.

"Jojo, this is marriage. You'll have obstacles in your path, but you have a responsibility to hurdle over them. For better or worse," my mother says, her manicured fingers tightly wrapped around her arms.

I grit my teeth; my molars are going to be dust after this interaction. "And in this case, the obstacle I'm expected to hurdle over is finding his secretary bent over his desk with his dick buried inside her?"

My mother narrows her icy blue eyes at me, "Well I don't really enjoy the phrasing, but I suppose yes."

"Well, I didn't really enjoy seeing it, so I'm sure you can understand why I can't just pretend like it didn't happen," I'm feeling bolder by the minute, my anger fueling me to say things I normally wouldn't.

"This is not the time or place to discuss this," my father reprimands, but my mom keeps going.

"We just want you to reconsider. Is all of this really worth it? Being stubborn is going to cost you your future, a comfortable life for you and your future children. You'll have everything at your disposal. No financial limits or burdens. You could move out of that studio apartment and stop working at that school where you're overworked and underpaid. Think of everything you built."

"You mean everything YOU built," I fire back.

"That is enough!" My father's baritone booms. Thank God

everyone is outside, so they probably didn't hear that little outburst.

"Josie Ann, you will consider what your mother is saying, and Laura for the love of God this is not the time," he grits.

"Fine." I say curtly before turning my back on them and walking into the kitchen. I fling the door to the refrigerator open and grab a bottle of wine. I quickly twist the top off before walking out onto the patio.

*I'll show them a disappointment alright...*I say to myself before drinking pinot straight from the bottle. I let the bitter dryness of the wine coat my throat before I can think about how much their words stung.

———

A few hours later the party is well under way. Tiki torches line the fence to keep out the bugs and all of the string lights Max and I hung earlier keep the backyard dimly lit in a warm glow. *Well, maybe that's the entire bottle of pinot I just drank.*

Unsure. Since my parents left, I was able to relax more, and therefore may have partaken in more drinks. I don't think Ella's yard has ever looked so beautiful, or fuzzy.

Max is currently spinning Stella around the backyard as they dance to "Time After Time" by Cyndi Lauper, her billowing purple sash nearly touching the grass as he dips her. *Why is that the cutest thing I've ever seen?*

As the words ring through my mind, he catches my gaze, and gives me a wink before pulling Stella back up. I quickly avert my gaze as I feel my face heat. *Yep, definitely the pinot.*

I turn to the snack table and quickly shove a pretzel in my mouth before I feel a strong hand splay between my shoulder blades. I turn to look, and gold and green flecked hazel eyes stare back at me. This close I can smell the subtle scent of citrus cologne that smells like I want to taste it. In the dim lighting his olive skin looks golden.

Son of a bitch he's hot. This is probably how poor innocent prey feel when they see the beautiful light of an angler fish; right before it unhinges its jaw and eats them alive.

Oh God. This is not good.

"Dance with me, Josie," not a question, a demand. The rumble of his words echo in my ears, the vibrations tightening my spine.

Don't fall for the beautiful light Josie. You remember what it's like to be eaten alive. I steel myself, "Absolutely not."

"There she is," he chuckles. "You've been so quiet all night. You haven't sniped at me once."

"I don't snipe," I scoff.

"You do," he narrows his eyes at me, a slight uptick at the corner of his mouth.

"It's not my fault I find you utterly repellant." I deadpan.

His tongue pokes at the inside of his cheek as he leans forward and cages me between his arms. "That's not how it looked earlier when you had to roll your tongue back up into your mouth like a cartoon dog after I walked in soaking wet."

The audacity of this man. His cockiness is unmatched. "Someone is full of themselves," I retort while rolling my eyes.

"I know what I saw Josie, and I know you aren't as unaffected as you claim. If I'm as repellant as you say, then what's the harm in dancing with me?"

"I don't dance," I say not meeting his eyes, opting to stare at my converse instead. I think being caged in by his arms, smelling his cologne, and also looking into his eyes would make me lose what little footing I have left.

"How about a wager? Let's play a game. Flip cup survivor. If my team wins, you dance with me. If your team wins, I'll leave you alone," his voice is low, and my heart skips a beat as his arms no longer cage me. He takes a step back.

"Fine, if no longer being in your presence is my reward I'll do anything," I retort.

A cocky smile plays on his lips, "Don't say *anything.*"

I glare in his direction as he gathers up teams of four and sets up a folding table with solo cups lining the edge. Me, Stella, Jack, and Ella on one team. Max, Lola, Nadia, and Liam on the other.

Everyone gathers around as Max explains the rules, "Okay everyone, Flip Cup Survivor. Each solo cup is filled halfway with beer, the object of the game is to chug it as fast as you can, and then once it's empty, flip it on its head. Then the next person in line does the same. You go down the line until the last person has finished. The first team to finish wins."

"Oh, fuck Jos, you're going down. Max and I used to play this at the dorm all the time. We're undefeated," Liam laughs while clapping Max on the back.

"So you're saying you hustled me?" I ask Max, trying and failing to hold back a laugh.

He smiles and shrugs, "Who knows, maybe I'll have an off night."

He didn't.

In fact, my team's defeat was embarrassing. Poor Stella, she tried, but I didn't even get to drink by the time Max finished his cup, sealing their victory.

I drink the beer anyway; I'll need the courage if I'm about to dance in front of everyone.

Max walks towards me and bends down to whisper in my ear. The citrus smell of him is intoxicating, his breath warm against the shell of my ear. "I hope you like the song I picked."

My breath hitches before I can stop myself as his strong tattooed arms wrap around my body. *Don't fall for it Josie...*

I steady myself. "Let's just get this over with," I grumble.

He holds me close as "At Last," by Etta James floats through the speaker. *Damn it. I love this song.*

Max leads me every step of the way, it feels like I'm barely moving my own limbs. As he grabs me with his firm hand against my back I feel like a puppet with all of my strings being pulled. His warm hand holds mine softly, and I feel like I could get whiplash with how one minute he's gentle and the next firm.

My head is swimming, and he smells so good. I make the mistake of looking up into his eyes, and the green and gold flecks are burning back at me. I feel his gaze all the way to the very core of me, flames licking in all the most sensitive places along my skin.

This is a ruse. I know this is all a show. He does all of this to reel you in. The dancing, the tattoos, the fucking smell of him, the eyes. It's a trap. One I'm falling right into.

This is insane. I'm like a mouse voluntarily walking into a cat's mouth, but I want him. I need to taste him. What little pride I have left is waging a literal war in my brain with the pheromone coup currently happening.

He grips me tighter, his body now flush with mine. It's just a dance, but as the hand once holding mine skates to the back of my neck and teases lightly at the curls on my nape, it feels like so much more.

As the last notes of the song play, he dips me. Somehow, even as my head is tilted downward, every other part of me is pressed against him. His hard muscles against the softness of my body is a delicious sensation vaporizing the last of my resolve.

He can sense it, I know he can, because as he pulls me upward his eyes don't leave mine. Green and gold fire is melting me from the inside out, and I know it then. He's going to kiss me.

And I'm going to let him.

The hand at the nape of my neck helps close the distance, and before I can think twice his lips are on mine. They're so soft I can't help but whimper against the plushness of them.

He swallows the sound, grunting in approval as my mouth opens wider for him. My whole body feels like it was stuffed with firecrackers, each one going off simultaneously as his tongue slicks against mine.

He tastes like every sin ever committed.

He tastes like every bad decision I've ever made.

He tastes like he could absolve every broken piece of me.

He tastes like a beautiful trap.

He nibbles my bottom lip, the small action making me clench

every intimate muscle I have before nuzzling my nose and pressing his forehead against mine. "Come home with me, Josie," he whispers, his voice rasping against panting breaths.

I walked into his trap. I'm a fucking idiot.

Anger floods me immediately. Not just from the foolishness of letting myself be tricked, but for my parents, for Trevor, for the moments that lead me up to this very point. I push away from him immediately, distancing myself so I can't get wrapped in him again.

"Oh, hell no! I'm going to stop you right there. Abso-fucking-loutely not!" I yell while clenching my fists at my side.

He straightens, seeming offended as if I slapped him. "Why not? You're clearly attracted to me."

That was not the right response, and it just makes me even angrier. "Because you're a cocky asshole whose own inflated ego could be a balloon in the Macy's Thanksgiving Parade. We kiss one fucking time, and you want me to go back to your place with you? I only kissed you because I was drunk!" I'm on the verge of screeching now, and it's not until this exact point that I realize everyone is gathered around, watching everything unfold.

Well fuck...

He folds his strong arms across his chest, his shoulder muscles pulling his shirt tight against him. I hate myself, because even in my rage I can't help but want him to wrap me back up in them.

His eyes narrow while he clenches his jaw. "You're lying to yourself. I heard that whimper in your throat."

All of the day's suppressed rage boils more and more to the surface. He may not be the cause of all my problems, but he's going to get the brunt of my anger. "Does it matter Max? If not me then it'd just be someone else right? Why don't you just go find some other girl to lure to your bed? Let's not pretend you don't see me as expendable."

His eyes flash with anger. I clearly struck a nerve because he turns to leave. "You know what? I'll go do that right now. Thanks for the suggestion." He retorts sarcastically before storming into the house.

He leaves me there, with everyone trying and failing to look everywhere but at me, like they didn't just see that entire saga unfold. I hear the muffler of his motorcycle as he backs out of the driveway, and I don't even have it in me to care. Max virtually lit me on fire, and now I'm just a husk of the leftover anger and desire left behind in the dust.

Chapter 2

Max

I wake up in bed Monday morning with the sun trying and failing to break through my black out curtains. I have no idea what time it is. I blindly feel for my phone on my night-stand, and I nearly drop it on my face when I see the time. It's 9:07am. and I told my boss Shawna I'd be in the office at 9am.

Fuck.

I run around my room and quickly throw on jeans and a black V-neck shirt. With one hand rapidly brushing my teeth and the other haphazardly running styling wax through my hair, I finish in record time. I run out the door with deodorant in my hand and resolve to throw it on at my first stop light.

I grab my keys and helmet off the counter and run down the stairs of my apartment to my orange Honda Fury chopper, praying to whatever saint is in charge of traffic patterns that Shawna won't notice I'm not there yet.

Today of all fucking days. Of course I'm late. I back out and let the feel of the wind hitting my chest calm me down. I'm never late. In fact, I hate it. When you're raised with a retired Army vet for a father, being late to anything is essentially inexcusable, so naturally I'm furious. Today is supposed to be the day I convince

Shawna to hand the Fiji project over to me. It'd be the biggest account of my career, and I've worked my ass off for it.

The company I work for, JetSet Excursions, reviews hotels, accommodations, restaurants, and experiences for incoming tourists. Hotels or businesses that want to advertise on our site have to first be reviewed and vetted by one of our employees and then the entire experience is documented for both the company and JetSet to promote. Basically, I get paid to eat and travel and then write about it. It's a literal dream job, and as much as I love it, I've been wanting a bigger assignment, and the Fiji project will give me just that.

Well, if I still even get it that is.

Is there really an excuse? No. Not unless you count that ever since I kissed Josie Jones two days ago nothing in my brain seems to function at its normal rate. Over a damn kiss.

A kiss. One that ruined me in the best way possible. Until I fucked it up tremendously, and I can't stop replaying it over and over again in my head like a movie hell bent on torturing me.

I don't know what happened. I'm usually a lot smoother than that. Just right then and there telling her to come home with me was brash even for myself. There's usually a lot more nuance that goes into that sort of thing, but all I could think about is how she smelled like coconut and tasted like wine laced with some sort of hallucinogenic drug and my grip on my self-control slipped. I don't think at that moment I'd ever wanted anything more than to taste every inch of her.

I've always enjoyed needling her, flirting with her because she's gorgeous and absolutely unattainable in my eyes. That is until I saw how she looked at me while I was soaking wet and dripping all over the kitchen floor. In that moment, I thought maybe I had a chance.

Someone like Josie doesn't give a guy like me the time of day. She's a relationship person, the kind that wouldn't know how to date or hook up without commitment. She wouldn't even know the meaning of no strings attached.

I, however, don't think I've ever had a string attached to anyone. Ever. Not romantically anyway.

When your father is in the Army, you spend a lot of your life traveling from base to base, never staying anywhere for too long. As a result, I'm great at making new relationships, but bad at maintaining them. Liam being the exception of course.

I mean, how many guys can say that nearly every girl he tried dating in middle and high school cheated on him? Just me, but what can you expect when you're dumb enough to think you're the exception to the long distance rule? Or worth being exclusive with? I don't exactly scream "date me" when not one single relationship I've had has lasted longer than two months.

After a while I just became accustomed to what I like to call the "nothing permanent lifestyle." I don't like anything that keeps me attached too long. I don't have to get heartbroken if I don't give it to anyone to break.

So yeah, Josie and I hooking up would never logically make sense. I'd be done after a few days, and she would want something I'm not capable of giving. I'm a lot of things, but I'm not a big enough dick to lead someone on like that. Especially if they're my best-friend's girlfriend's best-friend. Shit say that five times fast.

I park my bike in a spot before tapping my key card on the front entrance door rushing into the building. After running up the stairs to the second floor I stop right in front of Shawna's open office door.

I'm about to knock when she stops me, "You're late," she says, not even bothering to look up from her laptop. She's currently bouncing on a giant ball that supposedly relieves the pressure on her hips from the giant baby bump she's sporting.

"I know, I know, I'm sorry. There's no excuse, but if it's any consolation I am willing to grovel and kiss your feet," I pant as I recover from scaling the stairs at a rate I've never once been able to accomplish at the gym.

She finally deigns to look up from her computer at me, flipping her dark locs over her shoulder as she continues to rotate her hips on the ball. Her dark brown eyes are full of amusement as they meet mine, "Absolutely not, I have no idea where that mouth has been. Although the groveling does sound nice." She gestures for me to sit down.

"Do I need a ball, or can I sit in an actual chair?" I smirk.

She snickers before shooing me towards the chair on the other side of her desk, "Don't be cute. Now what did you want to meet with me about, Max?"

I sit in a chair across from Shawna and clear my throat like it could get rid of the anxiety in my stomach. "Okay, I'm not going to beat around the bush." I rest my forearms against the desk and look her straight in the eye. "I'm asking you to give me a chance. I want the Fiji assignment."

Her face pinches and her maroon painted lips pull towards one side. "No," she says bluntly.

"What! Why? You won't even think about it?" I ask in shock.

"You aren't right for the assignment," she says before turning back to type something on her laptop.

"And why is that?" I ask while trying to keep my irritation at bay.

She looks back up from the screen, like she didn't expect me to still even be here. "Because Max, I'm going on maternity leave soon. This is the biggest assignment our company has seen in the seven years I've worked here. It has to be perfect. I need to know that when I leave for four months my position will be held in the same regard as it was when I left."

"But isn't it illegal to not have your job waiting for you when you get back?" I ask, my confusion obvious.

She heaves a deep sigh, "Technically yes, but it's not the technical part I'm worried about. It's having to reacclimate, having to fight for assignment distributions again because once I'm gone I'll have to rebuild the trust of my capabilities all over again. Being not only a woman, but a black woman, I had to work my ass off to get this job. I'm sorry Max, but I have to make a big enough impression that the CEO doesn't forget about me while I'm gone."

"That makes sense," I reply while I pinch my nose. "But is there a reason why I'm not a good fit? Why do you think I won't make a good impression?"

She looks off to the side, as if she isn't sure whether to say what she's thinking or not. After a few moments she seems to have decided to just go for it, "The Fiji Tourism company is wanting to go for the romance angle. They're looking for a couple to go, and well, I've known you a long time Max and God knows you're not a relationship guy, so I figured I'd have Bobby and his wife do it."

On the outside I think I look calm, but on the inside I'm panicking. I've been dying for this assignment. I want it so badly I scramble for any lifeline I can think of to save myself. "But you can't stand Bobby or his wife! She tried to get you to join a pyramid scheme that sells holistic oils at the last company Christmas party. You know I write better than he does. You've told me. Multiple times. You say he's dry. If this is really supposed to leave a big impression, then why pick him?"

She sighs loudly and massages her temples, "Yes, while that is all true, the fact remains that he's the only available member of staff not currently on an assignment and also in a committed relationship."

Shit. My brain scrambles for a new strategy, anything to convince her to pick me. I'm the better choice and she knows it, there's just one tactic I haven't tried. Lying my ass off. "If that's really the only reason then, pick me. My girlfriend and I have been dating for a few months now and it's getting pretty serious."

Her back goes stick straight; her eyes full of shock. "You have a girlfriend?" I can tell she wants to call my bluff, her eyes zeroing in on me, "Interesting, I've never heard you mention her once until this very moment."

"We've been keeping it under wraps. Her parents don't

approve so we've been keeping it hush hush." I say, thinking on the fly.

The side of her eyebrow ticks up questioningly, "How convenient. What's her name?"

This part is way easier than it should be because there's been only one name on my mind for the past two days. "Josie. Her name is Josie."

I can't tell if she's buying it, her face is unreadable. "Wow you've really been holding out on me, Max. You're normally an open book. Tell you what, I'll hold off on the Fiji decision for a few more days. In the meantime, I would absolutely love to meet the woman who actually convinced you to commit. Melinda and I would love to join you two for dinner on Friday night. Does that work for you?" I feel like this is a test, but hell I've already come this far.

I give her the broadest smile I can manage, "I'll check and make sure Josie is free, but I'm sure she'd love to double date with you and your wife."

"Splendid," she says with a smile. "I'll see you then."

I turn tail and walk out of her office as fast as I can. This is fine, everything's fine. I can do this. I just have to convince Josie to go along with it, and if she doesn't agree then Shawna will know I'm a liar and fire me.

Absolutely no pressure at all. I mutter underneath my breath like the lunatic I am while walking towards the elevator and hitting the down arrow.

Chapter 3

Josie

Since it's summer break, I have a lot more free time on my hands. I take my time getting out of bed and letting my body wake up. The best part of not having a roommate? Walking around my house naked whenever I want, which I do. Frequently.

I exchange my bonnet for an orange silk scrunchie and tie up my curls in a giant bun on the top of my head. I have no plans for today, and I'm relishing every second of it. When I decided to leave Trevor and move into a place of my own, these are the mornings I dreamt of. This may not be a fancy downtown apartment, but it's all I could afford with a public-school guidance counselor salary. And I love it all the more for it.

I could ask my parents for the money for a bigger place, but that's just giving them another reason to keep me under their thumbs and control my life. This is the first place I've ever lived that really truly is my own, and I decorate it how I want and live how I want. If I want a giant bean bag in my living room, then there's no one to stop me.

I fill my espresso maker with the nectar of the Gods that is Lavazzato espresso and listen to the comforting trickle of the coffee, letting the rich smell fill my nose. There is no better smell than coffee, and that's a hill I'm willing to die on. Although I hate to admit that Max's cologne is a dangerously close second.

As I pour my Captain Crunch (the peanut butter kind because I enjoy having the skin on the roof of my mouth intact) in a bowl and fill it with almond milk, a disturbing amount of inappropriate images flood my brain.

How his strong tattooed hands gripped the back of my neck.

How the taste of his tongue against mine sent me to another dimension.

How much I absolutely hate him for that being the best kiss I've ever had.

I'll take that fact with me to the grave.

In all fairness to me I've only kissed three people in my whole life. My first boyfriend, Kyle, that I dated all through high school until we broke up amicably when we went our separate ways in college. Trevor, who I dated almost all of college after our parents set us up on a blind date and heavily pressured the outcome of our relationship. Then Max, the man whose kiss singed every inch of my lungs and stole my breath like I was exposed to smoke inhalation. Even though it's been great imagery for my Sucky Sucky, otherwise known as my rose suction vibrator, it can't happen.

IT *WON'T* HAPPEN AGAIN.

The man kissed me for only a minute and invited me back to his place. If that doesn't scream bad decision, I don't know what does. I set my coffee on my end table and turn on *A Pup Named Scooby-Doo* reruns before plopping into my giant bean bag and covering myself with a fluffy blanket. This is my happy place. No more thinking of a sexy Italian man with gorgeous hazel eyes and olive skin. Nope.

Just when Scooby and Shaggy start being chased by the cheese monster and I'm sufficiently distracted enough, my phone buzzes with a text from a number I don't recognize.

Unknown: Meet me for coffee at 2.

Josie: Who is this?

Max: Max.

Max: Do you seriously not have my number saved?

Josie: I only save numbers of people I actually talk to.

Josie: Also you could try asking instead of demanding.

Max: Josie, can you pretty please meet me for coffee at 2 p.m. in the year of our lord 2023, at my behest?

Josie: Why?

Max: I need to talk to you.

Josie: We're talking now.

Max: I think this is something you'll be more receptive to in person.

Josie: Considering it's coming from you I find that hard to believe.

Max: please please please...

Max: You can't see it, but I'm on my knees begging.

Max: I'm risking creasing my Jordan's as we speak.

Max: I'll buy your coffee.

Josie: That's the least you could do.

Max: I'll throw in a blueberry scone.

I take a bite of my now mushy cereal and wonder how he knows that blueberry scones are my favorite. Lucky guess? Stalker that saves the receipts I throw away in the trash can? Both?

Josie: Fine. See you at 2. Gold Leaf.

Max: Thank you thank you thank you!!!!

Max: You won't regret this.

Josie: I already do.

As I throw my phone down on the bean bag next to me I stifle a groan, covering my eyes with my hands. There goes my day of nothing. But who am I to pass up free coffee and a scone? He must be desperate. I have no idea why he would need to talk to me. Besides our mistake of a kiss two days ago, the only interaction we've had is through Ella and Liam.

And I like it that way.

———

I sling my cross-body over my shoulder and settle my aviators on top of my head as I open the door to Gold Leaf and inhale a greedy lung full of coffee scented air. Even though it's hotter than the devil's taint outside, I have on a long sleeve flannel that drapes loosely over my body and leggings. I don't know how long I'm going to be here, but I'm always prepared for the air conditioning to be on full blast.

I feel my cheeks flush as I look over to the corner booth and see Max sitting there with two coffee cups and a blueberry scone on a plate. As I approach the table, I see on the label that he got my exact drink order. An iced americano with almond milk and three pumps of classic syrup.

What the fuck?

I reach out a neon green painted nail to poke the scone. It's warm. How in the actual fuck does he know my order? I lift up the scone to further inspect it, and Max gives me a weird look, like he's wondering what I'm doing. I can't help but notice that his eyes are greener than usual today, and then I want to kick myself for paying attention in the first place.

Stop noticing your potential murderer's eyes, Josie.

I stand next to the table and cross my arms, "Are you going to murder me?"

His eyes grow wide, and I watch as the sleeves of his hunter green henley inch up his muscular arms. He throws them in exasperation, revealing a weeping willow tree growing up his forearm I've never noticed before. "What?"

"How do you know my coffee order?" I ask incredulously.

He steeples his hands together on the table before letting out a frustrated huff, "You yelled it at Liam when he got it for us the other day."

I'm skeptical at best, since when does Max do anything but try and piss me off? "And I'm supposed to believe you just happened to remember all of that from the one time it came up days ago? Because my current theory is that you've been stalking me and brought me here so you can kill me and wear me as a human suit."

"Jesus fuck Josie!" He mutters while sliding a big hand down his face. As he does I notice he has a rosary tattooed on his hand.

Why are you paying so much attention to him all of a sudden, Josie...?

He shakes his head and looks at me like I've already exhausted him before our conversation has even begun. Clearly, I irritate him as much as he does me.

"Sorry I watch a lot of true crime and *Scooby Doo*. Can never be too careful these days," I shrug.

"God forbid I try and do something nice..." I hear him say under his breath.

Once I decide I've sufficiently irritated him enough, I slide into the chair across from him. Sitting only a table length across from him is entirely too close. From here I can smell the citrus scent of his cologne, see the dark olive complexion of his skin in the small gaps between his tattoos, and see how not one hair is out of place. This man is so hot, and it's not even remotely fair.

He clears his throat, and I realize I've been staring at him for far too long. An annoyingly cocky grin tugs at the corner of his full lips, and the appraising feeling from moments before is replaced with a much more familiar one, irritation. "Why am I here, Max?"

He leans back and smirks, "What? We can't just get coffee together?"

"No," I reply curtly.

He rolls his eyes and finds an empty sugar wrapper on the table to fiddle with as he talks, looking self-conscious all of a sudden. "Okay fine. I need a favor. A big one."

I can feel myself glaring at him, "So ask someone else."

The wrapper has been crushed into a tiny ball before his eyes meet mine, "Well that's the problem. It has to be you."

"Why?"

"Let me talk for longer than two seconds and I'll explain," he replies in irritation.

I huff and roll my eyes before settling against the back of my seat, showing him I'm listening.

"How do you feel about a free trip to Fiji?" he asks.

"It sounds like something someone would spray paint on the side of a windowless white van before they tied me up and threw me inside," I deadpan.

I watch as he pinches the bridge of his nose, letting out a slow breath of air. "Do you think about anything other than murder?"

"Around you? No." I say cooly.

A dark chuckle rumbles from his chest, "Okay, I walked right into that one. I'm being serious though."

I take a long sip of my coffee before I ask the question I know he's anticipating, "Okay so what's the catch?"

"I need you to pretend to be my girlfriend," he says it so seriously I almost believe him, at least I would if this wasn't an absolutely ridiculous suggestion.

I snort, "Ha. Good one."

"I'm not joking Josie. I'm being serious," he says without a hint of amusement. His shoulders are squared, with the most earnest face I've ever seen him make.

"Oh my God. You really are serious..." I trail off while feeling like my eyes are so wide they'll pop out of my head.

"Yeah."

"Absolutely not," I say in a clipped voice.

"And why the hell not?" he scoffs.

"Because I've read a thousand romance novels with this exact trope, and they always get caught." I shrug.

"Jesus, you're dramatic. This isn't some smut book trope. This is the future of my career at stake! Who turns down a free trip to Fiji?" He looks honestly shocked that I wasn't willing to just drop everything and fawn over him. Self-absorbed idiot.

"Me, that's who! Are you having trouble remembering that I

can't stand you?" I grit. He's lucky we're in public or I'd yell at him.

"I seem to recall you not hating me very much the other night," he says with a cocky smile I wish I could smack right off of his face.

I reply through clenched teeth, "Don't bring that up. That was a mistake."

"A mistake you liked," he winks. I could kill him.

I make a dramatic show of gagging like the idea makes me want to barf. Something tells me it isn't as convincing as I want it to be though. "Why exactly am I doing this?"

He exhales a deep breath, "I might have accidentally told my boss you were my girlfriend so I could land this assignment I've been wanting."

"Why?" I yell loudly enough that all the hipsters writing their screen plays on their laptops look up and glare at us.

"Ask why one more time Josie," he says with irritation.

"I think I have more than enough reasons to ask why, and you at least owe me some sort of explanation if you want me to do you a favor," I say plainly.

He sighs, "Yeah, okay that's fair. I don't know. You just popped into my head. The Fiji Tourism Company is the most important assignment my company has ever had, and I wanted it. But they were only looking for a couple so..."

"So, you lied and told your boss you had a girlfriend, so they'd give it to you?" I finish.

"Yeah that's the gist of it."

"You realize no one is going to believe you're dating someone right?" I ask with genuine curiosity. I mean the guy is self-aware right?

He chuckles lightly, "Yeah about that. My boss didn't seem like she totally believed me, so she invited us to dinner with her and her wife. I'm guessing she's trying to see if I'm telling the truth or not."

I cross my arms and glare at him, "And at no point did you think, 'Hey maybe I should ask Josie before I volunteer her'?"

"I'm more of an action first, think later kind of person." he responds.

"Well that much is obvious," I say dismissively.

He forces a smile, and it's so beautiful it feels like being exposed to direct sunlight. I'm almost tempted to slide the aviators off my head and put them on. "Just come with me, Josie. It's a free trip! Once we get there we don't even have to see each other."

Well now we're talking. The possibility of a beautiful beach in a country I've never seen is all too appealing. I don't remember the last time I did anything that was even remotely reckless. I'm not much of a risk taker, but the appeal of getting away from my parents' constant pressure and Trevor's constant texts and phone calls is too good to pass up. Which is why before I even realize what I'm saying I'm agreeing to lie to his boss's face at dinner and travel to the other side of the world for a man I can't even stand.

CHAPTER 4

MAX

As I pull up to Josie's apartment complex and park my bike, I'm starting to understand the gravity of what I've gotten myself into. I'm twenty minutes away from lying directly to my boss's face, and I'm having second thoughts.

Josie can barely be around me for longer than fifteen minutes before something I say pisses her off, let alone an entire dinner where we're going to be forced to pretend we're together. When I told Liam how I actually got Josie to agree to this, he told me he'd give me twenty minutes into dinner before she stabs me with a steak knife and pours cabernet in the wound. I wasn't even going to bet him, because the reality is he's probably right.

I text Josie and let her know I'm out front, to which she responds that if this were a real date she wouldn't go because I didn't come to the door. Fair enough, thankfully none of this shit is real anyway.

At least that's what I tell myself on repeat when I watch her climb down the stairs of her apartment building, and my tongue goes numb just looking at her.

Holy fuck she's hot.

I'd like to say I'm keeping it cool and unaffected, but I have to physically keep my jaw from hitting the floor. My eyes travel all the way from the red pumps on her feet to the deep tan of her legs. She's wearing a dark red body-con dress that hugs every inch of her very ample curves. Her dress looks painted on as it hugs her breasts, showing a peak of cleavage.

It's not just her body that looks absolutely breathtaking, but everything about her makes me want to devour her whole. The way her curls are wild and free, the way her deep brown eyes are lightly dusted with gold eyeshadow, the way her lips are the same red as her dress.

I'm unwell. Very unwell.

"Quit looking at me like Scrooge McDuck looks at a pool full of gold coins," she says while trying to suppress a smile.

I'm trying to talk, but words are stuck in my throat. I was not prepared for this. I honestly thought she was going to be wearing a t-shirt and jeans like she always is when I see her and that I'd have to beg her to change.

Am I nervous? No. Absolutely not.

"I'm just shocked you aren't wearing a SpongeBob t-shirt and ripped jeans is all," smooth. *Deflect. Deflect. Deflect.*

"I own other clothes you know," she scoffs.

"Not that I've seen," I say while I shuffle my weight against my bike.

She narrows her eyes in annoyance, "You literally saw me in a dress a few days ago."

"I assumed that was a fluke," I shrug.

"We're already fighting. This should be convincing," she fires back while crossing her arms against her chest. I watch the movement push up her tits and make her cleavage even more pronounced. St. Margaret of Cortona give me strength...

I grab my spare helmet from the bike compartment and hand it to her, "Just put this on and get behind me. We're going to be late."

Josie's face blanches and I watch her eyes get wider by the second, "I'm not getting on that flaming metal death trap!" She screeches.

"Wait... are you scared?" I ask while messing with a loose string hanging from the cuff of my leather jacket.

"What do you mean? Of course I'm scared! Do you know how many people have died on those things? It's a car with no sides! Meaning when there's an accident instead of metal crushing metal, it's metal crushing me!" She's panicking now. That much is clear.

"You're safe with me, Josie. I won't let you get hurt," I soothe.

"You can't possibly know that. You don't control the cars around you and what they do!" she shrieks.

"We'll take side roads and go slow. It'll be fun, and if at any point there's a chance of us getting hurt, I will literally shield your body with mine. I refuse to let you be hurt." I hope my words are as convincing as I feel like they are. The sheer thought of Josie being in pain makes me feel like my insides are being burnt with acid, and I know that I'm not bullshitting her. If she isn't comfortable, I won't try to convince her anymore.

I watch her shuffle her weight from one heel to the other, and I can tell she's thinking deeply. "You've never been in an accident?"

"Never."

"You'll go slow?" she asks while worrying at her bottom lip.

"Of course. I would never do anything to put you at risk."

I watch her deep brown eyes turn reflective, and I give her a moment to work through whatever it is she needs to. "You know I have been telling myself I should try new things..." she trails off.

"This is a new thing," I coax.

"A new dangerous thing," she taps her neon orange nails against her chin. "Okay fine. I'll do it." she says while straightening her arms at her sides. "But if you try for one second to do any reckless shit like weaving in and out of traffic, I'm forcing you to pull over and this all ends. I refuse to die in uncomfortable shoes."

Her comment makes me snort, "Josie, I promise no funny business. Now take my jacket, you're going to freeze without your arms covered." It's a balmy summer night in humid as fuck Indiana, but the breeze while we ride is intense and I don't want her to be cold.

"Well to be fair I did think the car I was going in had sides attached to it," she says while gently taking my worn leather bomber jacket that my dad gave me. He told me once it was a lucky jacket, and as long as I wore it, I wouldn't get hurt. By that point I was too old to actually believe that sort of thing, but I wear it every ride just the same.

I watch her shove the riot of curls falling down her back into the helmet and shrug my jacket over her shoulders, and fuck. She looks so damn good in my jacket. The bright red lipstick, the leather jacket, the heels.

She looks like my wet dream. Wait no, a wet dream. Not mine. Fake mine.

I help her onto the bike, and she presses flush against my back. Her coconut scent envelops me, and I force my helmet over my head so I don't outright sniff her. This is just a business agreement; I can't get a boner the very first night we do this.

The back seat has an elevated bump, so she's able to rest her chin on my shoulder, and her voice turns slightly raspy. "Don't get any ideas, Max. I'm only pressed against you right now so if shit hits the fan, I can make sure you break my fall. That's it."

I smirk and flip the visor down over my eyes, "Don't worry *gattina*, I'd never dream that you'd actually lower yourself enough to touch me for anything other than self-preservation."

I start up my bike, the motor humming loudly around us, and I can't help but smile beneath my helmet as Josie shrieks in my ear.

This should be fun...

———

Much to Josie's shock, we make it safely to St. Elmo's, and the true benefit of riding my bike in downtown Indianapolis comes to light. I can park anywhere. Sure enough, I get a spot right in front of the restaurant.

I force Josie to retract the claws that are clutching my sides in a death grip, and she hops off the bike. "Okay that wasn't so bad," she says while shrugging off my jacket and handing it back to me.

"You screamed the entire way," I chuckle while pulling off my helmet. I bend down into the side mirror to make sure I don't have helmet hair and comb my fingers through it.

Josie takes off her helmet and shakes out her curls before thrusting it at me, "Considering the circumstances you're lucky your eardrums are intact. But I did it! New experience, check." she smiles while mimicking a check mark symbol in the air.

"What's the joy of a new experience if you can't check it off your list, am I right?" I smile before my hand lands on the small of her back to guide her inside.

Just a few inches lower and it'd be touching the curve of her ass..

I shake my head, attempting to get it on straight, before holding open the door so Josie can walk through. As we walk to the host stand, I'm more than a little impressed by the place that Shawna picked. St. Elmo's is probably one of the fanciest restaurants you can go to in Indianapolis, so naturally I've never been before.

The exterior of the building looks hundreds of years old, and it's probably been here since downtown was first built, but you wouldn't know it because of how well maintained it is. Plush old leather chairs and booths, wood paneling, the dim glow of the wall sconces and a couple neon signs somehow work together. In one second, it looks like it could both be a dive bar and a Michelin star restaurant, but according to the four-dollar signs posted on the google reviews I looked up before we came, it's the latter.

At a table tucked away in a corner I see Shawna and Melinda, and I let the host know our party is already seated before we go to join them. I grab Josie's hand behind me, and I feel her tense in surprise. "Come on baby, time to pretend like you enjoy my company."

She relaxes her grip into mine and rolls her eyes, "The greatest acting of my career and no one to acknowledge it except you."

When we approach the table Melinda stands to give me a quick hug before I tuck Josie and I's helmets underneath the table, "Max, so great to see you again! I haven't seen you since the Christmas party, and even then, we didn't get to really talk because of that dreadful woman and her oils." I've always liked Melinda; she tells it how it is. With her dark brown hair pulled back into a sleek bun and gray power suit she looks like she just got out of court, which considering she's a defense attorney, is probably the case.

I smirk at Shawna while she glares at me and tries to push her round belly up from the chair. In a terrifyingly fast change of facial expressions her glare morphs into a wide smile as she shakes Josie's hand, "You must be Josie! I've got to say I honestly didn't think you were real." Oh yeah, I knew Shawna smelled bullshit. She's known me way too long.

Josie chuckles, giving Shawna's hand a light squeeze before tossing her curls over her shoulder, exposing her long neck. "Believe it or not, you aren't the first person to tell me that!"

Should I be worried about how good of a liar she is...?

Shawna laughs lightly and orders a bottle of red wine for the table as the waiter comes by, which I find comical considering she can't even have any, before continuing. "All I ask is that one of you breathes in my face so I can imagine what the wine tastes like."

Melinda's green eyes land lovingly on Shawna as she holds her hand and gives it a kiss, "You're almost there sweetheart, the final stretch, and once he's born, I'll buy you an insanely expensive bottle of cab as a push present."

"What's a push present?" Josie asks before I can, just as confused as me.

"It's when the partner not shoving a watermelon out of a small hole in their body buys a gift for the one that is," Shawna answers, "But if Mel thinks she's getting away with only giving me a bottle of cabernet, then she's sorely mistaken," she says while cocking an eyebrow affectionately at her wife.

"I wouldn't dream of it," Melinda laughs.

The waiter comes by to take our order. We all get steak, and to my horror Shawna gets hers smothered in cocktail sauce. She pats her belly lovingly, "Sorry but that's why we chose a steakhouse in the first place. This little guy has a very particular palate."

"And an expensive one," Melinda nods in agreement.

"I'd shudder to know the number of cows I've single handedly caused the death of. The horseradish, well, I have no explanation for that." She responds with a shrug.

"My sister Eleanor has been pregnant three times, and each time the cravings get more and more bizarre. With my youngest niece she craved pickles covered in tajin and hot sauce." I can't help but laugh at the memory of seeing my sister balance a plate full of pickles on her belly. Josie looks at me softly, and I realize then that I don't think she even knew I had sisters, or nieces.

Shit I should've prepared her more...

And right on cue, Shawna looks between Josie and I and asks the question I should've been more prepared for, "So, how did you two meet?"

I try to keep the panic out of my voice as I take a sip of wine, "Oh you wouldn't want to hear that story. It's pretty boring," I say after the bitterness of the wine coats my tongue.

"Oh, come on Max, any story that involves you actually settling down with someone is worth hearing," Shawna says while leaning back and resting her hands on her belly.

I feel panic crawl up my spine. We never talked about this. How could we not talk about this? Did I really not think about how a double date always starts with this question?

You wouldn't know idiot, it's not like you've ever been on a double date in your entire life, I internally groan at myself.

"We actually met in the tampon aisle!" I hear from the chair next to me. I still. *The tampon aisle?* My eyes go wide and my back rigid as I realize I have no idea what the loose cannon next to me is going to spout from her mouth.

The women on the other side of the table laugh loudly, "Okay now I definitely need to know more."

Well. We had a good run. We didn't even make it to the entrée's before fucking up. Fake relationship time of death, fifteen minutes into dinner. I know I have no choice but to be a bystander as Josie either rambles to the point where she has no idea what she's saying, or she succeeds in embarrassing me.

Honestly, my money is on embarrassment.

I want to make it perfectly clear, there is nothing embarrassing about the female body or anything that it does. I grew up with two older sisters, so I know more about periods probably than a typical guy, but why the hell would a single guy be hanging out in the tampon aisle? I'm going to sound like a complete weirdo.

Josie gives me a smile that to the untrained eye probably looks loving, but up close I can see it for what it is, amusement. I was right, she wants to see me squirm. "He saw me grab a box of tampons and took it upon himself to ask me which one was the most absorbent."

Shawna and Melinda both give me a weird look. I knew it. No way am I going to come out of this story not looking like a total creep. *Okay. I've got to stop this now before it gets out of hand.*

"It's not what you think." I say, interrupting God only knows what is about to come out of Josie's mouth.

"I get nose bleeds," I supply. "I saw in a movie once that you could put them up your nose, so I figured I'd give it a try." I feel my face begin to heat, and I pray to the Saints I barely talk to that I just saved my ass from complete embarrassment.

"Yes! That movie *She's the Man*, with Amanda Bynes right?" Melinda says with excitement.

I can't help but internally give myself a high-five. I haven't seen that movie in over a decade, but that scene really stuck with me. "Yes! That's exactly the one."

Shawna chuckles, "I loved that movie. I'm pretty sure seeing

Amanda Bynes dressed as both a man and woman is what made me realize I was bisexual."

"I understand, I questioned my sexuality when I watched The Hex Girls sing on *Scooby Doo and the Witches Ghost* for the first time," Josie chuckles lightly while looking at me from the corner of her eye.

I genuinely thought I'd disappoint her when I stopped her from embarrassing me further, but she just seems slightly amused. The thought of her and I having a crush on the same characters from our childhood piques my interest more than it should, but I mean come on, Luna was fucking hot. At least she has good taste.

"Still though, Max, that was pretty bold of you, going up to a complete stranger and asking which tampons are the most absorbent," Shawna says as the waiter walks over with our plates and lays them out before us.

I smile widely, "Believe me I was surprised too," I reply before gripping the bare skin exposed on Josie's upper thigh where her dress has ridden, making her slightly jump. She plays it off by rubbing her arms and muttering something about it being cold under her breath.

Melinda begins to cut her steak before looking up at us from across the table, "And Josie you were just like, yep this is the man for me?"

"What can I say, I liked his candidness," she deadpans.

"Turns out our best friends were dating, and we kept running into each other at all their events. I just knew it was meant to be. What are the odds? My very own tampon angel showing up time and time again?" I say with the cheesiest grin I can muster.

"Don't call me a tampon angel you moron," Josie seethes quietly so only I can hear her.

"You started it, *gattina*." I retort.

I'm not done with Josie yet, if she thinks I'm not going to try and get her back for that little stunt, she's wrong. "Aw *gattina*,you should tell them about our first date," I purr.

Before she has the chance to respond I jump in, "Oh how

sweet, you know how much I love this story so you're letting me tell it. Okay I'll go."

Josie stares at me with horror before I take another sip of wine and continue, "I took Josie to this really nice sushi restaurant, the nicest one in Indy just to put it in perspective. I didn't know this before, but apparently, she'd never had anything other than a California roll. My sweet little *gattina* wanted to impress me, so she went in ordering blind and got a random roll on the menu. This one was apparently extremely spicy, and since she'd never had wasabi before she didn't know how to eat it. So, she takes the entire glob of wasabi and puts it all on one bite. All I could do is watch in horror as she immediately gagged so badly that she barfed all over the table." I can feel Josie burning a hole through me from the chair at my side. *Check and mate.*

"Wow your guy's stories really have a lot of bodily functions in them," Shawna says before taking a massive bite of her cocktail sauce covered steak.

My grip on Josie's thigh gets tighter as I feign a loving smile, "What can I say, we're very open people, aren't we, *gattina*?"

"Aw that's a cute nickname, what's it mean?" Melinda asks.

I suppress a smirk before I respond, "It's a pet name in Italian. She loves when I speak Italian to her, don't you, *gattina*?"

"So much," she grits between clenched teeth. I stifle a chuckle as she takes it upon herself to polish off her glass of wine.

Just to rub salt in the wound even more I grab her hand and place a gentle kiss on her knuckles, and fuck, it kind of backfired because she smells incredible, like a sun-ripened coconut. Her eyes meet mine, and I see a flicker of something I can't figure out behind them before pulling away.

Shawna looks lovingly towards Melinda, "That's so sweet. It reminds me of when we first came up with our pet names for each other. Right, melon?"

Melinda squeezes Shawna's hand, meeting her loving gaze right back, "Aw you're so right, gum drop."

Jesus, those nicknames are too much. The sweetness of it makes me feel like my teeth might fall out.

Shawna looks at Josie, "Do you have any nicknames for Max?"

Well fuck. Here we go. I see her mouth curl up in a smile that I don't trust in the slightest before she answers. "Donkey Kong."

Shawna and Melinda shoot a look at each other, completely perplexed. "Donkey Kong? As in the Nintendo character?" Melinda asks.

Josie's smile grows wider, "Yes well he's a total brute..."

"Okay I think they don't need you to continue." I say through clenched teeth, while my hand resting on her thigh goes still.

But does she stop? Of course not. She leans in and whispers, which I've got to say is not even close to a whisper, the whole restaurant could probably hear us. "And well ladies with the way he throws me around the bedroom I might as well be a barrel if you catch my drift."

I feel my face heat as Shawna and Melinda cackle loudly. I look over and see Josie looking far too pleased with herself, but I'm still trying to figure out if that was supposed to be a compliment or not.

After she catches her breath from laughing so hard she coughs, Shawna gives me a look, "Okay, Max, she's a keeper. You've got the job."

Well, I guess I can't complain about how we got to this point, because I got what I wanted. Josie looks over at me, completely beaming, and I'm stunned into silence because I don't have a fucking clue how we just pulled that off.

CHAPTER 5

JOSIE

I'm snuggled into my favorite corner of Ella's dilapidated cushy blue couch covered in my required two blankets. Our conversation from the other night gave me the urge to watch *Scooby-Doo and the Witches Ghost* for what is probably the hundredth time of my life, and Ella was more than willing to join me on one of our many movie and snack binging escapades. Better known to us as M^3 or Millennial Movie Marathon. I need to watch my girls, Luna especially, because dear God I was not joking the other night. She made me question a lot of things in my young life.

As we watch the townspeople all come out of the woodwork to admit that they're all behind the fake witch running amuck, Ella thrusts our giant bag of popcorn in my general direction after shoving a handful in her mouth.

"I feel inclined to once again tell you this seems like a bad idea," she says around a mouthful of popcorn, a piece falling out before she shoves it back in. She's currently using Liam's body as a pillow, sandwiched between him and me on the couch. It should be noted that Liam had a bigger and nicer couch at his place, and yet Ella forced him to sell his because she refused to get rid of this rinky dink blue one.

"God damn, El, you are so fine," Liam laughs sarcastically. She shoots him a death glare before snatching the bag back and grabbing a piece of popcorn to throw at him. They're so cute it's nauseating.

I ignore the fact that this bitch just stole back the bag of popcorn and I opt to go for the pack of Twizzlers resting on the coffee table. "I know how it seems, okay, but it's a free trip to Fiji. Free, El. *Free*," I say while ripping open the bag of licorice.

I look over in her general direction and watch as she then has the audacity to roll her eyes at me. "Jos, with the amount of rom coms we've both read and watched, how is this not a red flag to you?"

"Yeah well, he's a cocky asshole. It's not like I'm attracted to him anyway. Plus, he said when we get there we can just split up and do our own thing, so green flags all the way."

She pauses the movie and raises her eyebrow at me while crossing her arms over her giant blue hoodie, "You realize that's how at least half of them start. Don't act like he isn't hot. I saw the way you looked at him the other night. You wanted to crack him like a glowstick."

"It's true Josie, he's very hot," Liam laughs before pushing his wire-rimmed glasses back up his nose and grabbing a bag of Hot Cheetos.

"Ugh, please, he's not that good looking," I lie. I'm just straight up lying to my best friend. That man is unbearably hot, and even worse he both tastes and smells amazing. *God, I wish I didn't know that.*

Liam shakes his head and chuckles, "See now we both know that's not true. I may be biased, but that man is one fine looking Italian sausage."

So yeah, I'm not a good liar obviously.

"Ew, babe, the imagery with that is just, too much," Ella snorts.

"What? Am I not doing the girl talk thing right?" Liam asks. Poor guy, it's not his fault that he's the odd one out. Ella might be his girlfriend, but I think we both know when I'm around he's the third wheel.

Ella reaches up her arm and gently pats his face with her hand, "Oh no, babe, it's not that. It's just, um, do you mind giving Jos and I some space for a bit?"

"Shit, oh yeah sorry," he facepalms before gently lifting Ella off him and getting up. "I'll just go make us all lunch," he says while pointing his thumb in the direction of the kitchen and leaving.

"That man is a golden retriever. I need one." I laugh only to meet Ella's very serious face, and let me tell you, she doesn't make that face very often.

"This is a bad idea," she says curtly.

"So you've mentioned."

She throws up her hands in exasperation, "And yet you won't listen! You think you can go on a vacation with that hot ass man to a couple's resort in one of the most romantic places in the world while pretending to be his girlfriend and not catch feelings?"

I shake my head at just how ridiculous of a suggestion that is, "Woah, woah, woah, catch feelings? Okay, fucking him I could understand, but actually liking him is another thing entirely."

Her sharp gray eyes narrow at me, "Oh really? When have you ever had sex with someone you weren't in a relationship with?"

"I-"

"No," Ella interrupts, "We both know the answer. It's never. You're too much of a romantic. Hell, Trevor's dick is the only one you've ever let into your *Chamber of Secrets* and we both know he didn't exactly have a basilisk."

"I hate you," I deadpan.

"Not as much as I hate myself," she smiles brightly.

I snort, "Cute. Real cute."

Ella grabs my hand in hers and gives me a serious look, "I just don't want to see you hurt, Jos. Liam's told me about how much of a player he is. As fun as the potential for the whole double-dating possibilities that mash-up would create, it's not worth seeing you hurt. He's not a relationship type of guy. Many have tried, none of succeeded."

"Were you not the one trying to set me up with him at your party only a week ago?" I ask incredulously.

"Not seriously! I didn't know the promise of a romantic vacation was on the table, and I sure as hell didn't know you would be pretending to date the man!" She yells before stress eating another handful of popcorn.

I give her hand a squeeze, "I'm an adult, El. I'm perfectly capable of going on vacation with a man and not having sex with him. Like I said, he already told me that once we get there, we'll go our separate ways. Besides sharing a room, which let's be honest I'll be on the beach reading 90% of the time anyway, we won't have to see each other. Which is fine by me because I'll say it for the hundredth time, I'm not attracted to him."

"Famous last words," she says with a shrug.

"Jesus Christ just un-pause *Scooby-Doo* before I throw this Twizzler at your head," I say in exasperation.

She reaches for the remote with a snort, "Awfully defensive for someone who supposedly feels completely not attracted to someone."

I use this as an opportunity to take the Twizzler in my hand and whip it in her general direction. Much to my amusement the licorice lands square at her face and we both cackle. Deflection is key, and when I get home from the trip, I'll be the first one to tell Ella I told you so.

CHAPTER 6

MAX

This is going to work, you can pull this off. Get to the hotel, text Shawna, go our separate ways, write the article, make a name for myself, and shove it in Bobby's Leave-It-To-Beaver-face while I'm at it. This has been my mantra over the last twenty hours.

It was my mantra when Josie and I were going through security back in Indy and she looked fucking adorable in her giant Michigan Football hoodie and leggings that hugged the perfect curve of her ass.

I said it over and over to myself when she was annoyingly cute and shared her earbuds with me on the first plane ride and we listened to her favorite podcast, *My Favorite Murder*, for hours while the coconut scent of her invaded my lungs.

I fought back the urge to say it out loud when I brought her a blueberry scone and an iced americano with almond milk and three pumps of classic syrup from the Starbucks at the Los Angeles Airport where our connecting flight was, and her smile was so big it felt like someone had my heart in a vice grip.

I repeated it over and over again when we landed at the airport, and I watched her come out of the bathroom where she changed into a crop top that gripped her breasts perfectly and exposed a slice of deeply tanned skin on her belly before hitting her high-rise shorts.

I definitely had to say it when we were on the boat that took us to the island and I watched her curls blow back, exposing the long column of her neck and the piercings going up her ears.

And as we walk up the dock to our little villa and into our home for the next week, I'm tempted to tattoo it on my forearm when we walk in and see that there's only one bed.

Of course, there's only one bed you moron, this is supposed to be a romantic getaway...

I want to kick myself.

Why?

Because it's going to take every bit of strength I have not to want to fuck Josie on every single surface of this villa.

Because this place is so damn beautiful it doesn't even feel real.

There's a main building where all of the restaurants are located along with the bars and the front desk area. From there, several extremely long docks stretch out in all different directions with eight villas stretching from each of them. Once we walk into the villa there are hibiscus flowers scattered along the entryway, and a massive hollowed out pineapple filled with different fruits cut into artisanal shapes to welcome us. This place is unlike anywhere I've ever stayed before.

Sure, I've stayed in some really nice places before, hell the resort Liam and I stayed at when I forced him to come to Jamaica with me was really nice, but this is just next level. We have our own damn villa!

Immediately when we walk in, it's cozy, with a small bar and a loveseat across from the massive four-poster canopy bed with gauzy white curtains hanging over the top. Everything's all open concept, except for the toilet thank God, but it's becoming clear that the whole "going our separate ways" thing might be more difficult than I initially thought.

Unfortunately, when I realize that there's a giant jetted tub and a massive waterfall shower that's all glass, leaving nothing to the imagination, I know I'm fucked. If I see Josie naked, it'll be game over for any shred of self-control I have. We're going to have to do something about that, because I'm no martyr.

As hot as I think that Josie is, I'm not in the business of being a total asshole. I know I can't give her what she needs. She's not a casual fling kind of person, if we hooked-up she'd want more, and I can't be that person. The night I kissed her was a lapse in judgment, a mistake I made before realizing that she doesn't do casual.

Not to mention shit is already getting super convoluted with us pretending to be in a relationship. If we were pretending to date and hooking up, well that's not a fake relationship anymore, that's just a relationship. And once again I don't do those, and she only does those. Not a winning combination.

So here l am, in the most beautiful hotel room I've ever stayed in, with one of the most beautiful women I've ever seen, and I can do... nothing. This should be a fun week.

"Wow, this is absolutely breathtaking," Josie gasps while opening the back patio door to a deck with two white fold out chairs and a step ladder leading directly into the clear, cerulean ocean.

"Perfect for reading?" I ask, already knowing the answer.

She gives me a knowing smile, "Or listening to how a serial killer used a person's skin to make a lampshade."

"Jesus, fuck Josie, your brain is terrifying," I shake my head while walking back into our little bungalow. I'm thankful that what I thought would be an extremely long twenty hours of bickering between us hasn't happened at all. We've been getting along shockingly well, although I'm sure it won't take long before that changes. I enjoy getting a rise out of her and watching the spot between her eyebrows crinkle in frustration.

"Stay sexy, and don't get murdered," she winks while reciting the sign off from the podcast we listened to on the plane ride and shutting the sliding door behind her.

"Speaking of sexy..." I trail off, unsure of how to proceed, "We're going to have to figure out the shower and bed situation."

Josie eyes the all-glass shower and then the large bed before her eyes meet mine, and lightly clears her throat, "It's, um, definitely cozy."

I smile, but it falls flat, "I'll take the couch, and I suppose if one of us needs to shower we can just tell the other one to make themselves scarce while we do."

"Sounds good to me," she nods lightly, "I'm going to start unpacking."

"Yeah, I need to text Shawna and let her know we made it," I reply before pulling out my phone and texting my boss.

Max: We're here. The place is gorgeous.

Shawna: Perfect! I'm emailing you a link to the itinerary now.

Itinerary.... I've never had an itinerary before...

Max: What itinerary?

Shawna: The client wants a full scope review remember? I enclosed all the activities and instructions the client wants highlighted. I'm assuming your phone is more than capable of taking the appropriate picture and video content. I had a travel tripod sent to the hotel, and they should be bringing it by shortly.

Max: What videos...?

I have literally no idea what Shawna's talking about. I've never had to do anything but include pictures in my blog and social media posts before, and I've never had a strict schedule I had to follow.

Shawna: The videos for the daily posts... Are you like severely jet-lagged or something?

Max: You never mentioned any of this!

Shawna: I didn't?

Max: No!

Shawna: Oh whoops, baby brain. Ugh, getting up every two hours to pee has really taken its toll. This isn't your typical one article assignment. The client wants a travel blog style post that includes both pictures and videos that we can post on our socials for every day you're there.

Max: Oh my God, I can't believe you didn't tell me this.

Shawna: Hey you try thinking straight while you're getting constantly kicked in the bladder by a literal human being. So I forgot? Sue me. You're in Fiji with a ten of a woman and I'm in a cramped office in Indianapolis waiting for my mucus plug to fall out. No one feels sorry for you. Get this shit done Max, and don't fuck it up.

Well then...

I look up from my phone to see Josie pulling out a neon orange bikini and putting it away in a drawer. *Wouldn't mind seeing her in that...*

"Well, *gattina*, change of plans. Looks like we have an itinerary," I say while she looks up at me with growing wide eyes.

"I thought once we got here we could go our separate ways," she says, crossing her arms over her chest. I try not to focus on how the movement presses up her breasts in that crop top in a way that should be illegal in my presence, and fail.

I let out a long sigh and pinch the bridge of my nose, "So did I, but I guess my boss forgot to mention a little detail about how this assignment is supposed to be us doing a video diary of all the romantic excursions Fiji has to offer. When I thought this was going to be like any other assignment, I figured I'd just use some creative liberties on the romance aspect while I wrote the article, but I can't just pretend we did all this stuff like I could if I were writing it. They want video proof."

She cocks up an eyebrow and purses her lips before responding, "I fail to see how you lying is my problem."

Well, there goes our twenty-four hour no-bickering streak...

I need to figure out how to spin this. Fast. Otherwise, all of this was for nothing.

"Oh come on, *gattina*, have a heart. You got to go on this trip for free." I say in a low voice as I walk closer to her. I figure seductively pleading might work.

She tries to hide it, but I hear her intake a sharp breath as I use my index figure to tilt her chin up to meet my eyes. I think I might have her, but any resolve that I thought might crumble dissipates just as fast as it appears.

Instead, she hardens her gaze as she looks me square in the eye, "Only because it benefitted you. I held up my end of the deal." *Okay, so seductively pleading is a no go.*

But the word deal sticks with me.

Deal.

How could I make this work, so it benefits both of us?

Think Max, think.

And then it hits me. I've seen her ignoring phone calls and texts left and right. I overheard her talking with her parents at the party when they thought no one was listening, and I know they want her to give that asshole a second chance he doesn't deserve. You don't just have a complete knockout like Josie and think you can do better. Heads up, you can't. She's the kind of woman that if you have her, you do everything to keep her, and that's why I know she and I would never work.

But if we could convince her parents and dick bag that she's taken, that she's moved on for good, maybe she can finally get the peace I know she wants.

Only one way to find out...

I realize I'm still holding her gaze, and her dark brown eyes seem confused as she tries to figure out what's currently going through my brain.

"Are you having a stroke?" she asks, her eyes turning slightly worried.

I ignore her and prepare to unveil my best shot at convincing her to go along with this charade. I hope it works.

"What if I sweeten the deal?" I ask as the finger hooked under her chin slowly releases and traces down the column of her neck. I really need to stop touching her like this, I'm only making it harder. Literally. And the small noises she makes in the back of her throat and how she lightly leans into the touch (despite the fact that she hates herself for doing so) is like a drug to me.

Before I completely lose my senses, I let my hand fall to my side, and her breath is shaky. She lightly clears her throat, I'm assuming to make it seem as if she's unaffected by my touch, before she speaks.

"I'm listening," she says curtly.

I walk to the bar in the corner, because fuck do I need a drink, and pour myself two fingers of bourbon over ice and take a sip. I let the burn ripping down my throat focus me on feeling anything other than how soft Josie's skin is.

"Your ex has been bothering you again recently, right?"

"Yes..." she hedges.

"And your parents want you to get back with him?"

"How did you...?" she trails off, looking incredibly confused.

"The party Josie, you guys weren't nearly as quiet as you thought you were. I went inside to grab a beer and I overheard you talking. I had to hurry up and go back outside because I realized it was a private moment and I was inadvertently eavesdropping," I say. I hope she doesn't think I was trying to spy on them or anything.

Her cheeks slightly flush, "Oh. Well. That's embarrassing. How much did you hear?"

I wince, "I left right around the time you said something about how you walked into him bending his secretary over his desk... A total dick move by the way. You're right, he doesn't deserve you."

Her eyes grow wide with horror as her cheeks turn a deep red, "Splendid. I love that for me."

Oh god I didn't mean to embarrass her. "Please don't be embarrassed. I only bring all of this up because I have an idea. What if our deal extends past the trip? I'll meet your parents, charm them obviously because look at me, and they'll leave you alone about the bag of dicks stuffed into a Vineyard Vines shirt. You post pictures of us on Instagram, so he knows you're taken. Then he leaves you alone. Problem solved." I say before brushing off my hands.

She snorts, finding this idea apparently hilarious. "Bold of you to assume you could get my parents to like you more than they do him."

I don't like the idea of what that idiot did to her, and if her parents had any real class they would like someone that made Josie happy. They would want her to be with someone that was faithful to her. Someone she could trust. How could someone like that asshole be better for her than me? Or at least, the version of me I'm pretending to be. The Josie's besotted boyfriend role I'm playing.

Because my pride makes me do stupid things, I finish off the rest of my drink and set the glass on the bar before walking back towards Josie. I get close enough that I'm mere inches from her face, so close I can smell the coconut smell of her hair.

My voice is pure gravel as I raise my tattooed hand up towards her face and let my thumb gently tug on her bottom lip. "I'll just charm them like I did you."

She lets out a shakey breath, before realizing my game and swatting my hand away. "Okay fine. It's worth a shot, but my parents will never believe we're together."

I narrow my eyes at her, "And why is that?"

A smirk plays on her full lips before she shrugs, "Because I find you completely and utterly infuriating."

I chuckle darkly before walking towards the porch, "Now. *gattina,* is that any way to talk to your boyfriend?" I look over my shoulder and watch as she scoffs before unpacking the rest of her belongings, and I know that this trip is about to get a whole lot more interesting.

Chapter 7

Josie

I wake up the next morning and my eyes feel like they're going to pop out of my head from how exhausted I am. After an insane twenty hours of traveling and a sixteen-hour time difference, my body is extremely displeased with me. When Max and I unpacked and got settled in we immediately went to bed. The end result being that I have no idea what day or time it is, but as I force myself to pry open my eyes it's still dark out.

I'm tempted to just say fuck it and go back to sleep, but on a middle school guidance counselor salary who knows if I'll ever get to travel again, let alone to Fiji, so I force myself get out of what might be the most comfortable bed I've ever slept in.

Seriously, it feels like sleeping on a marshmallow, and the giant fluffy duvet and pillows are somehow magically cold and heavy at the same time. If it wasn't for the jet lag, I'm pretty sure I would feel like a new woman. The urge to ditch the entirety of the Fiji Islands and pull a sleeping beauty by staying in bed is far too tempting.

But I made a deal...

Not sure that was the best decision I've ever made if I'm being honest, but I'm a desperate woman at this stage, and if it means that my parents and Trevor will finally leave me alone, then I'm willing to do what it takes; including but not limited to, sticking my head into a shark's mouth while also simultaneously scooping my eyes out with a melon baller.

Jesus, I really need to stop watching 'Criminal Minds,' my brain is getting darker by the day...

I'm normally a morning person, but even I'm no match for a sixteen-hour time difference. As I drag my feet over to the sink, I squirt a blob of cinnamon toothpaste on my brush and see a very scrunched up Max looking insanely uncomfortable on the loveseat.

Looking at him makes me wince, and I feel guilty that he had to spend the night sleeping on a couch made for ants. Maybe I should just offer for him to share the bed with me...? I mean we're both adults.

I step a little closer and see that his neck is basically bent at a right angle, and I know that a few more days of this will leave him with a permanent head tilt. He'll just be walking around looking constantly confused and it'll be all my fault.

There should be no reason that two mature adults, well, one mature adult and one adult with the maturity of a frat boy on Viagra, can't share a bed platonically. Regardless of how hot said adult may or may not be.

After I spit my toothpaste into the sink, I take my bonnet off and style my hair before walking towards the closet to grab my flip flops. The closet happens to be near the couch, and I'm close enough to see how unfairly cute Max is when he sleeps.

My eyes trail all the way from his slightly mussed hair to his white t-shirt that clings to the muscles in his arms. The awkward angle he's laying at exposes where most people have a stomach, but he has a slab of marble with a perfect olive tone. His gray sweatpants hang loose on his hips, and I try not to look, I promise I do, but the pants are just tight enough that I can see a VERY prominent bulge. Like, I know I've only ever seen one penis before, but well, I can say this much, Trevor's dick did not look like that...

A basilisk indeed...
God damn it Ella.

I'm being a creeper right now, I acknowledge that, but my God this man's body is somehow making my mouth water and also go completely dry at the same time. As I'm busy marveling at a body that by all accounts deserves its own Italian fresco, Max stirs briefly, and it's enough to make me jump in fear that I've been caught being a stalker that watches innocent people sleep.

Thank God he's just slightly adjusting, and I use the moment while my heart is rapidly pounding in my chest to serve as a warning that I should not be ogling my fake boyfriend. Emphasis on the fake, and as attractive as this man clearly is I could not think of a worse idea than muddying the waters as far as I'm concerned.

I shake my head to get it on straight, quickly slip on my cheap ass Old Navy flip-flops that I got with Ella thrifting years ago, and grab my kindle so I can read my smut while the sun rises over the ocean in the background. I hope it distracts my brain from the marble sculpted abs and massive bulge currently asleep on the couch in our room.

———

I lose track of time, and I'm staring out towards the orange and gold sunrise over a cerulean ocean when I hear the sliding glass door behind me open. The loud sound of the door shutting startles me out of my trance, and I look up to see a very sleepy Max rubbing his neck.

His hair is still slightly mussed, and the man is so annoyingly perfect looking all the time that it irritates me even more that he makes messy hair look sexy. When he wakes up, he looks like a fairytale prince kissed him awake from his slumber while sprinkling fairy dust on him. When I wake up it looks like I had a long night of sleeping under a bridge and demanding riddles as currency. As if I need another reason for him to annoy me.

He drags a tattooed hand behind his neck and massages, lightly groaning as he does, "Morning... wow, this view is incredible!" His eyes grow wide as he takes in the golden rays and the way they sparkle against the ocean in front of us, but all I can seem to focus on is how beautiful his olive skin looks as it soaks in the sunlight.

I wince as I watch him roll his neck at different angles, "Is your neck bothering you from sleeping on that micro-couch?"

He uses one hand to stretch his neck over to the opposite side before smiling at me, "Aw, *gattina*, you worried about me?"

I bristle, because damn it he's right, I am. *Quick deflect, deflect, deflect...*

"No! I just don't want my 'boyfriend' to not be able to turn his head and then keep falling off things because he doesn't have any peripheral vision. That'd be crazy embarrassing."

Not my best work I'll admit...

He acknowledges my deflection with a small smirk that makes his eyes crinkle as he leans against the glass door, "Don't worry, whenever you're around my head seems to turn involuntarily anyway."

My cheeks heat, and I know it's not from being in the direct line of the sunrise, but from his words. They're just that though, words. Max may joke around and hit on me, but I don't take his praise seriously.

So I reply and try to hide the very obvious blush that's creeping into my cheeks by turning to look down at my kindle. "Not if you keep sleeping on that couch it won't"

A small smile plays on his lips as he walks towards the folding chair beside mine and sits down, close enough that I can smell the intoxicating aroma of his cologne. "Are you offering to share your bed with me, Josie?"

"Ummm..." *Think brain, think! Move your mouth and speak damn it.*

But before my brain can think of a logical response to his question, he keeps talking and closes the space between us even more, so that his face is only a few inches from mine. From here I can see the way the gold and green flecks of his hazel eyes reflect the light and they're so beautiful it hurts. "...because we both know I won't turn down the chance to sleep next to you. Especially because we both know if we're in that bed together, you won't be able to keep your hands off of me."

Wait, what did I miss? How long was I zoning out?

I scoff as I process the audacity that this man seems to have and shake my head while irritation claws at my throat, "I'm an adult that is more than capable of keeping my limbs to myself. Especially if you're the one next to me. God knows your ego would take up so much space I'll be sleeping on the edge of the bed anyways."

Ha! Thank you very much. Apparently as long as I don't drool over him and stay perpetually irritated at his general existence, I'll be able to retain my brain function.

He chuckles as he leans back in his chair so that he's facing towards the sun, "Fair enough."

"So, what's on the agenda for our romantic getaway today?" I ask in an effort to change the subject.

"Breakfast on the patio and then a mud bath at the hot springs. Ready to get dirty?" he says while facing me to suggestively wiggle his eyebrows.

I cringe, "Mud bath? How the fuck is a mud bath romantic?"

He shrugs before closing his eyes and leaning back once more, "Not my job to question that, just to document it and share my opinion."

I groan at his flippant attitude, "I'm already regretting this."

"That honestly doesn't surprise me, but too late! We're in this together now, *gattina*," he laughs.

"Call me kitten one more time..." I say behind clenched teeth.

His eyebrows shoot up as he looks over at me, "Ooh she knows Italian..."

"No dickhole, I just know how to use Google translate," I say while letting out an irritated groan and pinch the bridge of my nose.

"Alright, Josie," Max says curtly before folding his tattooed and muscular arms across his chest.

I reply with a small nod, "Better."

———

After we finish breakfast on the patio, and I drink the necessary dosage of caffeine for me to handle the fact that if I was still in Indy it would be yesterday, we pack up the tripod and meet the cab outside of the hotel. Mud, here we come.

The peak of romance, obviously.

Since we're working directly for the head of Fiji tourism, it's allotted us an absurd amount of special treatment, and besides the very obvious perks like the hotel stay, we also get our own private hot spring.

I'd be way more excited about the hot spring if it didn't also require me to bathe in mud beforehand, but that's neither here nor there.

After the guide gives us the spiel about how the mud is rejuvenating for the skin and gives us our designated buckets, he leaves us to our own devices. I know this is supposed to be romantic, but seriously, it's mud.

"Well, I guess we should go ahead and get some footage," Max says while unfolding the tripod and making sure the angle of the camera on his phone shows the entire hot spring.

"I guess so," I hedge before kicking off my sandals and letting my neon orange toenails sink into the earth. The ground here is different, slightly softer and springy. I take in a deep breath of humid air and close my eyes so I can truly appreciate the feeling of the warmth on my face as I listen to the trickling of the springs. This is paradise right here.

"Strip down *lover*," I hear Max's husky voice coast along my skin making me shiver, and I know that he must've gotten closer since I closed my eyes.

My eyes flip open, and I'm about to give him shit and tell him not to call me that, but the words get caught in my throat. Standing far too close to me is a shirtless and very muscular Maximiliano, and I'm too stunned to speak.

This man should not be this hot. It's not fair. How in the hell am I supposed to keep this man humble when he looks like that? For God's sake of course he's cocky. I would be too if I looked like the stunt double for a Hemsworth brother.

My eyes slowly drink him in, all the way from his toes, up muscular calves, towards gray swim trunks that hug his thighs before leading up to a V that points directly towards a place that just this morning made my mouth water. The problem though, is that when my eyes meet his hazel ones, he's smirking so fucking hard that the green flecks seem to shine brighter.

And that right there, is why the man drives me insane, he knows he's hot and I hate it.

"Like what you see, *gattina...*?" His voice is husky as he refuses to break eye contact with me.

"I thought I asked you not to call me that?" I ask, my voice coming out huskier than it should. I can't let him know how hot I think he is, my pride truly can't take the hit, so I decide right then and there that I refuse to be the one to break eye contact. I'm wearing a white crocheted cover up top and shorts, but I use this opportunity to cross my arms over one another and pull my top over my head before pushing down my shorts so that they pool at the ground around my feet.

I hear a low growl of breath and watch as Max's eyes slowly savor every inch of me in my bright red one piece that crisscrosses into a deep V, putting my cleavage on display. "Sorry, must've slipped out." He doesn't look the least bit sorry, that's for sure.

Needless to say, I got him to apologize, so the results speak for themselves.

His eyes refuse to leave mine, and I know I said I won't break eye contact first, but I can't do this. If only his gaze does this to me, I need to stop this before things get out of hand fast.

"So... now what?" I ask.

I make the mistake of looking out towards the hot spring, and as I do Max takes advantage of my vulnerability. All I get as a warning is the clanking of a bucket before I feel something cold and mushy make contact with my stomach.

I scream with shock as I look down and see a giant ball of mud sliding down my belly before watching Max double over with laughter.

That little asshole just threw a mud ball at me!

Oh, hell no.

While he's busy laughing so hard he looks like he might cry, I let my irritation fuel me and bend down towards my bucket before scooping a heaping handful of freezing cold mud and rubbing it into his annoyingly perfect hair.

"Ah! What the fuck," Max yells.

"That's what you get, you ass!" I shout back.

His eyes darken before he chuckles, "Oh you're going to pay for that," and lunges for me.

I quickly dodge his grasp and prepare to run. I'm obviously not thinking clearly because I don't run, like ever, and Max captures me instantly. As I've mentioned before, he's in peak physical condition, and I'm no match for him. Before the word 'fuck' can even fly out of my mouth he grabs me around my thighs and throws me over his shoulder.

I can't control my laughter as I hang upside down and my face is dangerously close to his ass. I feel the slimy cold mud as he smears it all over my thighs and calves before he spreads it across my back.

I squeal because I'm really fucking ticklish on my back and involuntarily kick my legs so hard that I accidentally knee him in the stomach. A whoosh of air escapes his lungs before he panics and sets me back on my feet.

Big mistake buddy.

If you're wondering if I have sympathy for him in his time of need, I don't. Instead I use it as an opportunity to scramble to my bucket and scoop up a handful of mud so I can smash it against his chest.

A good plan, in theory.

Except he's really fucking strong, and the small swell of pride I have for myself dissipates quickly when he gathers both of my wrists in his hand and locks them behind my back.

The movement startles me, and we both can't control our rapid breathing as we stare at one another. My chest shoves my breasts slightly forward with the way he restrains my hands behind my back.

The playful expression on his face is gone, and in its place is a look that I can only describe as pure desire.

Fuck.

I've never been restrained before, Trevor was never one to really experiment, but I can say that being on display under Max's burning gaze while I can do nothing to prevent the way his eyes rove over every inch of me does something to me. Something that makes me ache in places that should definitely not be aching right now.

My body is probably just sensitive because well... it's been a while since I've been touched by anyone but myself or my Sucky Sucky.

Yeah, that's definitely it. A natural, primal reaction to being touched by a man who is attractive in a purely scientific way that speaks to the suppressed cavewoman part of my brain. The rational part of my brain knows better though.

I shouldn't be enjoying the way he looks like he could devour me, it should irritate me because I know it's not like this small moment in time will make any difference in the grand scheme of things, but pride is a funny thing. I can't help but relish the way it feels to be looked at like this.

Using one hand to hold my hands behind my back, he looks slightly conflicted before reaching down to the bucket at his feet and taking a small handful of mud in his hand, spreading it out to his fingers. He uses the thumb covered in mud to grip my chin before tracing along my jaw and down the column of my throat at an unbearably slow pace. I shiver under his touch, and it's not because the mud is cold.

He's so gentle it feels like he's tracing me with a feather as his fingers trail down my arms, leaving streaks of mud in their wake. My breath hitches as his hand grips my thigh, massaging and smearing it into the skin there.

The ache between my legs grows more painful by the second as he worships my body, covering any exposed skin that he can.

"My turn," I say with a breathy moan. Honestly, I'm shocked I'm still breathing. I can still feel every part of my body prickle with awareness where he traced me.

"Okay," is Max's only response, his voice comes out as pure gravel and he releases my hands from behind my back.

I shake my shoulders out, the soreness of being restrained turning me on far too much to be normal.

"Don't move," I command before reaching into the bucket and grabbing a handful of mud. His eyes widen slightly, but I'm shocked when he doesn't reply with some pithy comeback. Instead, he just watches me as I coat my fingertips and trace along his sharp jawline framed in stubble.

He grunts quietly and I take both hands and drag them down his tattooed chest all the way to where his hips point inward at a V. The sound is so quiet I probably wouldn't have even heard if I wasn't hyper aware of every single noise and movement coming from him right now.

Just that small reaction has me preening, and I savor every sharp intake of breath or light moan that comes from him while I trace over his tattoos with mud. The weeping willow, the dove, the Zelda sword, and the rosary beads on his hand receive special attention. I've decided they're my favorite.

My gaze meets his, and I hate myself for feeling like this. Like pure temptation. I'm Eve and he's the snake with an apple obsession trying to get me to take just one bite.

I really want just one bite.

He looks very, very, biteable.

I'm about to say fuck it, but Max seems to come out of whatever spell we seem to be under and lightly clears his throat. "Cool, um, I think we got plenty of footage... let's let the mud dry and wash off in the hot springs," he says before walking over to the tripod and pausing the video.

I feel like whatever bubble was surrounding us popped, and I'm thankful that for once in his fucking life Max was the one with some restraint.

———

I know this is a fake date. Rationally I know it, so why does this not feel very fake?

Maybe it's because we had to play it up for the camera, but the look in his eyes really felt like desire. Burning hot, setting me on fire, rushed to the feral unit for fourth degree burns. My cheeks still feel inflamed.

I don't know if I've ever been touched like that before, even with Trevor. I guess it's just because I don't have experience with anyone besides him, so I don't have anyone else to compare to, or maybe, just maybe, Trevor and I didn't have as much chemistry as I thought we did.

Well that certainly explains why he felt the need to fuck his receptionist... Maybe it's me? What if... What if I'm bad a sex?

Maybe I pushed him to it.

Oh fuck. Maybe I'm like a fish that got pulled from the lake just flopping around like I'm gasping for breath.

Well, that's fucking humiliating.

Embarrassment seeps through the pores of my skin, but then I do what I do best when it comes to Trevor, shove the thoughts of him into a box in my brain and pack it away in the attic. Dwelling on my possibly awful bedroom habits will do nothing to help in this situation anyway because I'm not sleeping with Max. Just pretending to.

"Everything alright over there? You seem deep in thought," Max says as he moves the tripod to get a closer angle of the hot spring.

"Yep! Just ready to wash the mud off!" I say at an octave that could be mistaken for a bird call. I'm not subtle. Obviously.

"Alright..." he says while giving me a funny look. "Looks like the mud is dry enough, and clearly, you're very excited to rinse off. Let's get in."

"Splendid," I squeak. Just what I need, more touching and rinsing and seeing Max's tattooed skin dripping wet.

Max starts the video and takes the steps into the spring. "I want to get some footage of us washing each other off in the hot spring. Think you can manage touching me without gagging?" He gives me a knowing smile. I know what he's not saying, we're pretending that whatever the hell just happened with the mud buckets was a blip. Thank the lord.

I chuckle lightly, "No, but I'll persevere."

I grab my phone so I can take a selfie of us together. "Come here," I say as I wade into the spring. Good lord this feels incredible. Warm and fresh. I've been in the water for 2.5 seconds and I'm already feeling cleansed.

I move closer to him, both of us still caked in mud. "I figure today is as good a day as any to announce that we're 'dating.'" I say while making quotation marks with my fingers.

I hold the phone out, but he grabs me at the curve of my waist and presses our sides together. "No one is going to believe we're dating if you aren't even touching me," he explains.

"Fine," I huff. *Great. More touching.*

I lift the phone once more to take the picture, his body pressed firmly against mine, and right as I snap the picture he leans forward and kisses my cheek. A blush spreads across my face, the lingering feeling of his featherlight kiss over my mud-stained cheek making my stomach flutter.

He grabs the phone so he can see the picture, "Perfect." He says while we look at the photo. Both of us are covered in mud with streaks all over our faces. His hand grips the curve of my waist while I smile widely, my curls running wild behind me. It's the look on his face as he kissed me that I marvel at the most. Is it just me or does he look... besotted? That can't be right though. Maybe he just has some serious acting skills.

I need to break this moment immediately. I quickly wade farther into the spring and splash Max directly in the face.

"What the fuck, Josie!" he yells.

There we go. Playful I can do.

I cackle maniacally, "You said to help each other rinse off!"

"Yeah, sensually. Not like we're two kids fighting over a pool noodle!" he says with exasperation.

I can't stop laughing, his annoyed face is far too entertaining. Is this why he enjoys needling me so much? I don't blame him. It's pretty fun.

"Oh calm down, you're so dramatic. It's just water my sweet, sweet, Donkey Kong," I tease.

"So, we're really sticking with Donkey Kong huh?" he asks while narrowing his eyes at me.

"Yep," I say popping the P. "How exactly does one 'sensually' rinse someone?" I ask in the most neutral tone I'm capable of accomplishing. For the sake of honesty, it was most definitely not neutral at all.

His eyes darken, making my heartbeat stutter in my chest. "Would you like me to demonstrate?" he asks, his voice lowering an octave.

I bristle, "No."

A cocky smirk plays on his lips, "What's wrong, *gattina*? Afraid you'll like the way my hands feel?"

Yes. That's exactly what I'm afraid of. If the mud incident

taught me anything it's that I should be very, very, afraid of the way I'll react to his touch.

I steel myself, determined to make sure he doesn't see the fear in my eyes, so I smirk back at him. "No. I think you'll like touching me too much. Wouldn't want you to fall for your fake girlfriend now, would we?"

He inches closer to me, so close now that we're almost touching again. The green and gold flecks in his eyes turn molten, and the way he's looking at me makes me physically clench my thighs together.

He cups some water in his hand and lifts it to my cheek, letting the water droplets gently trickle down my face, washing away the mud. "Mmm... I definitely would like touching you entirely too much, but as for falling for you? Not going to happen," he says with a tone that's pure lust.

My mouth is so dry it feels like I shoved a ShamWow inside it. I bridge the few inches left between us, my breasts touching his chest, and glare up at him. "Oh? Should I be offended with how assuredly you said that?"

He meets my gaze, "No, Josie. It's just never happened. I don't work that way. I don't do commitment."

"Well, I guess it's a good thing we aren't actually together then."

Max cups more warm spring water in his hand and drags it up to my chin, gripping it while pinning my gaze in place as water runs down my neck. "Exactly. No risk of me falling for you, so what excuse will you come up with next?"

At this stage it feels like I have a point to prove. That I can handle doing this without catching feelings, just like he can. What's the harm really? I could use some fun in my life. I always do what's expected of me.

Well, except for refusing to study law and marry a cheating asshole.

I can feel something dormant in me stirring, adventure? The

urge to break this mold I've held myself in all my life. I don't want to be the same innocent, rule following, good girl I've always been. Maybe I should start taking more risks, and maybe, just maybe, I'm fake dating the perfect man to teach me just how it's done...

First things first, prove him wrong.

I put my hands on my hips, "Fine. Sensually rinse me then."

He chuckles and he slowly, painfully slowly, trails water droplets over my arms, caressing them. Once again, my body remembers all too well that only minutes earlier this same touch lit up my skin, and I'm right back where I was before. Needy and aching. I can't help wondering what actually fucking this man would do to me. He's only touching me for crying out loud.

He pushes me against him even more, and he traces his wet fingers up and down my spine, making me shiver.

A dark chuckle escapes him as he whispers in my ear, "Hmm... am I turning you on, *gattina*?"

His words are making me far too turned on. The ache and need for release just from his touch is becoming unbearable. This man does not play fair, that's for damn sure.

My voice comes out like a breathy moan, "No, just cold." I say smugly, "If anyone is turned on it's you." I'm not cold. I'm in a hot spring for fucks sake, but I can't just let him have this now, can I?

His fingers dance lightly at my tailbone, dangerously close to the curve of my ass. I can't help it, my breath hitches, making his ego get even bigger. I could kick myself. "Are you saying you turn me on more than I do you?"

I let out a shaky breath, "Yes, that's exactly what I'm saying."

He tilts my head to the side, exposing my neck to him before he trails water down the side, "I don't think so," he smirks.

The water slowly cascades down my neck, making me want to moan, but I suppress it, and my nipples pebble at his proximity, "That sounds like a challenge."

"Maybe it is," he shrugs.

I need to take back some semblance of control here. This just won't do. I trace my wet hands along his pecs, lightly dragging them over his nipples. He inhales sharply, and I smile to myself, before tracing the skin right about where his swim trunks hang low on his hips.

He closes his eyes, and I can tell he's trying to compose himself, which I refuse to allow, and I make sure my hardened nipples press lightly against his exposed chest. He growls at the feeling, and I drag my hands from the top of his back to the bottom, lightly scraping with my nails.

He shivers, and I'm close enough now that I can feel the very large bulge in his trunks press against my lower belly. The pure eroticism of it makes me want to melt into a puddle, and also conquer a small army. Seeing just how much I seem to affect the great Maximiliano makes me cockier than I have any right to be.

I've got him right where I want him. If I haven't mentioned it before, I'm very competitive. He challenged me, really, he gave me no choice. I play dirty, and I don't care.

I grip the dark hair at the nape of his neck roughly and force him to stare down at me. His eyes blaze, and I know I've won. I watch his throat work as he swallows, and he leans slightly forward.

I let him get close. Dangerously close. Close enough that I can feel his breath against my lips, and I can smell the intoxicating aroma of his skin.

Just as he's about to press his lips to mine, I grin wickedly before using my other hand to splash a giant wave of water at him, "I win," is all I say before sauntering towards the edge of the hot spring.

Chapter 8

Josie

After our little interlude at the hot springs the taxi ride back to the hotel was a quiet one. Neither of us acknowledged what happened and opted for what had to be the most tension-filled taxi ride in existence. My skin feels like it's sunburnt on every place he touched me, and the achy feeling between my legs refuses to ebb.

That same silence followed us back to our bungalow. When we walk into our room the cool from the air conditioning feels stark against my partially dry swimsuit. I hear Max grumble something about the gym before going into the closet and pulling on his athletic shorts and Nike's. Oh and he's shirtless of course. I swear this man lives to torture me. He grabs his gym bag without another word and all but runs out the door.

After he leaves, I go and lay out in a beach chair on the back porch so I can finish drying and will myself to calm down. My brain is full of jumbled thoughts of rippling tattooed muscles and cocky smirks that shoot sparks down my spine. And it needs to stop.

I grab my kindle and attempt to get lost in a billionaire marriage of convenience romance, but it doesn't work. If anything, it's just making me hornier, and it's taking me so long to finish the chapter that my kindle has all but given up on trying to learn my reading speed.

Maybe I should take care of myself since I'm finally alone...

I think that's the only way I'm going to be able to think of anything other than Max. The way the hard bulge of his cock pressed against my stomach was enough to make me lose my mind.

I make my way to the shower and grab my Curl Smith products out of my suitcase because I know there still has to be mud in my hair no matter how much I rinsed off in the spring.

It's times like these I really wish I would've brought my trusty Sucky Sucky with me, but I just felt too weird. Like what if he saw it? I don't know. I'm a grown woman with a vibrator like it's not a big deal, but that's just a part of me I don't feel the need for Max to somehow stumble upon.

I strip off my swimsuit and drape it over the glass door of the shower before stepping in. This shower is way bigger than it has any right to be, and the dark terracotta of the back wall has a seat carved into it with a massive rainfall showerhead off to the right. I'm convinced this shower is bigger than my entire bathroom in my little studio apartment.

I line up all of my products on a shelf by the showerhead and start my ritual, although I had to opt out of my coconut oil pre-wash treatment which I hope I don't pay for later. I'm on borrowed time and have no idea when Max will be back. Although he's probably one of those people that injects creatine and pre-workout into his veins before spending seven hours at the gym, so I'm sure I have plenty of time.

I turn on the showerhead and let the warm spray of the water wash over me. I take my time, making sure every inch of me feels clean, and when I run the washcloth all over my body, I pretend it's Max's strong hands roving over me.

I squirt a generous dollop of my coconut deep-conditioning treatment in my palms and run my hands through my curls, making sure to coat every inch and let it marinate for a bit.

Once my hair is sufficiently covered, I walk gingerly over to the seat and decide to make the most out of my conditioning time. Hell, I'm so worked up I probably won't even last three minutes anyway.

My body is slick with water as I run my hands down my stomach to the aching spot between my thighs. I use two fingers to run along my already wet folds, and I tease myself lightly before working my way up to my clit.

I let out a loud moan, and as I close my eyes, it's Max's fingers that I see rubbing small circles on my hardening clit instead of my own.

Suddenly a loud thud makes my eyes pop open, and what I see before me has me quickly removing my hands and using my arms to try and cover my breasts and vagina.

Embarrassment colors my cheeks as I look through the glass and see Max with his earbuds in, a gym bag dropped next to him on the floor, and wide eyes full of surprise. He's breathing so heavily that I can see the rise and fall of his chest. Neither of us moves, and to his credit his eyes never leave mine as he pulls the headphones out of his ears.

I don't know what's happening, but I feel paralyzed. Unable to move as his gaze turns from one of surprise to a darker one. I feel like I'm on display, and something in his unwavering stare makes me feel powerful. What was once embarrassment reddening my cheeks begins to feel a whole lot more like lust.

He must see my slight change in demeanor, and only then does he allow himself to drink me in, starting from my toes and slowly working their way upward. He's lazy with his perusal, taking as much time as he wants looking over every inch of me. I feel my pussy flood with want just from the weight of his stare.

Oh dear lord...

"I didn't tell you to stop," he says before sinking his teeth into his plush bottom lip.

"Wha--" I stutter.

The smirk I love to hate plays at his lips, "What's wrong with an orgasm amongst friends?"

My chest is heaving, and I scrape for any and all resolve I have left in me to reply. "We aren't friends, and even if we were, masturbating in front of them isn't usually one of the activities I'd participate in."

He chuckles darkly, "Good thing we aren't friends then, huh, *gattina?*"

My breathing picks up at a rapid pace, the place between my legs pulsing, begging for release. Am I really desperate enough to go through with this? I think maybe I am.

You're the one who said you wanted to take more risks...

And honestly, is there any greater risk than letting your hot-as-fuck fake boyfriend talk you through an orgasm when you know that's all there could ever be between you? Orgasms?

And you know it'd be good... says the little devil on my shoulder.

I watch Max stalk closer to the shower, peering at me through the glass, slightly fogged from the warm water. He traces a finger through the condensation before his eyes meet mine. "Now do what I say, and I'll help relieve the ache between those pretty legs."

His cockiness irritates me, but probably even more so because he's right. My first reaction is to argue with him, but fuck it. "Okay," I release on a shaky breath before uncovering my body.

"Holy shit, you are so fucking hot, Josie," he grits, and his reaction makes me feel all the more powerful. "Now hold up your hands."

I comply, and he continues, his voice lowering at an octave that makes my stomach somersault, "Now look at them. See those hands?"

"Yes," I reply softly.

"When those hands are touching you, they're mine," he growls, "Now show me what you want my hands to do to you."

I'm all but panting now, his filthy mouth sending shivers

through my body. I run my hands down my chest and head straight to my clit. I need release, and I need it now.

"I didn't say my hands could touch that pretty pussy yet," he says darkly.

"But you said--"

"I know what I said, but I want my hands teasing you first," he grunts. "Now move my hands over those perfect tits and roll your nipples between your fingers."

I do as he says, a jolt of electricity going straight to my center as I roll my sensitive nipples between my thumb and index finger, causing a breathy moan to fall from my lips. "You're so cocky. Who said anything about wanting your hands on me? I don't."

I'm lying. He knows it and I know it, but like I said, pride is a funny thing.

"Liar," his eyes smolder. "I know touching me earlier got you as hot as it did me. I had to run for five miles and bench until my arms gave out to try and stop thinking about those nipples rubbing against my chest. Even then I had to beat off in the gym shower to try and clear my head. Guess what? It still didn't work."

My hips begin to undulate against the slick tile of the shower, his words turning me on more and more. The thought of him jacking off while he thinks of me... *fuck that's so hot.*

"Does it turn you on thinking about me beating this dick to that perfect body pressed against mine?" he asks, his eyes boring into mine.

"Yes," I moan as I slide my fingers downward, desperate for relief.

"Did I say you could move my hands yet?" He grits.

"But I--" I begin to protest.

"Josie. Those hands are mine. They don't move unless I say so," he interrupts.

I can't breathe.

I can't think straight.

I'm losing control.

And I love it.

I'm just here, waiting for my next direction. Pressing my thighs together desperately trying to get at least a little friction to my clit.

"Good girl," he praises. "You can move my hand down now. Just one, I want the other one still pinching and rolling your nipple."

I do as he tells me to, slipping my hand between my thighs, leaning back on the elbow of the arm playing with my nipple. I open my legs so he can watch as my fingers play with my soaking wet folds.

"That's right, get my fingers nice and wet," he commands. "Now dip them inside. Push them in and out while tapping them against your G-spot."

As I slip my fingers, sorry HIS fingers, into my slick warmth, I angle his fingertips so they scrape along the spot inside me that drives me wild. I pulse in and out, my hips thrusting, needing more.

"Please Max--" I moan helplessly. What I'm asking him for, I don't know, but for some unknown reason I feel like he does.

I look and see his face completely wrapped up in me, his fists clenching at his sides. "My God, I think hearing you beg is my new favorite hobby."

I glare at him while continuing to pulse inside myself, "Don't be such a cocky little dick," I grind out.

"Oh Josie, you know I'm anything but little. I know you felt me pressed against you earlier." He chuckles, a sound coming deep from his throat, "I want my other hand on your clit. Move it down your body, slowly."

I do as he says, trail my fingertips down my sternum, to my stomach, to my mound, and finally my clit. I rest my hand there, waiting for him to tell me what to do next.

"That's my girl, waiting for me to tell you what to do. Such a fast learner. Go ahead, small tight circles on your clit. Do it now."

I can't even come up with a snarky remark because I just need to come so badly, I don't care about putting him in his place. I use one hand to draw tight circles around my hardening nub while my other fingers pulse in and out of me.

The feeling is electric, and I know I'm not long for this world. Between the constant touches and the way his filthy mouth talks, he's basically been edging me all day, and I'm definitely on edge.

"Are you close?" he asks with a grunt.

"Yes," I whine while picking up the pace of my hips swiveling up and down my fingers.

"Go ahead Josie, use my fingers to make yourself come," he commands.

Just like that, I'm undone. I all but shout as release coats my fingers and I see black and white spots behind my eyes. My heart rate spikes, and my legs shake as wave after wave of pleasure washes over me.

When I remove my fingers and lift myself up from the bench to look at Max, he's running his hands through his short dark locks and breathing heavily. He seems like he's in turmoil, and the look in his eyes is enough to make me want to invite him into the shower with me.

Before I can say anything though he grunts and picks up his gym bag once more, leaving the room, and me, empty.

CHAPTER 9

MAX

I wake up the next morning to sunlight pouring through the sheer curtains of our window and surrounded by the heady coconut scent of Josie laying on the other side of the bed. It sends my already rock-hard cock into a tailspin.

This is so fucked...

More like I'm fucked.

I thought I had a grip on myself, but when I walked into our room and saw that perfect body on display, I lost control. Seeing her run her hands up and down her caramel skin, perfect light brown nipples begging for me to suck them into my mouth, a small tuft of black curls covering the spot between her legs, begging to be filled.

I'm only human.

Honestly, if I wasn't so terrified of ruining everything, I would've bent her over that shower seat and fucked her the way she deserves to be fucked, but I know myself. I can't be what she needs. What she deserves.

She's worthy of someone much better than me.

Better than a fuck boy whose so afraid of commitment he'd rather deprive himself of love than risk hurting someone. Or getting hurt himself.

I wasn't always this way, but after the fifth military base I moved to, I just couldn't do it anymore. I learned at a young age that nothing in this life is permanent. Nothing. Just because you love something, or someone, doesn't mean you get to keep it. It just makes it all the more painful when it all inevitably goes away. They promise they'll call and text you every day, only to cheat on you with the guy you thought was your friend, hundreds of miles away.

The most committed relationship I've ever had is with Liam, my best friend. How sad is that? But shit, that little nerd got under my skin. With his constant Neil DeGrasse Tyson references and unironically wearing shirts with chemical bonds on them, he needed me as much as I did him. He struggled to come out of his shell enough to make friends on our floor, and I struggled with creating a bond that would stick with all the people I met. Together we were the perfect pair.

Or as Ella puts it, the perfect bromance.

She refers to the day that I moved into my dorm at IU to see the bunk below mine with a periodic table bedspread, and my outrage that he picked the bottom bunk, as our "meet cute".

Either way, besides my family, he's the only one who has been able to sneak past the guard I put up, and that is more than enough. I don't need to go around just letting another person in. Even if that person happens to be hot as hell and the perfect blend of sassy and funny.

She's fuckboy kryptonite.

Which is exactly why I need to focus on the fake part of the fake-girlfriend and stop fucking around. I can't forget why I'm doing this in the first place. I have a job to do.

I get up and take care of business before brushing my teeth and finger combing my hair, before I go find Josie where I know she'll be. Reading on the back patio seems to be her favorite thing here, and I can't blame her. The view is so beautiful it doesn't even look real.

As I open the sliding glass door, I see Josie bathed in morning sunlight, and she looks absolutely breathtaking. Like a glowing angel as her brown eyes hesitantly meet mine.

We haven't spoken since the shower episode yesterday. I didn't know what to do so I went back to the gym and ran on the treadmill until my legs felt like they were going to give out and then hid out at the bar until I figured Josie would be asleep. No better way to solve a problem than avoiding it exists... as I always say.

I don't know what her reaction is going to be though, and I'm bracing myself for any and all possibilities, including but not limited to, being pushed over the edge of our deck into the ocean.

Her eyes quickly flit from mine, "Um... good morning," she says quietly.

I give her a small smile, "Good morning, Josie."

She holds up her phone and waves it around at me, "Who are Eleanor and Vivian Rossi?"

Um... okay that's not where I thought this conversation was going to go...

I feel my face blanch, "My sisters... why?"

A wide smile spreads across her face, and if I didn't feel a giant pit of anxiety opening in my stomach, I'd be completely wrapped up in it. "Well, that explains the comments on our picture. Eleanor said, 'She's too pretty for you *scemo*.' What does *scemo* mean?" she asks innocently.

Son of a bitch.

I pinch the bridge of my nose in frustration, "It means dummy."

She chuckles lightly before continuing, "Vivian said, '*Dio santo* just wait until Ma finds out her *ometto* is actually dating someone.' *Ometto*?" she asks while saying the word with an upward inflection.

I feel my heart tug at the nickname my mom has always called me. "My Ma calls me '*ometto*', even though I'm a grown adult. It means little man. Comes with the youngest child territory I guess."

My eyes widen with fear, "Fuck! My mom!"

Terror strikes at the thought that if my sisters know, it's only a matter of time before my mom finds out, and if my mom finds out before I tell her...

Hell hath no fury like a Sicilian mother scorned.

I need to get ahead of this. Now.

"How did they find out?" I ask to no one in particular while I tug at the back of my neck.

I see Josie wince from the corner of my eye, "I may have tagged you in that picture so Trevor could see..."

I chuckle, not that this situation is funny, but because if I don't laugh, I'll spiral. "Ah, well. We've created quite the problem you see because at any moment my mom is going to call and--" before I can even finish the sentence my phone lights up with the word 'Ma' on the caller ID.

I wiggle my phone with the screen facing Josie as her eyes widen in shock, "Okay, that's just freaky."

I swipe to answer the call and put it on speakerphone, so Josie knows just what we're dealing with. "Ma, I can explain--"

"Maximiliano, am I a good mother?" she interrupts with what's left of her slight Boston accent. After my dad retired, we all settled in Indiana, which is where he was from, leaving only traces of what used to be a much stronger accent.

"Ma--" I try to answer, but that's a mistake. I should know by now that when she rants, any and all questions are rhetorical.

"I just want to know what I've done for you to betray me?" I look up to see Josie's eyes grow even wider. I wave my wrist at her to let her know that this is no big deal, my mother just has a flair for the dramatic.

I hear my Pop's deep rumble in the background along with the muffle of the weather channel, "Your mother is very distraught, Maximiliano."

I release a deep sigh, preparing the lies to fly off my tongue, "We just started dating, it's still new! You guys are being so dramatic."

Damn it Max. You know that was not the right response...

I wince as I hear the crackle through the phone, and I know she's probably pacing around the kitchen now, gesticulating wildly. "Dramatic? Dramatic! Is it so much to ask that the son I labored for twenty hours with, that I have loved and sacrificed for, tell me when he's met a woman? Finally met a woman and you didn't tell me! Not once have you ever brought a woman home!"

Oh great, we're already to the portion of the rant where she guilts me into submission by holding her long labor over my head. It won't be long now until she's done.

"Ma, there's never been anyone for me to bring home," I say with exasperation.

"My point exactly. When you get home, I'm meeting this girl that has stolen my *ometto's* heart," she says alternating back to her sweet and motherly tone.

"Ma, it's a little early for that..."

"Nonsense, you'll bring her over next Sunday. I'll make my sauce." she responds as if that's the end of the conversation.

"But--"

My Pop's deep rumble echoes through the phone, along with the volume of the weather channel growing louder. "Your mother is making her sauce, Maximiliano," he says gruffly.

My eyes meet Josie's, and we have a silent conversation about what to do before she flits her hand at me, telling me to do whatever it takes to appease her.

"Yeah, okay, I'll bring her," I groan.

Her tone is now as sweet as cream puff after getting her way, "Perfect, I'll let your sisters know. *Ti amo, ometto.*"

"*Ti amo, ma,*" I reply before hanging up the phone.

Josie's eyes keep moving back and forth between the phone and me, "Wow that was..."

"Unhinged?" I finish for her. "Yeah, well welcome to having an Italian mother."

She swallows a lump in her throat, "Now both of our families are going to think we're together. This is quickly getting away from us."

I respond with a curt nod, because she's right. This lie is getting more and more out of control by the minute.

She stands up and starts to pace the deck, "I should've fucking known. How many books have you read Josie, how many?" She's talking to herself. That can't be a good sign.

"What are you rambling about?"

She stops her pacing to glare at me, "Come on, Max. Of course this would get out of control. What the hell was I thinking letting you rope me into this?"

I fold my arms across my chest in irritation, "Hey don't act like you aren't getting anything out of this arrangement. You've been wanting your parents and that douche off your back for months now."

Her arms fling out wildly, "How would you even know? We barely even know each other! For Christ's sake I went to another country with you, and you know nothing about me!" She's spiraling now. That much is evident. I need to reign her in before she does something drastic, like call off the arrangement.

"That's not true," I respond.

"Oh yeah, what, because you kissed me once and watched me touch myself in the shower suddenly, you're an expert?" she scoffs.

The irritation I feel flares even more, and I close the distance between us, caging her in with my arms as she leans against the railing of the deck. "No, because I pay attention. I know you smell like coconut because of the curl cream you use. I know that you despise the taste of mint so much that you refuse to even brush your teeth with regular toothpaste, and you use the cinnamon flavor instead. I know that if given the choice you always choose the color orange, I know your exact coffee order and your favorite kind of scone, but most of all I know that you're tired of playing it safe. You want to stop our little charade because a part of you is afraid to see what life has in store for you if you actually stick it to that asshole."

She rears back from my words, but I've had enough of this

conversation. I move my arms from either side of her and stalk towards the sliding glass door.

"You're one to talk," she shouts back as I shut the door behind me. Because fuck, she's right. We're two sides of the same coin, we're both afraid of what will happen if we just take a chance.

CHAPTER 10

JOSIE

My irritation towards Max and his harsh words on the patio earlier doesn't seem to get any better as the cab driver drops us off at the lot for the Ecotrax tour. I want to say he's wrong, that he doesn't know me at all, but unfortunately it seems he knows a lot more than I gave him credit for.

As if sensing I'm already in turmoil, my mother messages me and tells me that she expects Max and I to have dinner at the house when they get back from the Hamptons.

At least one part of my plan is working out.

Considering letting Max watch me masturbate wasn't exactly on my itinerary for this trip, I'll take a win whenever I can get it. Especially the part where I liked it and haven't been able to stop thinking about how rough and low the octave of his voice would get as he talked me through the movements. The gruffness of his voice as I play the moments over and over again makes me wet just thinking about it.

My brain and my vagina are clearly not on the same page with what's best for us. My brain says he'll hurt us just like Trevor did, that we don't know how to have sex with someone without our emotions getting in the way. My vagina says dick me down first and ask questions later.

As you can see there's a lot to unpack there.

Which is why him knowing so much about me has me feeling confused. When I laid in bed last night alone, I knew what to expect. This is Max, fuck around and ask questions later was what I expected.

What I didn't expect was this morning and how he knew so much about me that I never even told him. He learned it all just from paying attention to me. I don't think to this day Trevor knows my favorite color is orange or that I use cinnamon toothpaste. Honestly, it's sad that a man could share a hotel room with me for less than 48 hours and already know so much about me. Things that a man I was engaged to couldn't even bother to learn.

I want to shove all the feelings that are duking it out like rock-em sock-em robots in my head into a box and kick it off a cliff.

"You okay over there? You seem deep in thought." Max asks as the gravel beneath our feet crunches while we walk towards the rental building. It's the first thing he's really said to me since our little disagreement this morning.

"I'm fine." I mutter curtly.

He gives me a look that says he doesn't believe me, but decides not to push the subject.

When we walk up to the window facing out from the building, Max lets the attendant know we're here for the private tour and have a reservation for the electric bicycle excursion before giving her the confirmation number.

Once she types in our information, she walks us through the safety procedures and what to expect once we get to the end of the tour. We have a private lesson of something that I've already forgotten the name of before we head back.

The tour is on what looks like converted train tracks, and our bikes are attached to one another side by side. We pedal along the tracks and eventually we'll end up on the other end, where our lesson of the thing I don't remember the name of is supposed to be. Simple enough you would think.

Wrong.

Max and I get on the electric carriage seats, and I put my feet on the pedals, only for them not to budge in the slightest. We haven't even started the tour and it's already not going how it's supposed to.

"How the hell do I make this thing go?" I groan while trying and failing once more to push the pedals forward.

"Have you tried setting it to wumbo?" Max asks.

"What?" I ask, my face contorted with confusion. Is he having some sort of episode?

"You know. I wumbo, you wumbo, he, she, me, wumbo." he deadpans.

I snort, realizing what he's doing now. "Oh, silly me, I had it set to mini."

"Oh my God did you actually smile at me?" he asks as his own smile spreads across his face. It's so beautiful it makes my lungs feel like all the air is slowly leaking out of them like a balloon.

"It's hard to believe I know, but I guess your *SpongeBob* reference caught me at a weak moment. I didn't take you for a fan." I smirk.

"Don't insult me. I could quote the first three seasons from memory," he replies. That smile lights up the green flecks in his eyes and it's just chipping away at my resolve by the minute.

"I just didn't peg you for a cartoon guy I guess," I say haughtily.

"Maybe you don't know everything about me then. I was a kid once you know," he retorts. If that's a dig or not from earlier, I can't be sure.

"Fair enough," I say raising my hands in defeat. "I guess I just assumed you were born watching *Spike T.V.* and competitive women's Jello wrestling."

He makes a noise that sounds like a mix between a laugh and a scoff that comes deep from his chest. "Wow, you think so highly of me. By the way, the reason the bike isn't working is because I'm not pedaling yet, you can't make the whole thing go with just one side."

I can feel my cheeks turn pink with embarrassment, "Right. Yeah, that makes sense."

We both push our feet down on the pedals and lo and behold, the bike starts to move. The muscles in my legs work harder at first to help make the cart move, but once we get a good rhythm going, it's an easy ride.

The tracks take us through a large forest, the trees a deep jade color that creates a canopy, shading us from the beating sun. Even though the air is thick with humidity I drag in a deep breath, letting the smell of greenery and vegetation fill my nostrils. I close my eyes so the combination of sun and a light breeze plays on my skin from the bike. The only sounds are the trickling of water in the distance, the chirping of birds up in the canopy, and the rustling of the trees.

It feels like peace.

There's a knowing prickle on my skin that happens when you know you're being watched, and I peek at Max from the corner of my eye to see him looking at me with a reverence I'm not able to place. "Can I help you sir?" I ask.

"You look beautiful like this," he replies with a breath. I look at his phone around his neck, recording the bike ride. *Oh, I see. He's playing it up for the camera...*

I smile, I might as well pretend that the compliment was genuine. "Thank you, my handsome Donkey Kong," I reply with a wink.

He rolls his eyes at me, but the smirk tugging at his lips tells me he's trying not to laugh. "I'm being serious. You're so Goddamn beautiful Josie." He squeezes his eyes shut momentarily before opening them again once more, "Seeing you like this, happy, at peace, I knew you were beautiful before. Obviously. Just fucking look at you, but with the sun on your face and the wind blowing your curls, it makes me feel like someone stole the air from my lungs."

Talk about stealing air, I can't breathe. There's a hammering in my chest that could crack a rib and I soon realize it's my rapid heartbeat. He can't say pretend things like this to me, fake girl-friend or not. I don't think my heart can take it. My skin heats as his eyes meet mine, and what I see there makes me all the more confused, because it doesn't look like he's pretending at all. This feels very, very, real.

"Thank you," I manage to choke out.

I'm desperate to change the subject quickly as we pedal over what looks like a large freshwater lake with algae growing across the top. I grip the handlebar until my knuckles turn white, desperate to ground myself back in my body. "So, what's this private lesson we're supposed to be getting again?"

He forces his face forward, and I can see the sharp cut of his jaw when I look at his profile. "It's called Shibari I believe," he answers.

"What's that?"

"I think it's a type of Yoga or something."

"Oh, cool. Beach yoga sounds nice and relaxing," I say awkwardly. Honestly, I think I need some Yoga right now; I swear every single muscle in my body is tied up in a knot and needs to be stretched out.

We pedal the rest of the time in the loudest silence I've ever heard, full of so many things being unspoken between us. We watch as the trees and random pockets of freshwater breeze pass until we reach the end of the tracks, which leads to a stone walkway through a break in the trees.

"I'm guessing we're supposed to walk through there," Max says as he points to a sign that says 'Private Beach Access' in bold red letters.

"Astute as always professor," I respond with a sarcastic smile that doesn't reach my eyes. I don't know how to act around this man right now. I'm floundering.

He raises an annoyed eyebrow at me, but much to my surprise doesn't comment, and instead he walks up the stone steps and through the opening in the tree line while I follow.

When we get to the other side, I see a view so beautiful my chest squeezes. My mouth hangs open in shock as I stare out at the clearest blue water I've ever seen brushing against white sand. Standing near the water with large blankets laid out in the sand is a blonde woman with a long braid that falls down her back and bangles climbing up both of her arms. She looks like Shoshanna's long-lost twin, and behind her looks like a swing set without the swing.... I'm confused.

We both take off our sandals as we sink our feet into sand so soft it feels like silk wrapping around my feet and walk towards the woman that I'm assuming is our instructor. She offers us a warm smile before extending out her hand and offering it to both of us, "Hello, you must be Josie and Max. My name is Sheila, and I'll be your Shibari instructor today. Please, take a seat on the blankets behind me."

We all sit facing one another on a blanket with a gold and red paisley pattern, "So, welcome to your private Shibari class. Have either of you taken a lesson before?" she asks with a bright smile.

Max and I share a look before I respond, "I took a goat yoga class once, but I don't feel like I really retained very much. One of the goats kept trying to eat my hair and I was constantly afraid one of them would pee on me."

Okay Josie maybe that's too much information for right now...

My cheeks heat slightly with embarrassment when Sheila gives me a polite smile and Max looks at me like I've grown two heads. "Oh... that's interesting, but I don't think this will be quite the same," Sheila says as she lightly pats my knee.

I chuckle lightly, "Well I mean yeah, there aren't any goats here."

Sheila twists her lips to the side, and she gives me a look I can't decipher, "Well yes, and that this is Shibari, the ancient form of Japanese knot tying, or as some call it, the art of bondage."

"Wait, what?" Max and I yell at the same time.

The awkwardness I felt initially has now gone away and is

replaced with white hot anger. Of fucking course Max would tell me this is a fucking Yoga class. He's probably relishing the fact that I'm naive enough to have no idea what's going on.

I bare my teeth and my eyes widen, "Oh my God Max you fucking liar!" I grind out as I shove him in the shoulder, and my anger only spikes more when I see the complete unabashed delight in Max's eyes. He thinks this is funny.

"I swear, Josie, I didn't know," he laughs so hard his shoulders shake. My face is beet red. I did not sign up for bondage. The last thing I need is for Maximiliano to tie me up and restrain me right now, or maybe for his own safety, he should.

Sheila's face is one full of concern. Bless this woman, she's just trying to do her job. "Is everything okay? I know the idea of bondage can be a lot for couples just starting out, but once they try it, it becomes quite liberating," she says reassuringly.

I turn so I'm looking Max directly in the eyes, "I'm not letting you use your meaty paws to tie me up you sadistic son of a b--"

"Ha! She's kidding. Insulting me is just one of our kinks. Love the humiliation. Just can't get enough of it." He lowers his face close to mine, eyes locking on me. "She loves being tied up, don't you, *mi gattina*?" he interrupts.

The proximity of his face to mine is dangerously close, and I can smell the intoxicating scent of his cologne. It's annoying how quickly just smelling him stirs something deep inside me that makes me less angry with him.

"I'm not..." I trail off, unable to finish my thought because his mouth is close to my ear.

He speaks softly, so he knows that I'm the only one who can hear him, even with Sheila only a few feet away. His voice is low, and the sound makes my heart thump wildly in my chest. "We have a deal, remember? And an audience," he says while pointing at the camera.

"Now be a good girl, and let me tie you up," he whispers as his index finger traces down my throat. His words skate on a shiver that moves through my body at a torturously slow pace.

I collect myself, because I don't want him seeing just how turned on his words made me. "Fine." I bite out.

He grins at me like he's Elmer Fudd and I'm Bugs Bunny before turning back to our instructor. "Hey Sheila, this exercise doesn't happen to include a gag, does it? Because I really feel like Josie could use one right about now."

Oh my God, I could throw him in the ocean right now if I thought I was physically able to lift him.

Sheila doesn't seem to pick up on Max's joke and instead looks at him like he's the perfectly curious student. "Sorry no gags today, but when applying the practices at home feel free to experiment. With the express consent of your partner of course."

Sheila gets up from the sitting position to grab a long silky red rope out of the basket. I use the opportunity while she has her back turned to shove Max hard in the shoulder. The bastard just laughs.

"Oh, I'm sure we'll be taking all sorts of creative liberties when we get home, won't we, *honey*?" He says with a grin before he goes to set up the tripod so it's facing the blankets.

I really and truly hate the way he says that, and it sounds like a promise even though I know it's not. I also hate the way his cockiness grates on my nerves and makes my panties wet in equal measure.

"Now who will be the one being tied?" Sheila asks.

"Josie will be... I have more experience with restraints than she does," he says with a wink. Something I have no doubt he's telling the truth about.

Sheila walks Max through a basic knot that will bind my hands together behind my back. My breath hitches as I feel the red silk rope wrap around my wrists and slide against my skin softly before biting from the pressure of Max tying the knot. My pulse has elevated, and my breathing stutters as the rope tugs again while he loops the fabric around my wrists.

I never thought this would be something that would turn me on. Hell, Trevor and I never did anything even remotely like this before, but as Max wraps the binding around my chest to make a harness, I feel more secure than I ever have before. He walks in front of me so he can wrap the rope in a crisscross motion, only a few inches separating us.

It looks like I'm not the only one affected by my bindings, because when my gaze meets Max's, his pupils have dilated to the point where his iris is almost completely gone.

Okay there is absolutely no way he's faking that...

I may not have a lot of experience with men, but I know what it means when my gaze lazily trails down his body and his shorts are bulging a lot more than they were previously in the crotch area. I smirk up at him, but all he does is flare his nostrils before Sheila has me lay on my stomach so Max can bind my legs.

Fingertips gingerly trace down my legs before lifting my thighs up slightly so the rope can slip underneath me. Max straddles my legs and I can feel the press of his erection against my thighs as he wraps me up. If the rope wasn't already binding my thighs, I'd have to clamp them together just to get relief to my pulsing clit.

He moves the bindings down my legs, the silk ties applying enough pressure that I can feel every heightened bind, but not so much that it's chafing my skin. He finishes tying around my ankles before Sheila walks him through how to attach the ankle binding to the wrist binding, making my back arch.

I'm pulled and wound tight, and at this point I know I'm so wet I'm probably soaking through my bathing suit. I've never felt this vulnerable, this safe, and when Max comes around to my front and crouches down so his eyes are level with mine, he pinches my chin so he can focus my gaze towards his.

"I've never seen a sexier rope model in my life," he whispers before his thumb traces along my bottom lip.

My breathing quickens, but Sheila interrupts before I have to scramble and come up with a response, *thank God.* "Well, that's all I have for today, but might I just say you two have a lot of chemistry. You understand the other's body language very well."

Max gives me a knowing look, a secret smile only I can see, before he crawls behind me and undoes the binding. A tension I didn't realize twining beneath my skin begins to fade, taking the feeling of security with it.

Chapter 11

MAX

When Josie and I got back to our room after our surprise BDSM session, I immediately threw on my gym clothes and forced myself to go run on a treadmill until my dick no longer felt like it was going to punch a hole through my shorts.

I wasn't lying to Josie, I really didn't know what Shibari was. It's not my first time with knots and rope by any means, but Shibari is more of an art form, and that's what she was. Art.

Fuck. Tied up in that silky red rope I could've busted in my pants just from looking at her hog tied and completely at my mercy. The trust it takes to let someone take control of your body in that way has always been a turn on for me, but seeing Josie like that, saying I was surprised at the flush of lust that spread all over her body would be an understatement.

I'm supposed to be splicing and editing the footage from our Shibari session and sending it to Shawna, but my laptop might as well be dead weight for all the work I've gotten done. If tying up Josie wasn't already enough to fist my cock to for the rest of my life, then reliving the footage over and over again is just pure torture.

We were clothed the entire time, both of us in our swimsuits, this is for advertising a romance package not a porn site, but that doesn't stop me from letting my mind fill in the blanks. Her little tie dye bikini didn't leave a lot to the imagination, not that I would ever forget how she looked completely naked in the shower.

Her mouth parted in pleasure.

Her pupils blown wide with lust.

The way her wide hips undulated against her fingers.

The way she listened to my every command like the good girl she is.

Fuck. Me.

My cock hardens in my pants and presses against my laptop just thinking about her in the shower right now. I sat out on the porch after I got ready for dinner to give her privacy since the shower that's all windows does the exact opposite, but the urge to join her and lay her out on the bench while I tongue fuck her to oblivion gets worse by the minute.

Not a good idea Max... don't blur the lines...

My flimsy resolve thins more and more by the day.

We're supposed to have a romantic candlelit dinner on the beach tonight, so I'm sure that will most definitely not complicate things in the slightest.

I hear the door behind me slide open and turn to see a sight so beautiful that any and all words I've ever learned get caught in my throat. She looks unreal. Glowing.

She's wearing a tight orange dress that clings to every inch of her curves, tightening in at her waist and hugging her breasts like a second skin. The dress looks as smooth as silk, dipping to show a hint of cleavage, exposing the gold pendant that shines against her deeply tanned skin. My perusal is anything but secretive, it's unabashed, as I start at the orange heels lengthening her already long legs and ending at beautiful deep brown eyes swept lightly with a gold eyeshadow, the curls I ache to sink my hands into falling perfectly around her shoulders.

She tries to break the tension by reaching up and fiddling with one of her gold hoops, "Ummm... ready for dinner?"

Words. Think. Words. You know them.

I clear my throat before rolling the sleeves of my dress shirt up to my elbows to give myself time to remember how to speak. "Absolutely."

Great job Max. You did it buddy. You remembered one whole word.

I feel anxious and giddy, both two emotions that don't really ever occur to me when I'm on a date. Except this isn't a date. It's all for show. I literally have a portable tripod I'm carrying as proof, but that doesn't curb whatever turmoil is going on in my stomach. The feeling is unwelcome to say the least.

Whatever conflict I was previously experiencing quadruples when Josie and I walk to our designated spot on the beach to a gazebo covered in gauzy white linens blowing with ocean air, bright white fairy lights twinkling along the frame, and a bottle of champagne chilling in a bucket.

Josie looks over her shoulder and gives me a megawatt smile that makes my heart do something weird in my chest, and I can't tell if the sight of her smile or the sun setting over a sapphire-colored ocean are more beautiful.

Actually, I do know, it's the smile.

After I set up the tripod and set the phone to record, we walk towards the gazebo, and I pull out Josie's chair before I sit down in my own. That's not for the camera or anything, if my mom saw me not pull out a chair for a date, she would throw a slipper at my head.

Once again Josie gives me a smile before unfolding her napkin and placing it in her lap. Our waiter comes by and pops the cork to our champagne, pouring our flutes halfway with the bubbling liquid. When he leaves, I take a sip of champagne and let the sweet bubbles burning down my throat distract me from the weird pinching feeling in my chest I get every time I look across the table.

She lifts her champagne glass so she can clink hers against mine, "Here's hoping we can make it through this dinner without you announcing to everyone within earshot that I like to stick tampons up my nose." I say with a smile.

She snorts before clasping her hand over her mouth, making her laugh even harder. "The least of what you deserved."

"That's fair," I chuckle.

I'm actually capable of speaking in full sentences now, and If I'm acting weirder than normal Josie doesn't say anything. Instead, she looks out at the ocean with a reverent look crossing her face. "For what it's worth, I get why you lied."

My eyebrows pinch in confusion, "What do you mean?"

She sweeps her arm out, gesturing to the ocean, "This. I wouldn't want to miss it either."

I look out at the ocean before fixing my gaze back on Josie, "It is breathtaking." I shake my head before she turns back around to face me, so she doesn't see me staring. "Plus, I couldn't give Bobby and his wife that came straight from Satan's ball sack the chance to come here instead."

"They're that bad?" she asks, her lips quirking up in a smile.

"Bobby adamantly believes the covid vaccine is a government conspiracy to microchip us, and at the last office Christmas party his wife Karla accused me of being 'a sheeple suckling Kool-Aid from the teat of Big Pharma' when they found out I got vaccinated," I laugh while steepling my fingers, because the idea is just completely absurd.

"Well, she's not wrong," Josie says, no emotion playing on her face.

"Wait... what?"

She leans forward, waving her hand towards me so that I lean in closer so she can whisper. "You're playing right into the lizard people's hands."

Horror creeps up my spine. Oh god, I knew the other shoe had to drop at some point. No woman is that perfect. "Lizard people," I choke out.

"Yes," she hisses through her teeth. "The ones who control the government. They've convinced us all that the earth is round and will microchip us into submission if we let them. They're controlling us all like puppets on a string from their inner sanctum at the earth's core."

"That doesn't even make--"

Josie busts out laughing, interrupting whatever I was going to say. She laughs so hard tears begin to well.

I narrow my eyes at her, "You're fucking with me, aren't you?"

I'm surprised she can even breathe with how hard she's laughing. "Oh my God, you should've seen your face."

"Yeah, you really had me going there for a second. I thought you were two minutes away from telling me that birds weren't real," I chuckle.

"That's not a thing," she laughs while taking a sip of her champagne.

"Oh, but it is. There are people out there that think birds are actually cameras and the government is using it as a way to spy on us," I laugh.

"And street cameras and smartphones, those aren't good enough? We have to rope the birds into it too?" she asks with a smirk.

"No definitely not, this is a conspiracy that goes all the way to the top." I deadpan.

"I see," she laughs and takes another drink.

Our menu is prefixed, so we don't even have to order before the waiter comes by and places our plates in front of us. My eyes widen at the beautiful arrangement of the steak and lobster, covered in glaze in an artful design. I almost don't want to eat it because it looks so nice, *almost*.

The waiter brings us two glasses of red wine to pair with the steak, and I lift my glass once more towards Josie. "To our fake relationship, may it end amicably."

She lifts her glass and the sound of a clink rings through the air as she touches hers to mine, "And may we be convincing while we do," she smiles.

We cheers, but something in the act feels hollow, like maybe my heart doesn't necessarily agree with the words coming out of my mouth.

Chapter 12

Josie

After we finish dinner, we walk along the beach towards the club that Max says the travel company wants featured on their website.

I had to ditch my shoes and carry them because wearing heels and walking on sand is basically asking for an early death, but I don't mind. Because when I walk alongside the beach and watch the ocean bleed into the night sky while the moon reflects off the water, it's ethereal. The sand sifting between my toes grounds me, which I'm thankful for because my brain is liable to float off my neck with the amount of thoughts spinning around in it.

I wasn't expecting this weird hollow and concrete feeling in my chest. It's unnerving, but when I look up at Max while the ocean breeze gently toys with his inky black hair and the moonlight shines off the green in his eyes, I feel my heart tug.

Oh no...

Do I... have feelings for Max?

Like more than I just think he's hot? Do I actually enjoy his personality?

Fuck me. This is not the time you stupid, stupid, heart. Maybe it's just a reaction to the romantic dinner, walk in the moonlight, and the bottle of champagne we polished off at dinner...

If memory serves, drunk Josie does find Max incredibly irre-sistible, but I don't know if it's really just only that.

I mean, who wouldn't find that dinner swoon-worthy? It's just a natural reaction that anyone in my position would have. I don't have real feelings for the man, I can't. He's the emphasis of fake in the term fake-boyfriend. This is just the result of a lifetime of reading and watching rom-coms. The aftermath of being engaged to a man that considered a romantic date him emailing clients while I stare at a glass of wine in various different restau-rant locations around Indianapolis week after week. They were always fancy dates with no substance. Of course, my brain and heart are confused.

Max places his hand at the small of my back as we enter the club entrance and flash our hotel key cards at the bouncer before entering. The club is packed, and Max is forced to push me flush against his side as we sift through the crowd towards the bar where he orders me a margarita on the rocks and himself a whiskey sour. I try not to think about the proximity of my skin and his while also trying not to think about how he knows my drink order. Just a whole lot of trying not to think.

The beat of the bass in the E.D.M. number playing thumps so hard it could alter the rhythm of my heartbeat, while the flashing multicolored lights illuminate what would otherwise be a pitch-black club. The air is thick and humid, almost sensual in the way it causes my dress to cling to my skin and moisture to pool in every pore of my body.

Max fishes out his phone to take a video for his assignment, "Dance with me?" he asks silkily.

My stomach twists, "Um... I'm not really much of a dancer, if you recall..."

"Well lucky for you, I'm a good enough dancer that I can carry the both of us, if you recall." He replies with a wink.

"I don't know how your head hasn't exploded with all the self-importance stuffed inside it," I scoff.

He chuckles lightly and bends down to whisper in my ear, or

rather, club whisper which is essentially shouting, "I guess I'll just have to prove it to you then." My body heats with how close his mouth is to me, and I have to suppress the urge to close the little space in between so his lips are on my neck.

In this case, suppressing is drinking an entire margarita on the rocks in thirty seconds, and that shit was so strong it tasted like Jose' Cuervo himself made it.

With my head slightly buzzy, Max guides me to the dance floor and finds us a spot in between two couples rhythmically dry humping each other to a Bad Bunny song. I feel a small pang of jealousy. I wish there was a time when I had been so attracted to someone that all I could think about is getting as close to them as I can and not caring who sees. A person that in a room full of people is the only one holding your attention.

I don't think I even had that with Trevor, and I was going to marry that man. Something that makes less and less sense the more I think about it.

Max's hand rests firmly on my lower back and he pulls me close so that one of my hands is clasped with his while the other rests at his neck. We're close enough that I can smell the mixture of cologne and salt from the sea air radiating from his neck. And I want so badly to lick him just to see if he tastes as good as he smells.

No, Josie. No. Stop that right now, I scold myself.

Max uses the hand on my lower back to guide my movements, and before I can even register what's happening, he's leading me through the motions to the thump of the bass in the music.

I lean in so I'm close enough for him to hear me as he guides my hips in a circular motion. "I hate that you're good at this too," I remark, my voice coming out huskier than I intend for it to.

He gives me a small grin, knowing that it must've been painful for me to give him any sort of compliment. "My mom and dad taught the three of us, my sisters and me, how to. They love to dance. My dad said it's the quickest way to a woman's heart, so naturally I wanted to learn as soon as I could walk."

I chuckle, at least he's self-aware. "That's sweet. I can just picture little Max dancing on his mom's feet. So cute."

He bends down to close the small distance between my lips and his ear, so that his face is flush with mine, setting my skin on fire. "Aw, *gattina*, did you just call me cute?"

"Never," I scoff with a hint of amusement in my voice.

His fingers play delicately at the base of my spine as the rhythm of the music turns more sensual, his voice lowering an octave and a smirk playing on his lips. "I think we both know, I'm a whole lot more than cute." The air between us crackles wildly, and heat pools in my belly.

I didn't realize we had any space between us, but we apparently did because he decides to fuse my body with his as his thigh parts my legs. My chest breaks out in a cold sweat while my heart beats wildly in my ribcage. We're so close I don't know where his body ends and mine begins, and still, I find myself wishing I could be closer. His air is my air as my chest rises and falls to the time of his own.

I dare to look him in the eyes, and what I see staring back at me are dark black pupils almost completely enveloping brown and green irises. Need flows through my body, burning my blood and heating my skin. Our movements are hurried, this isn't the romantic dancing from before. This is frantic.

Hips rotating and grinding against one another, firm tattooed hands grabbing my hips begging for more friction. I'm lost to the rhythm, lost in his body while my own is at his mercy.

When Max uses his hands to push my pelvis against his thigh a small moan escapes my throat, and my hips begin to have a mind of their own. Rotating and grinding down on his thigh, giving my clit the attention it's begging for, sending delicious shivers up and down my spine.

I've been reduced to my most base self, my only thoughts being the need for more movement. More friction. More heat. More of my body pressed against his.

Max's hands stay right where they were, never straying to my ass, and all I can think is how desperately I want him to.

He could touch me anywhere...

The thought startles me, breaking through my trance as the D.J. changes songs to one with a higher tempo. I feel like I'm a Russian spy who just had their secret phrase spoken, returning them back to their regular mental state with the way reality comes rushing back to me.

My body goes rigid as I realize that my vagina, covered by the very thin fabric of my panties, was pressed tightly against Max's thighs. I detach myself frantically before realizing there's a big wet patch on his pants where my pussy just was.

Horror grips me tightly, my eyes close to falling out of my sockets as they alternate back and forth between the wet spot and Max. A heated smirk plays on his lips as he looks at me intently.

I feel like every inch of me is on display.

Oh my god. I cannot believe I just got my vagina juices all over this man's pants. Embarrassment grabs me in a chokehold, and my skin flushes. "Um, I have to go." I say quickly before ducking my head and making a break for the exit.

"Josie, wait! Do you want me to go with you?" Max calls after me.

All I can think about doing is throwing every single blanket in our room over my head and hope that it buries me alive. I don't think I'll ever mentally recover from this kind of embarrassment.

"No, you stay. Have fun!" I shout behind me without stopping. I leave him in the dust as I hurry back to our little bungalow to take an ice-cold shower and hope that there's some sort of gas leak before Max gets back so I won't ever have to look him in the eyes again.

CHAPTER 13

JOSIE

When I wake up the following morning, there's a blissful ten seconds where I don't remember what happened last night. I stretch my legs like a cat and then snuggle into the cool sheets before the intrusive thoughts start pummeling me awake.

Max.

Sunset.

Beach.

Dancing.

Wet spot.

Oh my God... the wet spot.

Mortification claws at my neck and cheeks, resulting in a flush. Despite my best efforts, this entire scenario seems to be getting less and less fake by the hour. I'm spending the entire day with this man. I'm supposed to wake him up in ten minutes, and I can't for the life of me figure out how I'm supposed to approach Max or even look him in the eye after last night.

The man has seen me masturbate for God's sake, but somehow this is different. This wasn't something he volunteered for, and all the more embarrassing is the fact that I'd lost control of my faculties so much that I didn't even realize what was happening.

I don't want Max knowing the effect he has on me, because if he does, it really negates every single time I've ever said I wasn't attracted to him. It was a lie, obviously the man is objectively hot, but this is... different. Something is chipping away at him in my mind, and the mental guard I'd had up seems to be getting thinner.

I look at my phone and realize with a groan that it's time to wake him up and I still have no idea what I'm going to say to him. *Sorry I inked on you? My bad, you made my pussy cry? Sorry, I have a condition?*

Maybe I should ignore it...

Yes. Ignore it. Perfect plan, Josie.

I mentally give myself a high five for deciding on a plan of action and nudge Max in the shoulder telling him to wake up, earning me a grumble and the abrupt pull of sheets over his head.

I nudge him again, feeling the hard plains of his back muscles slightly strain against my touch. The flimsy green night shirt he's wearing clings in all the right places, or maybe the wrong places. I haven't decided if I'm acknowledging my attraction completely yet or if I'm stuffing it into the deep recesses of my brain along with Trevor and my parents' never ending disappointment.

"Maximiliano I-don't-know-your-middle-name Rossi wake your ass up, it's Sawa-I-Lau day," I say while continually trying to nudge him awake.

"It's Salvatore, now leave me alone you demon." he grumbles, irritation gripping his voice. *Not a morning person. Got it.*

I prop myself up on my elbow and grab a pillow, "I prefer succubus, now get the fuck up, the boat leaves in an hour," I say, matching his irritation, before throwing the pillow at his head.

Max turns over so he's facing me, narrowing his eyes before they alight with mischief, and I know it's coming. The mockery, the cocky attitude, the preening at my embarrassment, but something flickers in his eyes before he rolls back to get off the bed.

No mocking. Saying I'm shocked would be an understatement. We get ready in companionable silence, and I settle on a red halter top and jean shorts to wear over my swimsuit. We make it down to the breakfast buffet and I chug an amount of coffee that would probably be a lethal dosage to a small woodland creature before stuffing a croissant in my mouth and walking down to the docks.

At the end of one of the docks a man in all white attire and a captain's hat smiles broadly at us next to a catamaran with the phrase "Bulamarau" in blue script along the side. "Bula, friends, you must be Max and Josie?" he says with a smile that takes over his entire face. On most people it would seem fake, but it genuinely seems like this man is that happy.

Max grins and extends his hand, "Bula, yes we are!" he replies while our guide shakes his hand.

"Great, my name is Berenado and I'll be your captain and guide today," he says, still smiling. This guy must have powerful facial muscles.

I can't help but smile back, "It's great to meet you Berenado, thank you for showing us around today."

"Of course, Ms. Josie, it's a pleasure. When you're ready I'll help you board the boat and we'll set off toward Sawa-I-Lau." he responds before walking towards the catamaran and hopping over the gap between the dock and ledge that makes me riddled with anxiety.

Max being who he is and completely unafraid of anything, quickly hops over the gap and extends his arm out to me. The idea of falling through the crack in between and impaling myself on the dock is all too present in the forefront of my mind.

I squeeze my eyes tight and try to summon the strength to force myself to push through my fear, and when I open them, Max and Berenado are both staring back at me with their arms extended.

"I would never let you fall Josie," Max says calmly, his hazel eyes shining with sincerity.

I swallow the invisible lump in my throat and put one hand in Max's and the other in Berenado's, before putting one foot on a post jutting out of the dock and the other on the side of the boat. I use my supporting leg and push up, letting the momentum and the guys on the other side propel me forward.

Instant relief washes over me once my feet are on the solid floor of the boat. The interior is lush with all white furniture and gold accents, a stark bright white against the deep blue of the ocean.

Max and I settle into the corner cushions at the back of the catamaran, and he pulls out his phone in his waterproof case to start recording while Berenado brings us champagne and orange juice to make mimosas.

If Berenado were twenty years younger I'd ask if he was married, the man is an angel. A beautiful, alcohol delivering angel. Max makes quick work of filling our champagne flutes while I pull out my phone and snap a picture of us sipping our mimosas with the vibrant ocean behind us.

Once Berenado starts the boat, it lurches forward with a small pull, and we slowly pick up enough speed that when it's all said and done my curls are wildly flailing in the wind and Max pulls me closer to his side when I start to shiver. It's still early enough that the bright Fijian sun isn't out in full force just yet.

I snuggle down into the plush leather of the seats and huddle against Max for warmth before realizing he's filming the entire exchange in selfie mode. I'm acting like a girlfriend with him when I don't even know he's filming. That may be cause for concern, but I don't have time to think about it too much because heat is radiating from his skin and his smell glides over me like silk.

I'm at peace here, and it could be an hour, or five minutes, or three days when we arrive at the Sawa-I-Lau caves. I'm so engrossed in the smell and the feel of his hard muscles against my soft curves that the construct of time no longer exists.

Berenado docks the boat and ties it to a post before helping Max and me (basically just me) out onto the water-warped wood of the dock. As we walk off the dock and to the beach, the beauty of the lush emerald trees threatens to steal my breath from my lungs.

Max secures his waterproof case on a lanyard around his neck and hits record on his phone. Once we reach the stone steps that descend downward into the cave system, my heart begins to race, and the further we go, the heavier the invisible rock in my stomach gets. I don't know if I'm actually claustrophobic or if the reality of being underneath the earth is what frightens me more.

When we reach the bottom of the steps Berenado turns around to face us, and true to form, is grinning ear to ear. At least one of us isn't on the verge of an episode…"Okay, guys, I'm going to hand you goggles so you can get better acquainted with your surroundings. You can leave your clothes and any items you don't want to get wet off to the side right here and we'll retrieve it when we finish up. I'll go first. Once we wade in you'll go through a small dark tunnel. You'll swim through to the other side and--"

Poor Berenado doesn't even get to finish his sentence before I lose all sense of social decorum and interrupt him. "I'm sorry, did you say small dark tunnel?"

Berenado chuckles lightly, "Yes, that's how you get to the lagoon."

"Oh, hell no," I yell at an octave louder than I meant to as my heart begins to palpitate.

Max's strong hand laces his fingers through mine, "Don't worry baby, I'll protect you. You don't have to be afraid."

"Don't patronize me!" I yell. "Have you never seen a scary movie? I swim through the dark hole and a giant flesh-eating Alaskan Bull Worm comes from deep within the watery depths and swallows me whole."

Max chuckles. I cannot believe he finds my panic amusing. I want to kick him in the shin for it. He's apparently trying to tempt me to fake break-up this fake relationship, and I may not be a killer, but don't push me.

"That's not a scary movie, it's an episode of *SpongeBob*. This isn't Bikini Bottom and people do this literally all the time. Don't you think someone would've been eaten by now? Or are you so full of yourself that this supposed Alaskan Bull Worm would pick you out of the thousands of others that came before you?"

He's entirely too smirky right now. I can't stand it.

"Look at me! I'm sure I'd taste delicious!" I yell out before realizing the implication of what I just said. My cheeks flush crimson, and Berenado finds a spot on the wall to stare at. When my eyes land on Max, my cheeks threaten to flush for a completely different reason and gone is the embarrassment I felt only seconds ago, replaced with pure, gut-wrenching, lust.

The green in his eyes burn jade with heat, and with that one look alone I can feel the little clothing I have on become entirely too suffocating. His teeth graze his bottom lip, and the hunger in his eyes feels like it could be the death to my flimsy resolve.

He steels himself, and I know it's taking a lot of willpower for him not to respond to my slip up, "Tell you what. We'll go through the dark hole, and if an Alaskan Bull Worm jumps out and eats us, I'll let you say, 'I told you so.' I know how much you love that."

The heat from only a few seconds ago temporarily banks, "I don't see how that will ease the sting of death, but fine."

He grins wildly, and Berenado has conveniently stopped staring at the spot on the cave wall that had him enthralled only moments before. We all strip down to our bathing suits and leave our clothes in a pile off to the side of the cave.

Berenado wades in first, followed by Max, who guides me into the water slowly. I try to let my body acclimate to the temperature of the water as Berenado hands out our goggles.

I'm shivering, and I don't know if it's because of the temperature of the water, the fear of swimming through a dark tunnel, or the fact that Max watched me wade into the water with an innerving focus that made me feel naked. Probably a combination of all three, but the water is definitely cold enough that my stupid nipples are hard against my orange bikini top.

I notice Max's stare dips down to my chest, but thankfully he has enough decency not to say anything out loud. I've realized he can be a loose cannon sometimes and I genuinely have no idea what's going to come out of his mouth.

He pulls me farther into the water so I'm deep enough that I'm covered up to my neck, and I feel goose bumps burst all over my arms and legs. At this stage, my body has acclimated to the temperature of the water, so the shivering currently wracking my body is one hundred percent because I'm scared.

"*Gattina*, look at me." Max says quietly so that only I can hear and tucks his finger underneath my chin. His eyes flash with a certainty that makes me feel like time could stand still if he willed it to. "As long as you're with me, you're safe."

My heart gives a sharp thud against my rib cage and those words seem to melt away my fear because for some stupid reason I believe him. The earnestness in his eyes tells me everything I need to know. My trust isn't always given away easily, but somehow over the last few days Max has earned it. It makes me want to swoon and scream in terror in equal measure.

Ew, I did not just say swoon...

We strap on our goggles and Max gives Berenado his phone so he can take a quick picture of us before we swim through. Max throws his arm around my shoulders, and I snuggle into his chest while we give a thumbs up to the camera, getting ready to submerge ourselves completely.

We decide the best way to do this is for me to be in the middle, that way if I start to panic Max will be behind me and Berenado will be in front of me. The sad thing is that it's not even a long swim, and this might be the scariest thing I've ever done. Well, besides telling my parents I didn't want to be a lawyer. That was downright terrifying.

Berenado goes under first and I follow closely behind, letting the cold-water chill me from head to toe as I'm completely submerged. I feel the pressure of the water enveloping me and I follow Berenado up to the mouth of the hole in the cave wall, he pushes himself through, but I hesitate. I can't see all the way through to the other side and something similar to panic threatens to claw at my lungs along with the lack of oxygen.

I feel a warm hand press against my lower back, so different from the cold water surrounding us. Max gives me a warm smile and a small nod, as he gestures to the opening. He may not be able to speak to me, but I know what he's saying. His words from moments before flooding my brain, *"As long as you're with me, you're safe."*

I steel myself and gather the strength to crawl to the hole and push myself through. What I'm able to see is absolutely beautiful, and the sheer fact that I'm swimming through a cave would take my breath away, if I had any left that is.

Seconds later I'm on the other side, and I swim to the surface gasping for oxygen to refill my lungs. Only moments later Max pops up right next to me, grinning ear to ear, "Well, what do you know, not a Bull Worm in sight."

I see Berenado sitting on a rock jutting out of the cave wall, and we both start swimming towards him. "Don't get cocky, we haven't swum back through yet."

He rolls his eyes in mock annoyance, "If I didn't know any better, I'd think you wanted to get eaten just so you could be right."

"Honestly, that doesn't seem too out of character for me," I laugh while we reach the rock that Berenado is laying on.

The cavern we're in stretches high above our heads and jade moss lines the rock formations jutting out of the walls while water cascades over one side of the cavern. The water is crystalline, and so blue that it looks like I'm swimming through liquid sapphire. It's more beautiful than my mind could've ever pictured, and to think I almost didn't let go of my fear enough to see it.

We spend a good portion of time swimming in the crisp water and laying out on large rocks. Max looks ecstatic with the amount of footage he's gotten. I realize I haven't seen Berenado for a while, and I start to look around the cave for him.

What I find shocks me as I watch Berenado climb up the rock towards a larger one jutting out of the cave wall. Once he reaches it, he maneuvers himself to the top of the rock and walks towards the edge.

I look over to see Max studying our guide's every movement, and the look of wonder on his face does not bode well for the future me, I can already tell. Berenado jumps from the ledge and lands in the water effortlessly, as if he does this every day, which I guess he might.

Berenado pops back up to the surface with that same huge smile on his face. Max swims forward and claps him on the back, "Dude that was amazing! I have to try that."

"Oh yes, it's simple enough, there's distinct foot holds and everything. The hardest part is getting from the wall to the platform, but it's not too bad," Berenado replies modestly.

"*Gattina*, I bet that would be great footage if we jumped off the ledge together!" Max says excitedly. I don't know if I've ever seen this man as happy as when he's near danger, or convincing me to partake in said danger, and that really concerns me.

"Oh. Hell. No." I say curtly.

"Ugh, pick a new phrase already," he admonishes in a pouting tone. This adult man went to a pouting child at an alarmingly rapid rate.

I feel a heavy rock form in my stomach at the idea of climbing a literal cave wall, "What if I fall to my death and hit every rock on the way down?" I ask as I try to subdue the internal panic I'm feeling in my voice.

"Does everything have to end in death with you?" He asks while trying and failing to mask his irritation.

"You know, I do enjoy a good serial killer documentary every now and again," I reply with indifference.

A small smirk tugs at his lips, "So you're either watching cartoons or true crime documentaries?"

I lightly shrug my shoulders, "I believe life is about balance."

He chuckles lightly, and I can't help but watch the tattooed muscles in his arms flex as he treads water. "Fair enough, but this lagoon seems to be murderer free, so maybe put the death panic on hold and do something adventurous for once."

"Death Panic would be a great name for an emo band," I respond trying to change the subject.

He looks at me with narrowed eyes, "Josie, quit stalling. You're in Fiji for Christ's sake, live a little."

I hate him for it, but he's right. Not that I'd ever say that to his face, but I came on this trip because I needed a little crazy in my life, some adventure. I wanted to come away from this trip feeling like a new woman. A new woman who's in charge of her own life, one that lives for herself instead of others. This isn't the time to play it safe, it's the time for new experiences.

I inhale a deep breath through my nose before exhaling through my mouth, "Fine. But if I die, I'm coming back and haunting your ass."

His grin is so wide it threatens to melt my insides from just how adorable it is, "When I see redrum on my bathroom mirror, I'll remember you fondly."

I roll my eyes at him as he hands Berenado his phone to record, and we swim over to the rock's edge. We shake the excess water off our hands and feet and Max has me go first so he can walk me through the foot and hand holds our guide had showed him.

The rock is cool underneath my palms, and I'm shaking with nervousness once more as Max walks me step by step along the cavern wall. The rock can't be more than ten feet high, but that's still enough for me to regret ever attempting this when I make the stupid mistake of looking down as I climb.

"Josie, you're safe with me," Max reassures as he moves closely behind me. Once again his words soothe me, and I get to the hardest part, the junction between the cavern wall and the jutting rock that I have to climb onto in order to jump.

I steel my spine, and steady my hand. *I can't do this. Oh my God I'm not physically strong enough to do this. What was I think-*

ing? I hate exercise. There's no way I'm strong enough to brace my arms enough to hold me.

I look down once more, and I might as well be on top of the empire state building for how high up I feel like I am.

"Josie, are you okay?" Max asks, slight hesitation creeping into his voice.

"Um, I don't know if I have the upper body strength for this," I reply, not even trying to hide the tremble in my voice.

"Would it help if I was on the rock and pulled you over?"

"Umm... yes," I respond in a shaky voice.

"Okay, one second," he says before climbing upwards and is right behind me on the wall. His legs and arms are long, and I swear this man is part spider monkey with the way that he doesn't even break a sweat while climbing and swinging himself towards the ledge and pulling himself up.

When he lands on the platform he extends his arm out, and I grab hold of it as I maneuver myself to move onto the platform. I push down with my supporting leg, and Max helps me the rest of the way as I land on solid rock.

Oh my God... I actually did it.

Berenado gives us a thumbs up in reassurance as we walk to the edge of the platform, and I realize I never let go of Max's hand. He gives me a small reassuring smile, "Would it help if I held your hand?"

This entire experience is going to be enough adrenaline to last a lifetime, and all I can do is nod my head furiously as I look down at the water in the cavern below us. I'm unable to speak due to both fear and the beauty of the glittering water below us.

Max uses his hand to guide my gaze to meet his, "Josie, I know this is scary, but you're strong, you can do this. You climbed all the way up here; this is the easy part. All you have to do is jump. No matter what happens, I swear to you I will not let go of your hand. Okay?"

"Okay," I squeak.

"Alright, we jump on three," he says, giving my hand a quick squeeze.

"One," my heart is beating wildly in my chest.

"Two," I can hear the blood roaring in my ears.

"Three," I push down and jump outward. Feeling weightless, Max and I both scream as we hurtle towards the water. Max squeezes my hand one more time before impact and then I'm surrounded by cool crisp water.

It takes a second for me to get my bearings, and I feel the tug of Max's hand as he helps me towards the surface. When I break free, I suck in a lungful of air and shout wildly.

I feel untamed, giddy, euphoric. Now I understand what an adrenaline rush truly is, because this feeling is indescribable. My eyes find Max's and his face is full of pride, "Oh my God that was amazing!" I yell before throwing my arms around him in an embrace.

It must be a reaction to the insane amount of endorphins running through my bloodstream, but I don't care. I want to feel his skin pressed against mine. He pulls away just enough so his hazel eyes can meet mine. "See! I told you you could do it."

I nuzzle into his touch lightly, enjoying how warm he is despite the chill of the water. I realize that we've been holding each other for too long and force myself to push away from him. When I do, it's so cold. Too cold, without him pressed against me. I hate it.

"Let's go see the footage that Berenado got!" I say with entirely too much enthusiasm to be believable. Max looks like he might say something, but then thinks better of it and swims to the edge with me like he wasn't responsible for me feeling ten emotions in the span of five minutes.

Chapter 14

Max

The morning after Sawa-I-Lau I wake up with slightly sore muscles and the light smell of coconut drifting off the pillow next to me. Josie must be exhausted because this is the first time I've woken up before her.

I know it's probably weird that I'm staring at her, but I can't help myself. Even asleep she's so beautiful it hurts. Her purple bonnet has her curls swept up inside, leaving the slope of her neck exposed and I fight the urge to trail kisses along the smooth brown skin there.

Her thick lashes sweep across her cheeks, her lips slightly parted as she takes small even breaths. I'm in awe of her, and that fucking terrifies me. There are so many reasons why hooking up with Josie would be a terrible idea, and yet I find myself caring less and less about the consequences of my actions the more time I spend with her.

Maybe I'm just one of those idiots that wants what they can't have, and the moment I possess her body like I so desperately want to, I won't be interested in her anymore. I can't do that to her, not just because I'm not an asshole but also because there are way too many variables.

Her best friend and my best friend are all but married, and

Liam's already told me he plans on proposing in the next year. No matter how you spin it, Josie and I are going to be in it for the long hall. I can't fuck up the future of our relationship and make it awkward forever just because I can't stop thinking about how she would taste coming apart on my tongue.

The shower incident was bad enough, and I'm more than willing to admit it was a slip in my control, but we've been able to get past it so far. There are no guarantees that if we fucked it would be the same outcome though, and that's why I just need to get over myself and keep this relationship strictly in the realm of fake.

I feel Josie stir in the bed next to me before stretching like a cat and opening her eyes. Her soft brown irises have a tint of amusement in them, and I realize I've been caught admiring her. I can't even bring myself to be ashamed of it in all honesty.

"Good morning, Donkey Kong," she grumbles lightly before stretching some more.

"Good morning, *gattina*," I smile. "How'd you sleep?"

"Like a coma patient. I think all the adrenaline from yesterday gave me a hangover," she responds while turning on her side to look at me.

"Ah, yeah well get ready for round two, it's seventh heaven day." I say while trying not to stare at the sliver of skin that was exposed with her movement, making her sleep shirt ride upwards.

"Seventh heaven? Isn't that a game where you go into a dark closet for seven minutes and make out with someone?" her brows crinkle in confusion.

"No, that's seven minutes in heaven, but if you want to play that game, I'm sure I can find room in our busy schedule." I reply with a wink. *I haven't even made it five minutes without flirting with her, this is bad, very bad.*

I lightly clear my throat, "But uh, this is the floating restaurant where we'll go snorkeling at."

She rolls her eyes so dramatically I'm shocked they don't get stuck in the back of her head. She flings the covers off her body and walks toward the closet, slipping on a pair of yoga shorts underneath her sleep shirt much to my chagrin.

Josie walks over to the sink and starts what seems to be a never-ending skincare routine. She looks over at me with suds on her face, almost covering her shy expression. "Hey, I know we're leaving in a few hours, but I was wondering if we could just order breakfast to the room? My social battery is low, and if I'm going to be in a restaurant floating in the middle of the ocean, surrounded by strangers, I'll need to decompress beforehand. Yesterday was so fun, don't get me wrong, but it was a lot."

"Understandable. Do you want me to leave? I can go to the gym for a bit if you want." If she wants me to give her space I wouldn't be offended, this trip so far has been a lot, even for me. Normally my assignments aren't nearly this hands-on.

Her soft brown eyes flit over to mine, giving me a perplexed look. "Weirdly enough, no. Would you want to hang out and watch cartoons with me?" She looks like her own question shocked her while she asked it.

Honestly, I would love nothing more than to lay around on the couch and watch cartoons with her. A lazy morning with Josie sounds like perfection, but I can't seem too eager, so instead I respond, "Depends. What are the options?"

Josie grabs the remote and starts flipping through channels on the tv, "Looks like *SpongeBob* or..."

"*SpongeBob*."

She looks at me, her eyebrows lifting with amusement. "But you don't even know the other options?"

I shrug, "Doesn't matter. *SpongeBob* wins. *SpongeBob* always wins."

"Fair enough," she chuckles.

"If this is the Alaskan Bull Worm episode I'll know for sure we're in a simulation." I say with amusement.

She laughs, and the sound makes me smile like an idiot. "No, it's the jellyfish house party one," she replies.

"A true American classic," I chuckle.

I place our breakfast order on the hotel's website when a text pops up on my screen from Shawna.

Shawna: Love the footage so far, very cute, but I want to really sell the romance aspect. We need more passion, some heat. Definitely need at least one kissing picture. You know? I don't know, maybe it's the pregnancy hormones talking, but it needs more spice. We're supposed to be selling the romance of the island. I'm not saying whore yourself, but like... whore yourself.

Me: I honestly don't even know how to respond to that.

Shawna: Designers, make it work.

I groan loudly and pinch the bridge of my nose. I know when she says the phrase "Designers, make it work," that I'm supposed to basically figure out whatever creative nonsense words she throws out and make it make sense. Shawna is incredibly talented, and also incredibly obsessed with *Project Runway*, but sometimes she'll have visions in her head that are difficult for her to explain, so it's my job to take whatever feedback she throws my way and give her a finished project that matches what she's thinking.

Whore myself... but don't whore myself...that has to be the most nonsensical feedback she's ever given me.

Me: You sent me to a bondage class. How much spicier could this possibly get. Also how is that not some sort of HR violation?

Shawna: Oh, I'm sorry, I thought you wanted this assignment?

Me: Yeah, yeah, all right. I get it.

"Everything okay?" Josie asks, peeking over at me.

I laugh, but it's hollow. "Yeah, it's just my boss. She says she needs more spice. She wants footage of a kiss."

Her face contorts into a quizzical look, "Uhh... like what kind of kiss? Like a peck? Or like passionately?"

"Is that something you're comfortable with? A more than a peck kiss?" I question, trying to read the look on her face but falling short.

She shrugs, "I mean sure. We're adults and everything. No big deal."

Huh. Not the reaction I expected from her, that's for sure. "Well, if you really aren't bothered by it, tomorrow would probably be one of the best days to film something like that. Maybe under the waterfall?"

A wry grin plays along her lips, "Oh yeah, that's perfect. I mean what's more romantic or passionate than making out under a waterfall?" her eyes become reverent, and I wish I could know what she was thinking about right now.

I on the other hand have a head full of radio static, and the only words that I can hear are make out and waterfall. My dick threatens to harden just at the thought of it.

This is a professional arrangement. Not an actual make out. It needs to be clinical at best.

I extend my hand towards Josie, "Perfect, so I'll pencil you in for a 1:00 pm make out session for tomorrow afternoon under the waterfall."

She snorts and takes my hand in hers, shaking it lightly. "I look forward to our meeting."

———

Later that day we board the small speedboat we chartered to take us out to Seventh Heaven, and we dock against the restaurant. When they say this restaurant is in the middle of the ocean, they weren't kidding. There's literally nothing else around us, just the expanse of a teal-colored ocean and a bright blue sky with cotton ball clouds.

I climb up the small ladder to the restaurant first and hold out my hand to help Josie up. She has that same red bathing suit that cuts into a deep-V that she wore a couple days ago with a see-through white cover-up hanging from her shoulders and her coveted mirrored aviator sunglasses. I think I'm at the point where she could wear a potato sack and jewelry made from bread-ties and I'd think she was hot. Which is a very dangerous place to be in.

"Wow," Josie remarks on an exhale as we take in our surroundings. The boat is all wood paneling and multiple stories tall with a ledge jutting from the top floor to jump from. The bottom floor we're on now boasts a large bar area and tables where we'll order lunch.

There are swarms of people from all walks of life in this random little floating restaurant in the middle of the Pacific Ocean, and it amazes me that we all somehow found our way here.

As we move farther into the first floor, a smiling woman with a tray full of shot glasses that are half orange and half red greets us. "Bula! Welcome to Seventh Heaven, would you like one of our welcome shots?"

I look at Josie and she nods rapidly. I grab out my phone, realizing I should probably be recording this, and ask a random stranger nearby to take a video of us. We pluck the shots off the tray before clinking them together and downing them. The sugary sweetness of the alcohol and what I think is orange juice and grenadine makes my lips pucker.

I look over at Josie however, and she's doing a little happy dance after taking hers. "I could drink one hundred of these!" she muses while taking another one off the tray and downing it.

I grab my phone from the random stranger and start steering Josie towards the tables so we can order lunch before I end up cleaning up orange and red vomit when we haven't even made it fully into the restaurant yet. "Woah, slow down there," I say before she attempts to take a third shot glass from the tray.

She shoots me a glare before we sit at the table and order five variations of different dumplings and pot-stickers and share them all. She was annoyed when we first sat down that I steered her away from the shots that were basically just liquid sugar. But she seems perfectly content now doing the same happy dance from before, dipping a pot sticker in sauce and popping it into her mouth.

"I want to meet whoever made these pot stickers and give them a nice fuck," Josie says around a mouthful of food.

"Is it too late to tell you I made them?" I say wiggling my brows suggestively.

She snorts while picking up a dumpling and promptly shoveling it in her mouth, "You've been with me the entire time, so unfortunately I think your cover is blown."

"But just so I'm clear, if I was the one that made the dumplings, would I be the one that was blown?" I ask, suppressing a smile.

"Correct," she responds with a wink that makes my dick twitch underneath my purple swim trunks. I should've worn spandex underneath them apparently. If I stood up right now the little crush I'm starting to develop will be the least of my worries.

God, a crush? Jesus, Max, are you twelve?

Honestly, as pathetic as it sounds, I am a full adult man with a stupid fucking crush. My jaw flexes in irritation. Only my dumbass would shout out the name of the one woman that would actually affect me this way. I couldn't have picked any of the unnamed women I've had a casual hookup with?

Apparently not.

But seriously, who could blame me? That kiss defied all logic. I made her dance with me because I thought it'd be funny to annoy her. I knew she was hot, because obviously I have eyes, but I always thought she hated me.

Yeah, that kiss was... a cataclysm, the beginning and the ending of everything.

I feel like I've just been gaslighting myself into thinking this was like any other woman I've been attracted to, but Josie is different. The problem is though, am I able to be different? Am I even capable of being what she needs? Probably not.

In all the situations we've been put in, this is when I have the revelation? Not when I had her tied up and at my mercy. Not when she had wrapped her arms around me as we rode on my bike. Not when I watched her come undone while her fingers pumped in and out of her perfect pussy. It's when she's cramming her mouth full of dumplings.

Naturally.

I can't decide if Josie should be a model for *Dumpling Digest*, or if I really just have it so bad for her that I find her adorable like this. She seems at peace, surrounded by water and a couple shots deep, her skin glowing in the sunlight while she eats. Her curls are just how I like them, wild and untamed from the boat ride. Seeing Josie free and uninhibited is going to be death to my resolve.

Maybe this is a little more than a crush...

I don't know how long I've been spacing out, but Josie waves a hand in front of my face trying to get my attention. "Hello, Max, nice of you to join us back on planet Earth. While you were gone Kanye West became president and the thirty-seventh *Fast and the Furious* movie just came out."

"Is that the one where they steal hover cars?" I ask before grabbing a spring roll and dipping it in the peanut sauce.

"The very same. *The Fast and The Furious: Undercover Hover*," she deadpans.

I laugh so hard I almost choke on my spring roll. "I can't wait to hear what President West thinks of this."

She leans back in her chair, taking a sip of her water. "Rumor has it he stood up in the middle of the premier and said 'Yo, *Under Cover Hover*, I'm really happy for you, I'ma let you finish, but *Tokyo Drift* was one of the best movies of all time!'"

I laugh so hard my eyes start to water, "Just how many pop culture references can you fit in a five-minute span?" I say when I can finally breathe again.

"In the words of Cady Herron, 'the limit does not exist.'" she says, quoting the famous line from *Mean Girls*. My sisters and I watched that movie so many times I could quote the entire thing from start to finish.

"Okay, Snapple facts, are you done eating? It looks like the band is starting up. Maybe we can dance for a bit?" A very serious blush crosses her cheeks, and I know she's thinking about the other night.

I want to tell her that she doesn't need to be embarrassed, and that was probably the second sexiest fucking thing I've ever seen. The first being when I watched her follow my every command in the shower, but I feel like that's crossing a boundary. Even though I've thought about her dripping wet for me every day since then.

I quickly change the subject, hoping I didn't just make her feel awkward. "On second thought, maybe we should get some drinks and head up to the top deck and lay out for a bit?"

I see a small smile begin on her face, "That, um, sounds good. Let's do that. Alcohol... good." Her eyes go wide, and her face flushes hotter.

I'm going to go ahead and put her out of her misery and not comment on whatever that just was. We go to the bar and order a whiskey sour and tequila sunrise before we climb the two flights of stairs to the top deck.

We find two lounge chairs next to each other that face out towards the ocean and set our stuff down. Josie walks towards the railing and peers out over the enclosure. I can't see her eyes underneath her aviators, but I'd bet they're so wide they take up half of her face right now. Her gaze then slowly turns towards the platform where people are already jumping off into the water. She looks queasy.

"How do you feel about jumping from the platform before we go snorkeling?" I ask like I don't already know the answer.

Her head flits quickly in my direction, and I can see my smug reflection in her sunglasses. "Are you bat shit crazy? Look at that drop off!"

I walk towards her before leaning against the railing. "Let me guess, you're going to hit every floor on the way down, cracking your head open, only to land directly into a shark's mouth and be swallowed whole?"

She stiffens before giving me a knowing smile, "You laugh, but sharks can smell blood from a quarter of a mile away. I'm no fool."

"What if I offered to jump in front of a shark so it would eat me instead of you? What would you say to that?" I counter.

"I'd say you're an even bigger idiot than I previously thought," she fires back with a smile.

"What if I hold your hand? Would you jump then?" I probably sound pathetic, but when I offered yesterday to hold her hand, it helped convince her. I try not to let the warm feeling that she feels safe with me squeeze my chest too much.

I see her brows scrunch together, deep in thought, and not for the first time I wish I could hear what she's thinking. "This is taller than the cave jump," she whispers, and I can't tell if she's telling me that or herself.

"It is," I answer anyway. I know she's scared, so I inch my hand towards hers on the banister and link her pinkie finger with mine. "Josie, you're safe with me," my words from yesterday echoing back to the present.

She sucks in a sharp breath, the small touch of her pinkie finger curled against mine on the handrail is enough to spike my heart rate more than any jump from a platform ever could.

"Putting your fake girlfriend in near-death situations must be your kink," she retorts before steeling her spine.

"I'm pretty sure anything you do is my kink." The words fly out of my mouth before I have a chance to stop them. Her eyebrows are threatening to enter her hairline they shoot up so high.

Fuck. Fuck. Fuck. How do I even recover from this?
Can anyone even recover from this?
Doubtful.

I clear my throat; I'm just going to own it. It's not like it's not true anyway. Everything Josie does seems to have some sort of lust-inducing spell on me.

"So does this mean you're going to jump with me?" I know my exterior is a lot more confident than I'm currently feeling on the inside. Normally I have no issues in the confidence department, but for some reason Josie is the exception to the rule. I've come to the conclusion it's because I care more about what she thinks of me than any of the other women I've ever been with, and I haven't even fucked her.

I don't know who I am anymore.

She sighs deeply, "As long as you promise to offer yourself up as bait if a shark comes."

"I promise," I smile. "Are you ready to go now?"

"No, but we need to go now because if I have more time to think about it then I won't do it," she responds before moving back to our chairs and grabbing our snorkel masks.

Okay, I guess we're doing this then.

We walk towards the platform and make sure our masks are firmly in place. "Okay, just remember. I'll be holding your hand the entire time, and blow out through the snorkel before you breathe in."

"Yep. Gotcha. No water is getting in these lungs. Nope. No way." Even her babbling is cute.

I turn the camera on in the waterproof case around my neck before linking my fingers through hers. "Same as before, we go after three, okay?"

She nods and takes a deep breath.

"One," her fingers tighten with mine.

"Two," she looks over the towering edge into the blue abyss beneath her. That's a mistake.

"Three," her fingers tighten against mine before we jump feet first off the ledge.

I don't know what it says about me that I feel more adrenaline from her hand squeezing mine than I do from jumping off a ledge, but I think I'm developing a complex.

A loud yell comes from the woman whose hand is linked in mine as we're suspended in the air for mere seconds before hitting the water.

There's a moment where everything stills. The calm from beneath the water as the pressure pushes against our bodies is soothing, and I realize then that I can open my eyes thanks to my snorkel mask.

I look over at Josie, a smile radiating from ear to ear as we swim towards the surface, and she gives me a thumbs up.

When we break through, we both blow through the snorkel tube, so the water comes out and she wraps her arms around my neck. "That was fucking amazing!" she squeals into the space between my neck and shoulder.

My heart is pounding in my chest at the feel of her arms wrapped around me, breathing in her coconut scent mixed with salt water. She pulls away slightly, her beautiful doe brown eyes looking at me in earnest, "Thank you for convincing me to do that, Donkey Kong."

I chuckle before bringing her closer to me once more, not ready to let her go just yet. The urge to just kiss her right here in the middle of the Pacific Ocean is so strong it takes all of my restraint to stop myself. I want to. *Desperately.*

But instead of that, I squeeze her against me one last time before pulling away. "Anytime, *gattina*. Now let's go see some fish." That's all I say before lowering myself back into the water and swimming away from the deck. The entire time we're under water I can never bring myself to let go of her hand, and it seems like she can't either. We stay that way, in our own little under-water bubble, holding hands and marveling at the brightly colored fish and coral until our legs are sore and it's time to swim back to the dock.

CHAPTER 15

JOSIE

I wake up the morning after snorkeling and somehow my legs and arms are even more sore than they were the day before. I groan, flinging an arm over my face. This is why I don't exercise.

I slept like shit last night. I could blame it on the sore muscles if I wanted to lie to myself, but the real reason doesn't allude me. Today is Kiss Day.

Kiss Day, the one that my dumbass thought would be no big deal. Surely, I must've blacked out during that conversation because the Josie that thought this was a good idea cannot be the same Josie currently laying in bed next to a man she's trying and failing not to be attracted to.

Where is the Josie that wanted to kick a smug Maximiliano in the balls? Is she in the room with us? Because in her wake is a Josie that's been dormant so long, I forgot she existed.

The horny one.

The one that likes dick.

Somehow, she's been forgotten. Locked away deep in the recesses of my brain along with all the bad feelings that come along with thinking about He-Who-Shall-Not-Be-Named whose name rhymes with sever. As in, I would rather sever my own big toe off than go back to that man.

I can't believe I even considered it. I really should talk to a therapist about why I'm so desperate to appease my parents, because I almost went back to a man who cheated on me after only barely being engaged.

This trip has given me clarity in so many ways, and I know now that even before Trevor cheated on me, we would never have been a good fit. He's so uptight, and although I don't have experience having sex with someone else, I'm pretty sure it should be fun.

I want what Ella and Liam have. I want the rip your clothes off because you can't stand waiting one more second to remove your clothes properly, sex. I want the earth shattering, heart gripping, mind numbing orgasm that comes from entrusting your entire body to another person.

I want to fuck Maximiliano.

Very badly.

God fucking damn it, I say dragging myself out of bed and heading towards the closet to pick out my outfit for the day. This was not the plan.

It truly wasn't.

But since I'm considering trying all these new things... maybe I should try out someone new too?

That's probably a terrible idea, but the part of me that's been neglected for some time now, the horny one, thinks it's a great idea.

The truth is, I've never had great sex before. I'm not saying it's Trevor's fault or anything, because I was a willing participant obviously, but I think I'm finally ready to put that part of my life in the past. To try sex again and see if it's really all people make it out to be, because I've got to be honest, I didn't understand what the big deal was.

But who better to show me if sex can be good than my fake

boyfriend who, let's be honest, knows his way around a vagina, or so he says anyway.

As I move the hangers in the closet back and forth trying to figure out what to wear to the waterfall today, that's when I make the decision. One that has nothing to do with my clothing choice and everything to do with the attraction that's been building more and more each day of the trip towards the man platonically sleeping in bed with me.

I'm going to propose an arrangement, just a small extension of the one we currently have. One that includes playing naked twister where every part of the board is right hand on clit.

Could this blow up in my face? Potentially.

Let's just chalk this up in the new experience's column: Motorcycle riding, last minute trip to the other side of the world, cave diving, snorkeling, and getting dicked down by my fake boyfriend.

I slip on an orange swimsuit with a drastically deep V and a back that dips all the way to the bottom of my spine before slipping my crocheted cover up over the top. It's probably the sexiest swimsuit I own, even though it's a one-piece, and I've been too nervous to bust it out. If the crocheted cover-up doesn't really actually cover up anything, well it's a sacrifice I'm willing to make. For the greater good. The greater good being my vagina, in case that wasn't clear.

No better time than when you decide to proposition your fake boyfriend to add a booty-call clause to your previous agreement I suppose.

When I walk over to the sink and grab my toothbrush, I look over at the bed where Max is still sound asleep, snoring lightly. His hair is slightly mussed, and he's tossed and turned enough in his sleep now that his white t-shirt is riding up and exposing the V cut of his abdomen.

Oh yes... why did I not think of this before? I'm mentally high fiving myself for this brilliant idea and also kicking myself for not thinking of it sooner.

Well probably because you were too busy being the Josie that wanted to serve Max a humble pie where the main ingredient was a swift kick to the balls. I tell myself as I start to brush my teeth.

Right...

I take my time with my makeup, coating my lashes with water-proof mascara and a deep red lip stain that should last while I swim. I pump my curl cream into my palm and rub my hands together before carefully coating my curls until they're ready to be styled. I separate my hair into two parts and braid each side until I have a set of pigtail braids.

I swipe on some deodorant and tropical body spray, feeling as confident on the outside as I can muster, and it's all I can do to tame the stomach full of butterflies on steroids I'm currently enduring.

Now if I can only be as confident on the inside as I am on the outside when I tell Max about my idea.

Easier said than done.

———

How does one exactly convince their fake boyfriend to become an active participant in the furthering of your sexual experiences? It's a question that plagued me the entire cab ride and subsequent boat ride to the island where we're hiking to the waterfall. The waterfall where we agreed we'd give Shawna the spice she's been looking for.

When we dock and get off the boat, I've gotten pretty good at not being afraid of falling down the crack now, we follow the directions our guide/captain gave us towards the waterfall. It's not difficult by any means, and there's a walking path the entire way, but I don't think the travel company Max is working on an assign-ment for wants the liability of us getting lost. Especially since the guide won't actually be walking back with us.

Nope. Just us two. *Alone.*

As we enter the forest, the canopy of trees is so thick that it blocks out any direct sunlight, and brightly colored birds flit back and forth between the trees. All of the shade gives off a light chill in the air, and for the first time since being in Fiji I wish I had a jacket. I rub my hands up and down my arms, cursing myself for wearing my most revealing clothing if only because now I'm cold.

"Are you cold?" Max asks as we step over vines that are growing across the path.

"A little…" I reply, doubling my efforts to scrub at my arms.

Without a second thought Max hooks a thumb in the back of the collar of his black t-shirt before pulling it off, handing it to me. I can't help it. I stop in my tracks and let my eyes drink in the man in front of me, all thick muscles and tattoos and olive skin that looks painfully lick-able. Honestly, all of this man is lick-able. How I ever thought I stood a chance against him is laughable.

I clear my throat lightly, "Um, thank you…" I say before taking the shirt and sticking my arms through the center so they're completely covered.

"Of course, *gattina*," he says with a smile of white teeth that are in contrast with the dark stubble that's grown since he last shaved.

I've never liked facial hair on a guy, but something about the way it looks on Max makes me want to feel it scrape the skin between my thighs.

God, what has gotten into me?

Then an idea of sheer brilliance strikes me. A question for a question. That's how I'll get my opening. We have a decent walk ahead of us, so this is sure to give me enough time to weasel in my proposition.

"Hey, want to play a game?" I ask nonchalantly as we move farther into the forest.

He looks back at me with an arched eyebrow, "A game?"

"Like a question for a question. Since we're pretending to date, maybe we should learn more about each other. Really sell it, you know?"

Josie Jones you brilliant little puppeteer.

"Yeah sure, why not?" he says while looking back at me with a smile as we walk farther down the dirt path.

"Okay, I'll go first. Favorite color?" I ask.

"Black."

I roll my eyes, "Why does that not surprise me."

"Well, I'd ask you what your favorite color is, but I already know it's orange." he says matter-of-factly. I smile to myself while he's not looking, his back slightly in front of me as we walk. Why do I love that he knows that about me without me even having to say it?

"Okay, your turn," I tell him.

"Favorite food?" he asks over his shoulder.

"Fish sticks."

He stops walking, turning around to look at me with his eyebrows scrunched together in confusion. "Are you joking?"

I fold my arms close to my chest as I keep walking, passing him. "No. Have you ever had a fish stick from the air fryer? Alternate between ketchup and tartar sauce and its chef's kiss." I say while doing the motion that goes along with the saying.

"No one's favorite food is fish sticks. Didn't you grow up rich? I figured it'd be caviar or some steak that comes from cows who are given a Swedish massage before they die or something."

"My family wasn't always this well off," I say quietly. "For the first eight years of my life we lived like a normal suburban family. Little ranch house. My parents worked their asses off trying to get their own law firm up and running. Scraping any and all money they could muster to get it started. They met at a law firm, fell in love immediately, and got pregnant with me. My grandparents and my mom are estranged, so they eloped at the courthouse downtown before they decided to build an empire all on their own. We ate fish sticks a lot growing up because my parents just needed something quick they could make before getting back to work. Somehow even though they were working constantly, we were happier then. I guess that's how I know that I'd rather have a happy middle-class life, than an empty rich one. When I eat them now it reminds me of a simpler time before money ruined everything."

He catches up to me with a few long strides, "Oh... that makes sense. Sorry if I came off... well..."

"Don't apologize," I say waving him off. "I didn't mean to emotionally divulge my entire life to you when we were having a simple conversation about fish sticks." I say with a smile.

"Don't be. I like it. When you open up to me, I mean. Much better than you hating me that's for sure," he says with a grin as we walk side by side on the narrow pathway.

"Who said I don't still hate you?" I reply with a smirk.

He chuckles, "Oh no you don't, *gattina*. You can't fool me. I've worn you down. Dare I say you might even enjoy my company now."

"God, help me, I think I actually do." I reply with a facepalm.

He gives me a devious grin, "Okay, your turn. You ask a question."

Do I do it now? Just go for it? I have a lot of unearned confidence apparently, because what comes out of my mouth next shocks even me. "Do you like eating out? Not like, at an Applebee's, but like a vagina?"

Once again, I've stopped the man in his tracks, his eyes growing wider by the second. "I'm sorry, the first question you asked me was what my favorite color is. The second one, naturally the progression went to 'do I like eating out, but not like Applebees'?'"

My face heats, I might as well lean into it. I give a little shrug. "I'm just curious if guys actually like that or if it's something that's only in my romance books? I mean Ella and I talk and everything, and she's told me, well everything, but I wondered if maybe Liam was just a fluke..."

His eyes narrow slightly and look even more confused than before. "Why would that be something only reserved for your romance novels and Liam?" He starts to smirk at the mention of his friend. Does he think my confusion is amusing?

My eyes drift upwards to the canopy above us, not wanting to look at him when I mention this. I'm so inexperienced compared to this man it's laughable. "Well, it's just never happened to me before. Trevor didn't like doing it. So, I thought maybe, that was how most guys are?"

His eyes grow hard as I finally meet his gaze. I can't believe we're standing on a dirt path in the middle of a damn forest having this conversation. "Are you saying no one's ever eaten you out before?" He seems genuinely perplexed at the idea.

"Well, no. I've only been with one guy before, Trevor, and he said it was gross, but maybe it was me that was gross." I start to feel that foreboding in my stomach. The one that reminds me I'm not good enough, not perfect enough. My eyes squeeze shut, willing the feeling to go away.

Shove it in a box in the corner of my head... Just shove it in the box.

"I love it," he says bluntly. My eyes fly open in response, and he's looking directly at me, like he can see right down to the very core of me. "In fact, there's almost nothing I love more than having a woman come on my face and making it so wet I spend the rest of the day tasting her. Fuck, I would willingly drown doing it. The only thing better is feeling a woman come on my cock."

I have no words. I'm completely incapable of speaking, my mouth is so dry it feels like I stuffed it with cotton balls. A warm feeling melts in my lower belly, heating my blood and making an ache bloom in my core.

But that's not all, he has more to say apparently. "If that asshole actually thinks that eating a woman out is gross then he's even more of an idiot than I thought. He should be honored you even wanted to let him lick you to an orgasm."

I shift uncomfortably, not sure how to explain that wasn't even an option anyway, but how do you explain you can't get an orgasm from another person to the man you're trying to casually proposition a situationship with?

"Wait, he has given you an orgasm before, right?" *Now how the fuck?* Did he read my mind or something?

"Is that your question?" I ask anxiously before I start walking again.

"Yes. Now answer it," he says in a hard tone, once again catching up with me in a few quick strides so we're walking side by side.

I let out a deep sigh, "No. I've never had an orgasm with anyone other than myself. Unless you count my Sucky Sucky, which is the name of my vibrator."

My eyes flit to his, and there's a hunger there that threatens to curl my toes. "No, that doesn't count," he responds, his voice sounding rougher than before.

I wave the thought away with my hand, "It's fine. I guess I'm just one of those women who can't orgasm from sex. It is what it is." My tone is a lot more flippant than I actually feel.

"Or you just haven't found the right man to put that theory to the test with yet," his voice is impossibly low now, and the heat in my lower belly grows exponentially at what sounds like a proposition.

This is it Josie, this is your opening. Take it!

"What if I was looking for someone to potentially test that theory with? For scientific purposes of course." I look everywhere but in his eyes, afraid of what I might find there.

He doesn't give me an option though as we approach the roaring waterfall now in our line of sight. He grabs my wrist still covered in his shirt and pulls me against his chest so that my breasts press against him. My breathing turns shallow as my eyes trail up his bare chest, to his neck, to his lush mouth that says such dirty things it makes me shiver, until they land on his burning eyes.

I let the shirt hanging from my arms drop to the brush at our feet, as his thumb gently tugs on my lower lip. "Are you asking me for an orgasm, *gattina*?"

I swallow an invisible lump in my throat, "I have a proposition for you," I say as my voice grows husky.

"I'm listening," he replies as that same thumb lightly traces down my neck to where my pulse is thumping wildly in my throat.

"What if we expanded the parameters of our relationship into a category that includes more... benefits?"

"Benefits?" He says with a smile that's all Cheshire Cat leading Alice astray.

I clear my throat lightly, letting the small action give me time to build my confidence for what I'm about to say next. "Well, you've been helping me try new things, and well... This would be something new, for me, anyway. I've never had a friends with benefits situation before, and my sex life has been pretty vanilla, well really more like flour, up until this point. I need more... experience."

A look I can't decipher passes through his eyes, but it's gone so quickly I question whether I even saw it at all. "And who better to test it out with, than me?" He smiles then, all cocky smirk.

"Well, yeah." I reply as the sound of water gushing from the waterfall ahead of us grows louder.

His eyes harden slightly, "I don't do relationships though. You know that. I don't want you to get confused. Pretending to date me and then fucking me, that wouldn't be confusing for you?"

"I'm a grown woman. I can handle having sex without catching feelings." I say this with more confidence than I feel, but I want this. Desperately. The more I think about it, the more I crave it.

"Okay, *gattina*, let's do it," his voice is reduced to rubble now.

I audibly gulp, "Like now? Here?" I look at our surroundings. All trees and no people. The only sounds are the rustling of the wind on the leaves, the rushing of the waterfall, and the chirps of birds flying overhead. We're completely alone. *It looks like there are rocks behind the waterfall that could hide us beneath it...*

His fingers trail the divot of my collarbone, making my skin tingle with every drag. "Why not? There's no one else around. Unless you're having second thoughts?"

It shocks me, but I trust him. I know if I wanted to stop this right now, say I had a momentary lapse of judgment, he would stop. He wouldn't pressure me.

Somewhere along the line I actually started to trust Maximiliano Salvatore Rossi, and that fact alone might be more terrifying than what might happen next.

I inch my face closer to his, our noses almost touching. My voice comes out a little shaky, revealing my nerves. "No second thoughts, Maximiliano."

He inhales sharply before rubbing a tattooed thumb along my bottom lip, "Fuck, my name sounds so good coming out of that pretty little mouth."

I think he'll kiss me then, but instead he sets up the tripod with the camera facing towards the waterfall, turns around and kicks off his shoes at the lip of the water and wades in, throwing a smirk at me over his shoulder. "Come swim with me, *gattina*."

"But I thought...?" I trail off. I don't know what I thought exactly.

"Be patient, Josie. Sometimes the tension is the best part," he grins while pushing the wet hair out of his eyes with his tattooed hand. The motion makes his arm flex slightly and I swear I feel all my intimate muscles clench.

Jesus, Josie get ahold of yourself...

"Like foreplay?"

"Yes, baby, like foreplay."

"Oh, Trevor was never one for that," I say while sliding my sandals off my feet and kicking them to the side. I'm starting to realize Trevor wasn't one for much of anything but golfing and bitcoin.

His eyes grow hard, "Why does that not surprise me."

I shrug my shoulder and peel off my crocheted cover-up and shorts, leaving me in my very revealing swimsuit. I feel like I'm under a microscope with the way his hazel eyes study every inch of me. An action that might normally make me feel self-conscious, but with him just makes me feel sexy. Like he wants to devour me.

God, I hope he does.

His promise of an orgasm may end up equating to a Faustian deal, but the temptation is far too strong to ignore. If he really loves giving head as much as he says, I might finally know what it feels like to be eaten out, something that the me from a year ago just figured would never be in the cards for me.

Maybe even an orgasm I didn't give myself...

I won't hold my breath on that one, but if there was ever a hope of it happening, I feel like Max would be the one that could get me there.

By all accounts we don't make sense together. He's every bit of the bad boy vibes my parents always told me to avoid: tattoos, motorcycle, and a man whore. I'm the bubbly "innocent" girl with lofty expectations from my parents on marrying someone well-off and clean-cut so that I can have 2.5 kids and carry on their legacy.

He's everything they never wanted for me. They'll be pissed.

Why does that make me want to do this even more? Don't most people have their rebellious years in their teens, not when they're well into their twenties? Sounds like questions for my next therapy session.

Either way, this is the perfect scenario. I have a fake boyfriend my parents will hate, one that will show them just how serious I am about not going back to that bag of douchery, and I'll get to have fun while doing it. Maybe even an orgasm.

A win is a win.

My first situationship. Let's do this.

My inner sex goddess is high fiving the rational part of my brain. Great, we're all on board with this.

I step into the water slowly, until I'm wading waist deep, and I swear his eyes don't leave my body the entire time. I never knew not touching someone could be so intimate. That someone could make me wet with just the way they look at me.

It's possible, and it's happening right now as he crooks a finger telling me to meet him in the middle of the water. His smile is devious, and I lick my lips at the sheer thought of what that mouth could do to me.

I'm close to him now, my breasts grazing his chest with every rapid inhale of breath. The tension is thick, and I don't know who's supposed to make the first move in this scenario. I mean are we just going to stand a hair's breadth away from each other for the rest of eternity? How long have I been standing here now?

A millisecond?

Ten years?

I truly have no idea. I might as well be in a wormhole.

The unbearable tension breaks as his head bends towards mine, and I can't wait any longer as I meet him the rest of the way. Mere centimeters, but still, no more waiting for his mouth on mine.

When our lips meet, the kiss devours my soul. His lips are soft and warm, and he tastes like something that I could only describe as Max. A taste I never thought I would have again, but I'm remembering just how good it is.

A groan comes from deep in his chest as he presses me against him, one hand grabbing my ass and the other sinking into my hair as his tongue slips out and licks along my bottom lip, seeking to gain entrance. I open to him willingly, letting my tongue tangle with his as my hands grasp at him to try and somehow get him even closer.

I don't know if he could ever be close enough, but I arch my hips up to meet his, desperate to feel the hardness of him against my center. I gasp when I feel him, already so hard, adding delicious pressure to my clit.

It feels so good.

Better than I ever anticipated.

"Fuck, baby, you taste so good, and I haven't even had that pussy on my face yet," he whispers between kisses as he hooks his hands underneath my ass and lifts me. I wrap my legs around his hips, adding even more pressure.

He cups my ass to leverage me against him, moving me up and down on the hard length of him. I feel sparks behind my eyes, as he moves me against him in tandem, kissing down my throat and nibbling at my collar bone. The hard ridge and friction of him against me builds an ache at my core so strong that if he wasn't holding me, my knees would buckle.

I need more.

Skin.

Friction.

Pressure.

More *him*.

"Maximiliano, please," I whisper into his mouth when he brings his lips back to mine.

I've decided Max is the man I've been with the past five days. The one pushing me to new limits, testing my resolve, watching *SpongeBob* on the couch while we eat breakfast together, the soft snores coming from the spot on the bed beside me.

Who I have now is Maximiliano. Setting my skin on fire, tangling his hand in my braids and gripping my ass tight enough to leave marks. He's the one whose lips are devouring mine. His cock is the one pressing against my clit through our bathing suits. His voice is the one who talked me through a mind-numbing orgasm using just his words in the shower.

And if part of me has come to enjoy both Max and Maximiliano's company, well that's not a thought I really want to delve into as his heated skin is pressed against mine.

He nibbles my bottom lip, his voice a rough chuckle, "You're so pretty when you beg."

I squirm against him as he carries me across the water to the rocks hidden behind the waterfall while I kiss and lick down his throat.

I've become incensed. My hands, my mouth, my tongue. I want them to play against every part of him. I've become so quickly unraveled and begging for more. The man hasn't even proven my orgasm theory yet.

The world seems quieter behind the waterfall as he lays me out on a wide rock, panting and whining at the distance he's put between us. My skin feels itchy without the weight of him. The rush of the water cocoons us, drowning out the outside world.

"Swimsuit. Off. Now." He commands. I don't argue, reveling in the way he takes charge of me, and I dispose of my swimsuit on the rock next to us. His eyes spark with desire, my entire body on display for him, as he drinks me in.

My bare back is hot against the cold rock, the sensations of hot and cold lick at my skin. I'm writhing underneath his gaze, my body needing his on mine, not caring about a shred of pride or dignity I might want to hang on to.

No, that ship has long sailed, crashed into a body of rocks, and marooned all the passengers.

I should feel shame, embarrassment, any kind of anxiety at all, but I don't. All I feel is the desperate need to know what happens next.

"So are you going to do something, or just stare at me?" I quip.

His eyes narrow at me, "Be patient, Josie. If you try to rush me, I'll bend you over this rock and spank that perfect ass."

I feel my body grow hotter. Why does that not feel like a threat I would mind? The thought of his hand smacking against my behind and the twinge of pain that would go along with it sounds delicious.

Wow. I'm super fucked.

His thumb tugs at my bottom lip as he hovers over me, before making a slow descent down my body. "Mmm... Does my *gattina* want to be spanked?"

I shiver, his thumb gliding slowly down my throat. His perusal of me is torture, and I'm ninety percent sure my heartbeat is in my clit. "I fucking knew it. Such a *good girl*, but she wants that ass to be red."

I arch my back, begging his thumb to trail lower, but he doesn't succumb. He's at my collarbone.

My clavicle.

Dipping in the valley of my breasts.

My breathing is erratic as I watch his every move.

Instead of trailing lower, his fingers move to the side and roll my nipples between them. My back arches off the rock, a loud moan ripping from my throat at the shock of the new sensation.

"You're so responsive baby. Fuck, these nipples are begging for my mouth," he groans.

"Please," I beg pathetically.

His eyes flare, "That's my girl, begging so politely." His voice is playful but filled with lust and need like mine. However, his is on a leash. I'm on the verge of melting into a puddle if he doesn't give me more.

He leans forward, his lips so close to my pebbled nipple that when he speaks I can feel his breath against it. "Lucky for you, I was going to anyway," he groans before his mouth parts around my nipple. Laving and gently sucking around it while his other hand goes to roll my other between his fingers.

Fuck, it feels too good. The tandem motion of the sucking and licking causes a rush of wetness coating my thighs. I press them firmly together just to get pressure to my clit.

Can people come from nipple play? Because I think I just might. My body is craving his so badly that at this point any extra attention sends me reeling.

"Fuck, your tits are so perfect. Perfect for my hands, my mouth. One day I'm going to tie up your arms and legs so those pretty nipples are on display for me, and I can suck them for as long as I want."

I moan deeply as I get wetter just from the promise of his words. "Mmm... my good girl wants to be tied up and spanked? I knew you fucking liked it. Liked being at my mercy. I'm starting to think you're not much of a *good girl* at all."

He alternates between nipples, sucking and licking at one

while rolling the other between his fingers until I'm a squirming mess of need. I arch my hips upward, begging for him to give attention to the lower half of my body.

A dark chuckle emerges from his lips as his fingers trail lower, "Okay, baby. You've earned it."

He's at the bottom of my rib cage.

My soft belly.

My pubic bone.

So close.

His thumb glides through my folds, gathering wetness there before moving to my clit. Adding pressure and small circles that make me see stars.

"You're so wet for me, *gattina*." He says with rapt attention. "I haven't even begun to do everything I want to that beautiful body of yours. I've been thinking about what I want to do to you for weeks now."

"Weeks?" I ask between gasps as he circles my clit with his thumb and uses his other hand to separate the lips of my labia.

"Ever since that kiss. I've craved you. Tried to fight it, deny it, but when you came to me, I couldn't say no. Thank God, I didn't because this pussy baby? This pussy right here is fucking beautiful, and I'm going to enjoy every second of you coming on my face."

That's the only warning I get before he lowers his head and licks all the way from the bottom of my cunt and dipping into my entrance before circling my clit.

I could scream. Oh wait, I do scream. That's me, screaming.

I don't know what I expected getting head to feel like, but this is next level. I couldn't even begin to describe just how good his tongue feels gliding through me.

I'm so wet at this point I swear he could drown down there. In an instant I'm riding his face, arching my hips upward as I grind against his tongue. Seeking friction and moving in any way that will get me more of it.

I think this is the peak of pleasure, that there's no way anything could ever feel better than this.

"You taste like the best thing I've ever eaten," he moans into my clit while his finger slides inside me, filling me in a way I didn't even realize I needed, playing with my G-spot.

I was wrong. Surely this is the best it could ever be. His finger works my G-spot while his tongue licks circles around my clit.

Then he slides two fingers inside me, and I could fly off this rock right now. My hips grinding down onto his fingers, his tongue, his face as pressure builds hot in my core.

Fuck. I know this feeling.

The building, the cresting, the climbing feeling towards the top of the rollercoaster before you free-fall downward. I'm about to have an orgasm. An actual orgasm given to me by someone other than myself.

"You're close, aren't you, baby?" he says between licks. I claw at the rock at my sides, trying to find anything to hold on to. Something to ground me. Something to keep me from flying off this rock into another dimension.

"Come for me, *gattina*. I want to feel you gripping my fingers nice and tight," he says, his voice low and gravelly.

His words are all I need. My hands grip his hair trying to pull him off me because the feeling is too good, but he holds steady. Licking and sucking my clit while his fingers fuck me.

"Fuck, I'm coming," I yell as my hips grind down hard on his fingers.

"That's right, baby, you come on my face. I want you dripping down my chin." The sensation is pure ecstasy. Unlike any orgasm I've ever given myself. It doesn't even feel real. There is absolutely no describing the feeling of floating and also being electrocuted at the same time.

I ride the high as I ride his face, slowing the movement of my hips as he slows the motions of his tongue and fingers. He's helping me come back to earth, gently tethering me back to reality before I'm left boneless against the rock.

A cocky smile plays on his lips, "So, about you being one of those women who doesn't orgasm..."

I fling an arm over my eyes, the overstimulation of my surroundings and an earth-shattering orgasm too much all at once.

"You were right. I was wrong," I groan.

He climbs up on the rock next to me, a very angry looking bulge pressing against my thigh as he lifts my arm from my eyes and wraps it around his neck. "That must've been painful for you to admit," he deadpans.

I giggle. Fucking *giggle*. Lord help me, "It truly was."

I wonder if maybe he wants me to return the favor. Honestly, I would love to, the way he just ripped apart my every fiber and put it back together I want to make him feel good too.

My hand plays with the V-cut of his hips. Trailing downward to where his shorts hang low on his hips.

"*Gattina,* I don't expect you to do anything back."

"But... that looks painful, and I want to. Like really want to."

He smiles before kissing me gently on the lips. "The first time I come with you, it'll be in that pretty pussy." He says between pressing light kisses to my lips.

"So, you don't want a blow job?" I ask. I'm genuinely curious. I figured... Well, he'd expect it.

He arches an eyebrow, "Have you ever given a blowjob before?"

"Well yeah. I was with Trevor for a long time."

He interrupts me, "Wait. So, you're saying that fucker who never ate you out, not once, got blowjobs?"

Huh. I've never really thought of it that way.

"Um, yeah. Pretty frequently actually."

He huffs loudly, "Jesus fuck I'm glad you aren't with that idiot anymore."

I smile to myself blissfully and ride an endorphin high unlike any I've ever felt before. I lay my head on his chest, tracing the tattoos on his arms with my fingers.

"Yeah, me too." I reply, and I realize right here, right now, I really truly mean it.

Chapter 16

MAX

I'm only human.

That's what I keep telling myself.

I tried not to blur the lines with Josie, I really did, but fuck, how do you look at a woman that beautiful asking you to give her an orgasm and say no? The answer is you don't. You can't.

I've been fighting my attraction to Josie for weeks now. That first kiss already chipped away at me, replaying over and over again in my mind like a song stuck in my head. The taste of her lips left an imprint I could never forget.

It was easy enough not to pursue her at first because she by all accounts couldn't stand to be near me, but something's changed. Day by day I've seen her annoyance of my general being dwindling more and more, and that's when I decided I needed to try and keep this as platonic as possible.

My attraction to her can't be anything other than temporary. Permanence has never been anything I've been able to offer someone, and Josie deserves more than that. Especially after everything she's been through. She doesn't need another heartbreak, and that's all I could offer her. I don't know how to be any different than how I am, and I told myself I wasn't enough of an asshole to inflict that on her.

I was wrong. I may not be enough of an asshole to inflict that on her, but I am enough of an asshole to not tell her no when she offers a mutually beneficial fake-relationship with benefits.

Josie is a drug, and I knew it. I knew that if I got to taste her again, I wouldn't be able to stay away, and yet I did it anyway.

But I fucked up. How exactly? Because I'm addicted, one taste will never be enough. I know how good being with her feels and I won't be able to stop coming back for more. Before I know it I'll become so crazed that I'll be living under a bridge and talking to pigeons like they're my roommates.

I'm not enough of an idiot to think that I'd fuck Josie once just to get her out of my system and then move on. I knew I'd come back for more, and it's confusing as shit because that's not something I do.

In the cab on the way back to the hotel, she snuggled into the crook of my arm and if felt so damn good having her body huddled against mine and smelling the coconut scent of her hair while I could still taste her on my lips. She's literal perfection.

Fuck, the taste of her. I don't think I'll ever be able to stop thinking about it. The way she would mewl and wiggle with every filthy word that left my mouth was enough to make me come in my pants right then and there.

I could've had her laid out on that rock for hours, licking and sucking and tongue fucking her until we both passed out from exhaustion. She deserves that. She deserves the world, and that's why we have to have an end date, because I know I won't be able to give it to her.

We haven't even had sex yet and I'm regretting when all this will inevitably end, but I have to set boundaries with her. I know she said she's a grown woman that can handle a no strings attached situation, but I can't risk hurting her.

It would gut me.

As we walk up the dock towards our bungalow, I grab our key

card out of my wallet and get ready to tap it against the lock. There's a thickness in the air. A tension both carnal and all consuming, and I know we need to have this conversation before I open the door, because once I do, it's on.

We know once we pass the threshold and the door shuts behind us, clothes are coming off and all I'm going to be able to do is think about all the different ways I can fuck her against all the different surfaces of our room.

I clear the gravel from my throat, "*Gattina*, I think we should talk about something before we go in there."

She eyes me tentatively, "Okay…"

"I think maybe we should add a few ground rules now that we've decided to make adjustments to our arrangement." I don't know why I sound so business-like. I guess maybe I just want her to know that I take this seriously.

"Yeah, okay, that makes sense… Can we not do that inside though?" she asks curiously.

A rough chuckle comes from my throat, "I'm afraid once I get in there all I'm going to be able to do is think about fucking that pretty pussy of yours and I'll forget all about the conversation we need to have."

Her eyes widen and breath quickens as she gives me a small nod, "Okay."

I feel a cocky smirk creep on my lips. She's so damn responsive. I fucking love it. "First, we're agreeing this is just sex, just you trying and learning new things. No emotional connection at all. We aren't actually dating."

She does her typical Josie eyeroll, "Yes, Max. Believe it or not I'll be able to resist your 'charms.' I'm not delusional enough to think you would ever want to date me. I know this is just sex."

For some reason, hearing the truth from her causes a painful pang in my chest at the idea that she would have to be delusional to think we could date each other. Probably best not to dig too deeply into that one.

"Right. Okay, and since we'll be trying a lot of new things, I think it'd be best if we had a safe word. One that you could say if things get to be too much. We're not going to be doing anything crazy, but I don't want you to do something you aren't one-hundred percent comfortable with doing."

She looks pensive, like she's really giving this concept a thorough walk-through. "Yoshi." She replies with a smile.

I can't help but laugh, "One day maybe we should really dive into what happened in your childhood that resulted in so many sexual Nintendo game references."

She shrugs with a smile, "I just figured, why go off theme you know?"

"And how will we be preventing pregnancy this evening?" I say in my best maître-d voice.

"I have an IUD," she chuckles.

"Condoms?"

"Are you clean?" she asks with an arched brow.

"Scouts honor," I reply, making the hand symbol.

"Yeah, I don't believe for one second you were ever a boy scout," she says with a laugh. "But if I'm clean and so are you then they aren't necessary."

"Well, that's really all I felt like we needed to cover. Anything else you want to add?" I ask while reaching out to lace her fingers with mine.

She taps her chin thoughtfully with her free hand and smiles broadly. "You absolutely cannot fall in love with me," she says matter-of-factly.

I chuckle at the *A Walk to Remember* reference, "Okay, *gattina*. I absolutely cannot fall in love with you. Now if that's all, there's a tongue in my mouth dying to taste you again."

She shivers slightly as I turn the knob and tug her inside so I can press her up against the closed door. I eat up what little distance we have between us and pin her between the cool metal of the door and my heated body.

My lips are on hers in an instant, and I moan at the taste of her. I can't get enough of it. Her tongue slips between my lips and massages against mine before I open my mouth wider to deepen the kiss.

Even with my body flush against hers, I can't touch enough of her. I need more. My hands coast up the soft skin of her thighs before pulling her legs up to wrap around my waist. I don't even have her naked yet, and I feel the heat of her pressing against my already hard dick, which is still tucked in my pants.

A small cry slips from her lips as she tilts her hips to sit on the ridge of me so it hits the perfect spot and gives pressure to her clit.

My voice comes out rough and gravelly, "If you think that feels good, imagine how good it'll feel when my dick is inside you."

She whines and I brush the curls off her neck so I can trail kisses down the skin there and nibble at the base of her throat. My girl must like the bites, because as my teeth gently sink into her skin she tangles her hands through my hair so she can grip the strands and press me into her even more.

"Oh, god," she cries when I sink my teeth into the skin of her neck once more. It's sure to leave a mark, and why does that turn me on even more? Knowing that people will see where I've marked her. It does unspeakable things to a caveman part of me I didn't know I had.

"Mmm... my pretty girl likes to be bit. Maybe I should leave marks all over your skin so you can remember every place I've owned this body," I say tightly before lightly licking the place on her neck where I bit her, soothing it.

She arches into me, "Something tells me I'm not at risk of forgetting that."

I can't help but chuckle as I pull her off the door and walk her to the bed with her legs wrapped around my waist. "Good answer."

She has far too many clothes on still. I toss her into the middle of the bed, letting the plush white bedding sink around her. I should've made that a rule, if you're on the bed, no clothes.

I kneel on the bedspread, straddling her thighs before lifting her shirt up over her head and untying the knot to her swimsuit. Honestly a fucking swimsuit should not hold as much power over me as this one does. It's a work of art against her soft brown skin, sculpting against all of her best features and curves.

Instead of letting her lay back down I grip her chin so she can look me directly in the eyes. This close I notice there are little flecks of gold in the beautiful brown of her eyes. My lips ghost over hers while I speak, "Now how does my pretty girl want to come first?"

Those beautiful eyes widen at my words, and her voice comes out shaky, "How I want to... come... first?"

I can't help but laugh as I nip at her bottom lip, "You didn't honestly think I would let you have only one orgasm did you?"

Her eyes look at me curiously, "I had my first orgasm with another person only a few hours ago. I wasn't going to be greedy enough to think orgasming more than once was even possible."

I smile into her neck where I'm nuzzling her, letting the timbre of my voice echo against her skin there. "*Gattina*, your tight little cunt being greedy for more of me is an expectation. Making you come more than once is a reward for me as much as it is you."

She laughs lightly as my fingers move downward to hook onto what remains of her swimsuit and shimmy it down her body. "Somehow, I doubt that."

I look up at her after throwing her swimsuit across the room, leaving her bare against the comforter. "It's true. Orgasms are like Pokemon, gotta catch 'em all," I waggle my eyebrows suggestively at her.

She laughs so loud her hand comes up to cover her mouth, and it makes me smile. I don't know if I've ever been with someone that made me laugh while we were in bed together. I didn't know laughing and still having a rock hard dick was even a possibility until I met Josie.

It's a pleasant surprise. It means she's comfortable with me, and hell if that doesn't make me unnaturally happy at the concept.

I'm still straddling her thighs while she props herself up with her arms behind her. I let my thumb tug down on her bottom lip while the rest of my hand tattooed with a rosary grips her chin. "Answer my question, *Josie*. How do you want to come? Do you want me to lick circles around your clit until you can't speak? Do you want to fuck my fingers while I taste just how much you want me? I could let you rub your clit along the ridge of my dick, getting it wet before it even goes inside you. I could make you wear a rosary around your throat. So many options, and fuck if I can't decide which one I want the most."

It's true. It all sounds so good I can't decide. My body wants every inch of her body all at once. Shit, I'm the one that's greedy for her. I don't know if the burning sensation under my skin would even be satisfied once I've had every part of her. It's alarming.

Plus, it's such a fucking turn on when a woman tells me the filthy things she wants me to do to her body. I may like being in control, but it drives me insane to hear what a woman wants from me, craves from me.

And then I get to decide if I'm going to give it to her or not.

Her doe eyes look at me, innocent and sweet, before I see a small spark fire off behind them. "I really liked fucking your fingers while your tongue licked my clit..." She smiles at me sweetly.

Fuuuuckkkk.

I of course would love nothing more than to taste her again. I lightly push on Josie's chest so she lays back down on the sheets, marveling at those perfect tits that are too big even for my hands to hold.

I bend my head towards her ear, tugging on it gently. "My good girl deserves a reward for using her words so well."

She whimpers and wiggles beneath me at my words while I

kiss my way down her body, stopping only at her nipples so I can suck and lick them before trailing farther downward.

I take her legs and drape them over my shoulders, opening her up so I can see her perfectly gleaming before me, already wet and needy.

I get close enough for her to feel my breath, and my words vibrate off the sensitive flesh, but not making contact quite yet. Like I told her before, the build-up is the best part.

I whisper against her, looking up at her with what I know are heavy-lidded eyes. She's panting already, looking directly at me. She wiggles her hips upward, her body telling me what it desperately wants without me even having to hear the words from her mouth.

"So responsive, *gattina*. You're already so fucking wet for me. I love it."

She gasps at my words, wiggling her hips even more until I pin them down with my forearm. "Maximiliano, please. I need you."

I think I growl at her words, literally growl like a fucking feral animal. She needs me, and shit I need her too.

"Have I told you how pretty you are when you beg?" I whisper before I flatten my tongue and descend upon her.

She tastes so fucking good. I wasn't lying earlier when I told her she tasted like the best thing I've ever eaten, it's true. When we're long over, and she's married to some wealthy lawyer guy with 2.5 kids and a golden retriever, I'll still remember the taste of her.

A loud moan rips from her throat as my tongue dips into her, tasting her right from the source. I harden my tongue while my hands grip her ass on each side and force her to grind against my face. I want my tongue to go as deep as it can.

"Maximiliano, fuck." she whines as her hands grip my hair and forces my face even closer to her, making my tongue go even deeper. I can barely breathe, and I don't even care. If I suffocate, at least I'll die happy, doing what I love.

My dick is so hard I have to adjust myself on the bed to alleviate some of the pressure as I slip my tongue out of her, replacing them with my fingers. I crook them against her G-spot, stroking it while she impales herself on them.

Her hands tighten their grip on my hair while I fuck her with my fingers, coaxing me back downward towards her clit. My pretty girl knows what she wants, and she's silently begging me for more.

And I think we know by now how I feel about that.

I lower my head directly towards her clit, flattening my tongue and circling it rapidly. I can feel her pussy begin to tighten, and I know she's close. I reach up with the hand that's not occupied and roll her nipple between my fingers.

"Come for me, *gattina*," I grit. "Soak my face."

My words seem to be her undoing, and she clamps down on my fingers, flooding them. She lets out a sharp cry as her body trembles. I don't let up, not yet, and continue the circles with my tongue and the crooking of my fingers.

"You're so pretty when you come," I say in reverence.

Josie really is. A weird observation maybe, but that's the only explanation I have as I see how her skin glows with a light flush and glistening sweat. How her curls are wild and her eyes hooded while she pants heavily lifting her breasts with every breath.

Josie sits up on her elbows, and her gaze turns hungrily towards my dick as she licks her lips. "*Please*," she whimpers. She's getting far too good at that.

"Don't worry, I'm not done with you yet. That was just the first one, remember?" She sinks back on the bed and stretches her legs and arms like a cat.

My *gattina*.

I walk back towards the bed, stripping off my shirt and swim trunks. "On your knees," I command. She does it without a second thought.

While I climb up the bed I smile at how willing she is to listen to me in bed, but how feisty she is everywhere else.

"Bend over," I say while putting a pillow underneath her, so she lays against it with her hips lifted up. That perfect ass is up in the air as I spread her thighs and settle between them while she wiggles in anticipation.

I give her ass a light tap, and she moans. I'm going to store that information away for later, that's for sure. I take my thumb and run it down the center of her, making her shiver and press back into me, forcing it inside her.

"Maximiliano please. I need more. I'm begging."She already knows what words will get her what she wants, and we haven't even fucked yet. I can't tell if that's a good or bad sign, but I don't have time to really dwell too much on that. Right now, my girl is begging, and I'm a generous man.

I grip the base of my cock and lightly drag it against her drenched pussy, it glides easily against her as I rub her clit with the head.

Now that I've collected some of her wetness, I place the head of my cock at her entrance as my impatient girl pushes against it. She wants this dick? My greedy girl will get it.

Without any further warning I slide myself in all the way to the hilt, and she cries out while a trail of expletives escape my lips, because she feels so fucking good.

Warm, wet, tight. Perfect.

She bucks against me, and I begin to move with her slowly, letting her adjust. Once I feel like she's comfortable I pick up the pace, pulsing in and out in deep, intentional, grinding thrusts.

I give her ass a light smack, "Jesus, fuck, that pussy feels so good, Josie, just like I knew it would."

Her only reply to my words are more moans and thrusts backward that get rougher by the second. Loud enough that I can hear the slapping of skin and the sound of my cock dragging her wetness in and out of her.

I'm not long for this world, and she feels too fucking good. I need her to come again. I refuse to embarrass myself but fuck, I don't think anything in the entire world has ever felt as good as Josie feels wrapped around me.

I use one hand to grip her hip so I can slam her down on my dick in short and rapid thrusts while I reach the other hand around to rub small circles around her clit. "That pussy is too good, Josie. You need to come for me baby because you're going to make me bust."

I know her ego is probably on ten right now, and she throws her ass back at me even harder. I feel her core begin to tighten, and it's going to be a photo finish as I feel my balls tighten in response.

She's panting loudly, only being interrupted by her moans and whines. She's so fucking close and so am I.

Just when I think I won't make it, she clamps down on my dick and the sensation is too much as my orgasm rips through me.

She screams out and my pitch probably matches hers because I see fucking stars. I don't even think I'm on this planet anymore because there's no way anything on Earth could ever feel this good.

Once we come down from our high, I pull out of her and grab a washcloth from under the sink. I wet it with warm water before bringing it over to her so she can clean herself up.

I lay down in the bed, utterly spent. I feel boneless.

Josie throws the washcloth across the room, hitting the bathroom sink. "Good job, LeBron," I smirk at her.

She smiles up at me before snuggling into the crook of my arm. My hand immediately goes up to her, and my fingers delicately play with the tendrils falling from her braids as our breathing evens out.

I have a feeling Josie is minutes away from falling asleep, which is confirmed in the next minute when I hear soft little snores coming where her head lays on my chest.

I'm exhausted, but I can't sleep. My mind is thinking at the speed of sound and won't shut off. My body wants sleep, but my brain won't stop running through the events of today on a never-ending loop.

My chest feels tight, and as I lay there with Josie on my chest, I wonder if I may be well and truly fucked, and not in the sexy kind of way.

CHAPTER 17

JOSIE

Have you ever woken up to a tongue on your clit? Until this morning, I never had, and I've got to say, it's my preferred way to greet the day. Forget Folgers, the best part of waking up is Max's tongue in your cunt.

Yesterday went better than I could've ever imagined. At one point I had strongly considered that I'd bring the idea to Max, and he'd straight up laugh in my face. But to my surprise, he was even more eager than I ever anticipated. Some might even say enthusiastic.

I had a lot of firsts yesterday. First time someone's ever gone down on me. First time I've ever had an orgasm that someone else gave me. First time I've ever had someone I was pretending to date agree to fuck me for funsies.

Like I said. A lot of firsts.

I woke up blissfully sore between my legs, and I'm kind of loving it. It's been a while since my vagina has made contact with someone from the outside world, and she's feeling it today.

When I woke up this morning with Max's tongue gently licking my clit, whatever soreness I may have been feeling was quickly disregarded for more pleasure.

I mean, he said he liked me greedy right?

Ask and ye shall receive.

I'm sure that's not how that bible verse was meant to be used, but I digress.

As I lay here curled against Max's chest while he absentmindedly draws lines up and down my thigh, I can't bring myself to get out of bed yet, even with the promise of a spa day in my future.

It's our last full day in Fiji, and I'm really contemplating skipping out on the spa day for rolling around in this luxurious four-poster bed with a man I couldn't even stand at the beginning of this trip.

So much has changed.

I feel like maybe I've changed.

I've done things I never thought I would do. Swam through a cave, dove off a cliff, jumped from the second story of a restaurant, snorkeled, and masturbated while a man that annoyed me watched.

Growing up with parents that worked constantly, we didn't travel much. It was all about the grind: fulfilling expectations, meeting goals, smiling at fancy dinners, and being the spokes-family for my parents' law firm.

No kinks in the armor, no breaks in the chain. That is until I got the courage to tell my parents my passion was in helping children, working in schools, not in law. Trevor was my consolation prize. If I wasn't going to be a lawyer, well then for appearances sake I better marry one.

Man, are they in for a shock when they meet Max. The small defiant part of me is maniacally rubbing her hands together in delight, however, the other part of me that is terrified of disappointing my parents is cowering in fear.

There's a lot going on in my brain right now but taking it one day at a time and enjoying myself is what I'm most focused on. As my fingers gently run through Max's mussed up sex hair, I know I'm definitely enjoying myself.

He gives me a small warm smile and places a small kiss on my forehead, "Good morning, *gattina*," he rumbles.

I grin widely, "Good morning to you, Mr. Donkey Kong."

He chuckles as he pulls me farther into his chest, "It's time to get up. It's our last day, and our spa appointment is in twenty minutes."

I groan loudly and secretly inhale the scent of his chest, good lord the man smells good. "Can't we just stay naked in bed all day?" I whine.

"Believe me, I would love nothing more than to fuck you on every inch of this bed, but they want the spa featured, and this is the last day to do it." He replies before scooting his arm from underneath me and getting out of bed.

"Ugh, fine," I complain before dragging my naked ass out of bed.

"Aren't you supposed to be the morning person out of the two of us?" He jokes while putting my cinnamon toothpaste on his toothbrush.

I raise an eyebrow questioningly, and he gives me a shy smile. "I didn't want you to have to taste mint while I kiss you."

My heart gives a sharp tug against my ribcage. He can't say and do things like this. My heart won't be able to sustain it.

Just keep talking, Josie. Don't stop and think about how sweet he is.

"I'm feeling very unmotivated this morning. There was a parasitic worm in my bed that sucked out all my energy last night," I reply while following him to the sink to brush my teeth.

He snorts and talks around his toothbrush, "Babe, please don't refer to my dick as a parasitic worm. The least you could do is call it an Alaskan Bull Worm."

I giggle around my cinnamon toothpaste, "There ain't nothin, too big or too ornery, for me to catch," I wink at him.

We both laugh so hard we almost choke, and the odd domesticity of it makes my chest ache even more.

Why can I picture this?

Why am I picturing this?

Waking up every morning and getting ready while laughing together... that's not in our future. We both know it.

It's temporary.

It's fake.

So why am I feeling so confused?

We get ready in silence the rest of the time and rush out the door and down the dock to the main building so we're not late for our appointment.

Max gets some short videos of the reception area before a cheery woman running the front desk of the spa gives us a big smile. "Bula! Rossi appointment for two right?" she asks.

"That's us," he replies with a smile. Here I am hyperventilating trying to catch my breath so I can speak, and this guy doesn't even look like he took a brisk walk.

The woman at the front desk seems to realize the man in front of her is fine as hell and starts to blush. Poor girl, she didn't stand a chance. I used to think I could fight it and look where that got me.

I over-corrected apparently.

"Right, follow me!" she squeaks, before leading us down a bright hallway that's all windows on one side that leads to a dimly lit room.

When we enter, the only light is from the candles placed throughout the small space, and the smell of sandalwood and some essential oils I couldn't name if I tried, permeate the air.

In the middle of the room is a copper tub, large enough to hold a throuple if it needed to. Although between me, Max, and Max's ego it's probably the perfect size.

Okay so maybe I like his cocky-as-shit attitude now. Sue me. It's fucking hot when he uses it to prove to you just how far confidence can get you when he's in your bed.

Turns out it's pretty far.

The woman from the front desk gives us a warm smile, "We encourage our couples to get a relaxing soak in before starting the spa-treatments. Please help yourself to the scented soaps and oils alongside the tub. I'll be back for you both in thirty minutes to take you to your massage. There are freshly warmed robes hanging in the closet for you to change into. Can I offer you any cucumber aloe water?"

I have no idea what aloe tastes like, and I've got to be honest, I have no intention of ever finding out. The woman is so sweet, and I don't want to offend her, so I just politely shake my head and tell her no thank you and Max does the same.

"Very well," she says brightly. "If there's anything I can help you with, all you have to do is press the call button next to the door. It will light up and let me know if you require assistance. I'll leave you to it," she winks, shutting the door before we can even tell her thank you.

Then it's just us. Alone. In a candle lit room with a giant bathtub and what sounds like a white noise machine playing Tibetan sound bowls while someone deeply hums in the background.

I feel like I'm supposed to be relaxed right now, but the air is thick. I can feel Max's lazy perusal of my body and it makes me feel like someone is tracing my skin with a sparkler.

How is this going to be relaxing exactly? Because right now all I can think about is Max and I naked with images from yesterday and this morning playing on repeat in my head.

He quickly takes a video of the room, zooming in on the bath before pocketing his phone and turning his green-flecked gaze back at me. Somehow, I keep forgetting why we're even here anymore. I feel like somewhere along the way this became an actual vacation and not an assignment.

He closes the space between us and traces his thumb along my bottom lip. He lowers his lips to my ear and growls, "Strip for me, *gattina.*"

My blood immediately gets heavy, and I don't even question it anymore. I succumb to his orders quickly, as if my body knows the promise his heady words contain.

I want to tease him. The past couple days it's felt like he's had the upper hand, and that just won't do. That's not how our relationship works.

Well. Fake relationship.

I grab the hem of my lime green tank top and slowly pull it over my head, revealing my lacy black strapless bra. His gaze darkens, like he could rip my clothing off with his teeth faster.

I give him a sly smirk and wiggle my jean shorts over my ass and thighs before letting them pool at my feet. He licks his lips, and all I can think about is how badly I want those lips on mine. That's not my goal though.

I want him to beg.

I want to know if he wants me as badly as I want him.

It's only fair.

I turn so my back is facing him. Looking over my shoulder I unclasp my bra and let it fall to the floor. His eyes haven't left my body once. At this point I feel like the Ying Yang Twins could bust through the door and tell me to shake it like a salt shaker and he wouldn't even notice it.

The thought gives me even more confidence, and I hook my thumbs into my lacy black thong, bending over in front of him and slowly peeling it down my legs, giving him a full view of my ass.

He sucks in a sharp breath, just the reaction I wanted.

I slowly turn to face him and let my hands reach up to lightly play with my nipples, forcing a moan from my throat.

"Fuck me, you are so beautiful," he says in a low voice. He leans forward, so close to sucking my nipple between his lips.

I want him to, desperately, but I want to win even more.

I don't know when this became a game he doesn't even know about, but I'm four minutes in, so now I'm committed.

I press my palm against his chest and lightly push him back a step before walking towards the tub. I sink one foot in at a time, hissing slightly as my body adjusts to the warmth of the bath. The water feels slightly thicker, like it's been mixed with oils, and smells like oranges and lilacs. My shoulders lower, the tension in my muscles already relaxing and I'm not even fully submerged.

Once I've bent down and my thighs cross the bubbly water threshold it becomes easier to sink the rest of the way. Before I realize it, I've sunk into my shoulders and my neck rests gingerly against the side of the copper tub.

The warmth of the water and smell of the oils envelops my skin like a cocoon, and I finally let myself look over at Max.

He looks rigid, and it makes me almost as cocky as he is with how I've affected him. Is this how he feels all the time? All this unearned confidence? No wonder he is the way he is. If I knew I affected men like this all the time I'd be cocky too.

"Well? Are you going to just stand there gawking, or are you going to get in the tub with me?" I say with a smile.

Who even am I right now? This cannot be the same me that got so self-conscious in front of Trevor while trying to give him a strip tease that I stopped half-way and ran to the bed so I could hide under the sheets.

I'm so different now. He's made me different, in a way that Trevor never did. With Max I don't know the meaning of the word shame. In the two days that we've added the benefits clause to our fake relationship I'm already more comfortable with him than I ever was with Trevor.

That should probably signal a red flag to me, but oh well.

I watch as Max hurriedly takes off his clothes and lets them sit at a puddle on the floor. For once he's not running his mouth. I don't know what to make of that, although I'm sure it'll be short lived.

What's left behind in the wake of his hurried clothing removal is a beautiful sight to behold. If you've ever wondered what it would look like if a Greek statue fucked an Italian fresco and got it pregnant, then I have news for you. All you have to do is see Maximiliano Rossi naked and you would know the outcome.

No matter how many times I see him, the pure beauty of his

sculpted body will never stop taking my breath away. His olive-skinned abs cut into a deep V, drawing my attention to the main attraction, standing fully erect and begging for a mouth to swallow it.

Whoever said God doesn't gift with both hands has clearly never met Max. When the man was made it's very obvious that when the fine-as-fuck elixir was being added someone tripped, fell, and accidentally threw the whole bottle in.

I lift my hand from beneath the water and crook my finger at him.

Thankfully he doesn't keep me waiting any longer, and he closes the gap between himself and the bathtub, sinking in quickly. He lets out a small moan, the only inclination that he feels the heat of the water at all, before he settles his shoulders underneath the bubbles and leans his neck back against the side of the tub. I watch his body going slack, mimicking mine.

"Holy fuck, this feels so good," he moans. The sound of his voice is gravelly, and if I wasn't already submerged under water the timbre of his voice would make me crazy wet.

I close my eyes, letting the warmth of the water, smell of the oils, and the proximity of Max's body to mine lull me into a purgatory of relaxation and hypersexual frustration.

I'm still in that sense of relaxation and security when I feel the trail of a finger start at my knee and then lazily work its way towards my upper thigh. I open one eye, looking at Max incredulously before he gently turns me so my back is facing his front and I'm leaning against him instead of the lip of the tub. I notice that along the wall is a wide mirror, and in it I watch how his hard muscles cage me in.

His skin is warm against mine, the heady smell of his cologne mixing with the oils in the water making my body somehow tense and relaxed all at once. I've noticed that he has that effect on me. I'm somehow both calm and on edge when he's around

I watch Max reach toward the shelf near the tub and pump a liquid into his palm. Instantly his warm hands are on my shoulders, working an orange scented oil into my muscles and rubbing out the tender knots.

The motion of his deft fingers into my tense muscles makes me moan. "Of course, you're good at this too," I remark. If he was facing me, he would see a massive eye roll.

A throaty chuckle passes his lips, "If it involves my hands or my mouth, it's safe to say I'm good at it."

His hands on my skin and pressing into my sore muscles feels so good it takes all my energy to stop myself from moaning so loud that the poor innocent lady at the front desk hears me.

I'm sure even if he can't see my eye roll, he can hear it in the inflection of my voice, "How could I forget how incredibly humble you are?"

I feel his shoulders shrug behind me as he unravels a knot in my right shoulder blade, "Being humble is just another form of self-loathing to me, and I think you and I both know how much I love myself."

His words make me do something that's between laughter and a full-blown scoff, "Oh yes, of that much I know."

He removes his hands from my shoulders, and I groan at their absence. His fingers slowly move forwards, massaging my breasts. His voice is low in my ear, "And yet my confidence never stopped you from being attracted to me."

There's a lilt to his voice that sounds dangerously close to mocking me. Even though I know my pride when it comes to this man is long gone, I can gaslight myself all I want until I'm ready to face it. "That seems like a stretch." I snort.

His fingers trail past my breasts and down farther towards my soft belly. "So, it doesn't turn you on when my fingers trail down your skin?"

I know I'm lying. He knows I'm lying. Like I said though, I've already committed. "No," I say bluntly.

He growls lowly in my ear, and without him directly calling me out I know he's saying I'm a liar. "Then I guess you won't feel anything if every word I say, I moan against your ear?"

I stiffen my spine even though every part of my body wants to sink into his and succumb to the deep throaty sound of his voice. "I feel nothing," I say smugly.

He closes the small distance between his lips and my ear, "Liar," he hisses before lowering his mouth to the crook my neck where it meets my shoulder and licks all the way up. I watch the whole thing unfold in the mirror in front of me, and it just turns me on more.

I can't help it, my body shudders at the feel of his slick tongue against the sensitive skin of my neck. Even if my body betrays me, my words won't. "Sorry, you just don't seem to affect me as much as I do you."

A dark chuckle escapes his throat, "Oh, I seriously doubt that. I bet by the time this day is over you'll be begging me to put you out of your misery and fuck you against any surface I can."

A twinge of annoyance pricks at my spine. I spent years with a man where I always wanted him more than he wanted me. There were times where I felt absolutely insane because I wanted a physical connection with a boyfriend when it seemed like he couldn't care less either way.

I'll be damned if I'm doomed to repeat it with my fake boyfriend with benefits.

Good lord, we really need to find a way to shorten that phrase. It's unnecessarily long winded.

Even as his fingers trail up the column of my neck, his lips at my ear, I'm not ready to cave. I double down and pretend to readjust myself in his lap and wiggle my ass against dick, forcing a grunt from his throat.

"I don't think so," I smirk.

The hand tracing the column of my throat wraps around my neck, forcing me to watch us in the mirror. His grip doesn't cut off air but adds a small bit of pressure at the base of my throat. I inhale sharply, the thought of being at his mercy already threatening to undo me.

I notice then the hand applying pressure to my throat is the tattooed one with the rosary. The way he grips me makes it look like I'm wearing it. Oh fuck. I get it now.

He grins wickedly, watching my every facial expression in the mirror. "I always knew you'd wear it perfectly," he whispers against my ear.

My hips have a mind of their own, and wiggle against him, desperate for friction. No matter what words come out of my mouth, my body will always give me away. It responds to him in a way that I have no control over. I both hate and love it in equal measure.

"Oh, gattina, when will you let go of the control you love so much and admit you don't hate me as much as you let on?"

I glare at him through the mirror. "And when will you realize you're not as irresistible as you think you are?" He wants to talk about my control issues? I'll show him just how much control I can have.

Now I just have to force my body to get on board.

He releases his grip on my neck, a dark chuckle escaping his lips, "I guess we'll find out who's right soon enough."

Just then there's a light tap at the door, "The massage thera-pists are ready when you two are," the woman from the front desk says through the door.

"Thank you, we'll be right out!" I squeak. Oh God, did she hear anything? How long has she been at the door? For the love of God, I hope these doors are thick.

Max gets out first and helps me out of the tub. We wrap ourselves in warm fluffy towels and dry off before putting on our robes.

We're met in the hallway by two women, one with a long dark French-braid falling down her back, and the other with big light brown curls pinned up in a clip. "We have the room ready for you," the braid woman smiles brightly.

I don't know what's in the water here, but everyone seems extremely happy. I guess if you live in paradise that's pretty common.

We follow the women to another darkly lit room with two large massage beds in the middle tucked in white linens. The only light is from the candles flickering along the shelving on the back wall, and I'm starting to think this place is sponsored by a Tibetan sound bowl company because the tinkling music hums through this room too. The smell of oranges fills my nostrils, and it helps calm the part of me still all worked up from my bath with Max.

I wonder if the woman massaging me will see how tense I am and somehow know. No, that's crazy. Why am I spiraling right now? I'm acting like Ella.

The idea makes me smirk, because the thought of her reaction when I tell her everything that happened is sure to be comedic, and also there's going to be a lot of "I told you so's" that will be decidedly less funny.

"We'll give you a moment to disrobe and cover yourselves with the sheets on the bed, we'll start face down." says the clip woman before they walk out the door to give us our privacy.

We undress and hang up our robes before getting underneath the warm sheets of the massage bed. "Oh God…" I hear a throaty moan come from the bed next to me. The sound makes the buzzing feeling in my blood instantly come back. So much for the relaxing massage.

I lift my head to glare at Max, who has a big shit-eating grin on his face. "What?" he asks with fake innocence. "The warm sheets feel good on my dick."

"For the love of God please refrain from making any noises or talking about your dick while those poor innocent women are in this room," I beg.

He snorts, "Jesus, give me some credit. I wouldn't talk about my dick to strangers."

I narrow my eyes at him, "Oh, so that luxury is something only I get to enjoy," I respond sarcastically.

"Currently there's a lot of things about me only you get to enjoy," he says while waggling his eyebrows suggestively.

I can't help but laugh, "I'm starting to think the only two settings you have are sexual innuendo and needling me."

"I do get an insane amount of enjoyment out of both of those things," he quips while setting up the tripod to start filming. That earns him a glare, which just makes him even happier.

A light knock at the door tells us that they're about to come in. They both give us a quick smile before walking towards the back wall lined with various bottles that I assume contain different oils or lotion.

It all starts out innocently enough. Hair Clip has magic hands and I feel like I could cry from sheer joy when the warm oil is rubbed into my skin. Finally, I can feel myself relaxing and I snuggle down into the warm sheets even more.

I'm not sure how much time has passed, it's possible I fell asleep. At some point I know she had me flip over but I only vaguely remember doing that. Suddenly, I hear French-braid's gentle voice over the Tibetan sound bowl music. "Okay you two, now it's time to take what you've learned and apply it to your partner."

Apply it to your partner? Like right now?

Max looks up and his face matches mine in confusion, "You mean when we get home?"

French-braid replies sweetly, "Oh, did they not tell you this was an instructional massage? The first half we apply techniques, the second half we watch you perform the techniques specific to your partner so when you get home, you'll know how to use them."

"Oh..." I trail off.

"Now who would like to be massaged first?" Hair Clip asks.

Is this resort just one giant forced sexual encounter after another? Did I miss something and this is like some sort of package for couples struggling with intimacy? Although I guess I can't say anything after Max literally had me tied up on the beach. No amount of massaging would be able to compare to the awkwardness of that entire encounter. We weren't even hooking up then, but I'd be lying if I said I didn't consider it while he had me tied and bound.

"Come here, *gattina*," Max's voice is husky as he crooks his finger, motioning for me to come to him.

Our massage therapists step out so I can get the robe on and then come back in once I'm dressed. "Okay, now you'll want to start with some oil. Rub it between your hands to warm it and then start where your partner feels the most tension."

"Where do you have the most tension?" I ask Max, regretting the question the minute it flies out of my mouth. My eyes grow wide, and he looks up at me from the table and gives me a wink, "I like where your head's at ,Jos, but I was going to say my lower back."

"Perfect! Mr. Rossi if you could flip over onto your stomach for us," Hair Clip (who I just noticed has her name stitched on her uniform(it's Jessica)) says while motioning for him to flip over.

I pump the oil in my hands and rub them together to emulsify it while Leona (French-braid, I'm really kicking myself for not seeing it sooner) demonstrates the motion to use on his lower back.

My hands repeat the motion on his warm skin, and since he can't see me staring, I take the time to fully appreciate and ogle the man on the table in front of me. His back muscles ripple even when he's relaxed, and he has two adorable dimples at the base of his spine. He has a large back tattoo of a cloaked figure holding a sword stretched between his shoulder blades to his mid-back, and I can't help but get lost in the detail of it. It's both beautiful and haunting.

I never thought I'd find tattoos hot. In all honesty I was always attracted to the clean-cut-suit-jacket-I-invested-in-bitcoin-type, but as I stare unabashedly at the beautiful man before me, I had no idea what I was missing out on. He's so fucking hot, but there's something else heavy in my chest when I look at him. A small ache that cannot and should not be there.

Pack it away, Josie. Shove it way back into the attic of your brain. He'd never be interested in you that way. You're just going to get hurt again.

"Fuck, *gattina* your hands feel so good," he rumbles. His voice is smoky and trails against my skin, making me even wetter than I already am from the way he's been edging me for hours now. I'm starting to care less and less about winning, and that concerns me greatly.

I swear he's doing this on purpose. His moans are just a ploy to turn me on and make me admit that he affects me more than I do him. We've played this game before and it's a dangerous one. I know him well enough now that I can tell when he's trying to needle me.

By the time Max turns off the camera and it's my turn to lay on the bed, my entire body feels so sensitive that just one small touch might burn me alive. Max changes into his robe and a small (okay a big) part of me is disappointed because it covers entirely too much of him.

Jessica and Leona leave so I can undress, so it's just Max and I in the room, alone. The tension is so thick it makes my heart race. As I lay face up on the table, completely naked underneath the sheets, I try to calm my erratic breathing. Was this supposed to be relaxing? Not one part of me feels relaxed right now.

Max bends down so his nose is almost touching mine, his hazel eyes simmering, "Where do you feel the most tension?" he rasps.

"I think you know the answer to that," I respond, my voice breathier than I intended.

"Are you caving yet, Josie?" He rumbles.

A knock sounds on the door before Jessica and Leona come back into the room. The knock breaks me from my Max induced trance, and I feel like I was hypnotized and someone said my trigger word.

If I thought massaging him was bad enough, Max massaging me is far worse. The way his hands feel on my body are both soothing and possessive. Somehow, he knows exactly where to touch me and when, even when we aren't doing anything sexual.

By the time the massage is over, I'll be lucky if there isn't a giant wet spot on the bed from where I was laying. I don't think my ego could handle the embarrassment of that happening twice in one trip.

I get dressed back into my robe, and we're led into another room where we're wrapped in eucalyptus, laid out in chairs, and given water. It's supposed to help us before our last stop, the sauna

"You know, I've never seen someone look so hot wrapped up in leaves before," Max muses.

"Oh, really? How many times have you been in this exact scenario?" I retort.

"This is the first time, but I could confidently say if it happened before you'd still be hotter," he says while looking at me from the corner of his eyes.

"I'm sure you'd say that to anyone who was nearly naked sitting next to you," I scoff, trying to hide the way his words make a small part of me grow heart eyes.

His face takes on an expression I don't recognize, but it almost looks pained. "I wouldn't actually," he responds before facing forward, effectively ending our conversation.

I wish I could tell what it was about what I said that bothered him. I mean, it's not like it's anything other than the truth. I know if I wasn't here, he could've replaced me with literally any other woman and had the same outcome. I'm not naïve enough to think that I'm special. It's exactly why the small ache in my chest is entirely unwelcome. I'd never expect Max to be any different than he's ever been: completely adverse to any type of commitment.

When we're unwrapped and lead to the sauna, we're left alone in our silence. I sit on a cedar bench across from Max, who is by all accounts still brooding, and I try to let the steam melt away the annoyance I feel.

It doesn't work. I can't take the silence anymore. It's driving me nuts. I stand up from my seat and drop my towel, so I'm in front of him completely naked. "Did I say something to make you mad?"

His eyes are wide, trailing from my toes all the way up to my head, drinking me in. I can tell he's at war with himself. Torn between whether or not to tell me what he's thinking.

Fine. I can be more convincing if I need to be.

I straddle his lap and wrap my arms around his neck, making sure my eyes are looking directly into his. "Tell me."

I want to get past whatever weirdness happened, and the bulge underneath his towel connecting with my center is sending shivers up my spine despite the heat and humidity of the sauna. I feel myself sink further downward, so more pressure is on my clit, and my hips rock slightly.

Max groans at the contact and moves his hands from his sides to grip my ass and help me rock back and forth harder against his ridge. Just the feeling of the heat from his body and the air surrounding us is enough to consume me.

I lean over and kiss his lips, licking the seam of them, and he opens up for me willingly, his tongue seeking mine to deepen the kiss. He still tastes like cinnamon, and the sharp tug from this morning is back.

"Tell me," I moan into his mouth before he swallows my words against his lips.

I break away and grab either side of his face, forcing him to look at me. He's avoiding the subject. It's obvious. His hands grip my ass harder, and I whimper at how good it feels. He's an expert at deflecting, I'll give him that.

"You're not going to make me forget you know," I moan as he undoes his towel from his waist so I'm straddling his dick directly. He's so beautifully hard I can already feel myself dripping on him.

"Fine," he groans. His eyes look downward, and he moves his hand to the little space separating us, touching the most sensitive part of me and rubbing circles on my clit.

I cry out at how good it feels. My clit has been begging for attention for hours now. I know he's doing this to try and distract me. Max isn't one for serious emotion, and if he can distract me while he tells me what he's thinking then he's barely having to acknowledge it. Not that I'm complaining by any means.

"Maybe I don't love that you think so little of me," he grunts as he slips two fingers inside me while working my clit with his thumb.

I use my arms wrapped around his neck to help me leverage myself while riding his fingers, "I don't think little of you." I say with a moan.

He crooks his fingers against my G-spot, causing sweat to trickle down my spine with how good it feels. "Oh, really? Then why when I tell you how beautiful you are do you brush it off like I just say that shit to any woman I can lure in?"

The hand that's fingers aren't currently inside me grip my ass and force me to ride his fingers even harder. I already feel so close to orgasm I see spots. I'm vulnerable like this. It's only fair I guess. If I'm forcing him to talk I can't very well not do the same. Plus, my brain can barely put two words together right now, let alone come up with a convincing lie.

"Because," I pant. "If I can brush it off, then it helps me convince myself that this is just sex."

"As opposed to what?" he grunts before taking his fingers out of me. I cry out, feeling empty after just moments ago feeling so full.

I rock against him before he lifts me up just enough to line himself up against my entrance. The fingers that were just inside me wrap around my throat, forcing me to wear the rosary, and he slams me down all the way to the hilt.

It feels too good. I'm unprepared for how good riding his dick feels. Nothing good for you feels like this. This isn't romantic. We aren't confessing our feelings for each other, but we're saying a lot without saying anything at all.

This right here we can understand.

"As opposed to what, *Josie*?" he grits out while lifting me up and down his cock in rapid succession. The spots in my eyes are back, and I'm so close.

"Tell me, or I won't let you come," he commands.

No. Please, no. I need to. I can't think of a torture worse than withholding my orgasm at this point.

"Because maybe I'm starting to possibly feel more than fake feelings okay? Now please, let me come." I cry out. Fuck, I can't believe I said that. He's going to end this right now and then I'll be stuck in this purgatory of need for an eternity.

"Good girl. That's what I wanted to hear. Now come for me," he commands before moving the hand gripping my ass to my clit and rubbing it once more. In an instant I feel the sharp ecstasy flood my veins as he pulses in and out of me while applying the perfect amount of pressure to my clit. I fall over the edge, seeing spots as my pussy clamps down on his cock and I orgasm into oblivion.

He's close behind, and he cries out as he empties inside me. We're covered in sweat. Between the sauna and the sex, I feel it trickling down my rib cage, my spine, my hair. I feel cleansed all right, more from telling Max what I've been thinking about all day than anything, but I didn't miss how I ended up spilling my guts and he didn't.

CHAPTER 18

JOSIE

Well, back to reality, or fake reality, I guess.

As we board the plane for the flight home, it's bittersweet, and not just because I'm pretty sure Frodo's journey to Middle Earth took less time, but because so much has changed in just a week. I'm not the same Josie from a week ago, and part of me is worried that all of this newfound self-assurance will disappear the moment we land back in Indy.

Can a place technically change you? I think so, but I also think a big part was sharing this experience with Max. That changed me too. I swam through a cave, jumped off a two-story building, and had the best sex of my life.

That wasn't Fiji, that was Max.

Infuriating, beautiful, sweet Max. I felt safer jumping off a cave wall with him than I did sitting on a couch with the doors locked next to Trevor.

There's a lot to unpack in that last statement, but on a plane next to the man in question isn't the time to sift through it.

In true us fashion, after Max fucked a confession out of me that I might, possibly, maybe, have a slight crush on him, he didn't bring it up again. I refuse to be the one that both admitted to what I was feeling, and also be the one to bring it up again.

Now it's his turn.

Unfortunately for me, he's an expert deflector.

We settle in, and he lets me have the window seat while he takes the middle. I bend over and grab my headphones. When I sit back up, I feel a warm hand settle on my upper thigh, his fingers lightly tapping against the fabric of my leggings.

When I look at Max's face, it's unreadable, and I so wish I could figure out what he's thinking. Does he want to end our agreement early because I fucked up and have a stupid little crush on him?

I can suppress it.

I'm good at that.

This is me packing away any and all romantic feelings right now. *Yep, zero feelings at all.*

Max shirtless? *Meh, I'm pleasantly neutral.*

Max turning his lethally beautiful smile with perfect white teeth on me? *Mid.*

Max gripping my neck with a tattooed hand and growling low in my ear? My heart beats rapidly at that thought.

Okay maybe that one goes in the don't think about it ever category...

I can't take the silence, and at this point I'm very close to bridging the gap and just telling him it was just something dumb I said while his dick was inside me and I was desperate to come, but he speaks first.

"So, you ready to meet my parents?" There's that lethally beautiful smile, stay strong, Josie, stay strong.

The idea of meeting his parents makes me chuckle. "You mean lie to a group of strangers I'll probably never see again? No. I'm really not."

A sexy grin spreads across his lips. *No, not sexy. Nope. Just a regular human face smiling, a mediocre smile that makes me feel nothing.* "Don't think of it as lying. Think of it as briefly making an Italian mother very happy."

I feel my eyes roll involuntarily at that, "Somehow that

doesn't make the pit in my stomach any smaller. What if she hates me?"

He adjusts in his seat, his eyes flitting to meet mine, and shrugs. "Well first of all, she would like a serial killer that wears people's skin like a human suit if it meant I was actually serious about them. But, in the very unlikely chance that she doesn't like you, it's not like you'll see her again after Sunday."

Well, that answers the doubts in my head of how he feels about me, this is still very much a fake relationship. If that's the case, then why make me admit anything at all? Is it just some sick game he plays? He wants me to bare my soul to him so he can pull the rug out from underneath me while he leaves unscated? If that sentiment stings, I wouldn't know because I've already shut it down. It's packed away, along with everything else I don't want to think about.

I smirk, "Wow, such a vivid, murdery picture you paint."

"I guess listening to all those murder podcasts really had an effect on me," he laughs.

"Hopefully not the murdering part. I'd hate to think I played a role in your villain origin story," I chuckle.

He waves his hand nonchalantly while the pilot goes on the intercom and announces we're preparing for take-off. "Oh no worries on that front. I've long learned to suppress the blood lust." he deadpans.

Right about now is when I notice there's a man sitting on the other side of Max, who chooses to readjust in his seat and face towards the aisle away from us. I laugh so hard I snort, and Max suppresses a smirk.

"What about you? Are you ready to meet my family?" I ask between bouts of laughter.

When Max is finally done laughing, he shrugs, "Easy enough. I just need them to like me enough that they lay off about the douche bag, right?"

"Trevor, yes."

Max rolls his eyes while making a sound of disgust, "I prefer douchebag." *Yeah believe me, so do I.*

"You sound like Ella," I reply.

"That's because Ella is right," he huffs.

"No arguments there. So, you aren't even remotely nervous then?" I hedge.

He grins, "Of course not. Parents love me."

"Of course you'd say that. As always, your confidence is both unshakeable and completely unfounded." I roll my eyes at that. I'd start taking a shot for every time this man forces me to roll my eyes, but then I'd probably need my stomach pumped.

"Well one of us has to be able to get through a dinner without being so nervous they bring up shoving tampons up noses," he scoffs.

I narrow my eyes at him, "You're never going to stop bringing that up, are you?"

"Nope," he replies while popping the P.

As the plane begins to taxi and get ready for takeoff, I prepare myself for the insanely long day ahead of us. I'm at least thankful that Max and I are talking and it's not awkward. Even if I desperately wish he'd at least bring up the sauna incident so I could know what he was thinking.

"I'm sorry. You what?" Ella shrieks.

After going through one hell of a jet lag adjustment and sleeping for fourteen hours straight when I finally arrived home, I knew I had to divulge every last detail of this trip to Ella. We tell each other everything, even if I know there's an 'I told you so' coming my way.

We've huddled up on the little blue couch more times than I could count. Hell, the cushions are probably filled with more secrets than Gretchen Wiener's hair. Despite the summer heat I yank a folded blanket off the back of the couch and cover myself up like it'll shield me from questions.

Thank God Liam is out playing basketball with Max as we speak because I would absolutely not be admitting to anything if he was here. Max is his best friend, and he has a loyalty to him. I don't know what would get back to him if he overheard. I don't even have any idea if Max plans on mentioning any of this to Liam.

This is exactly the tangled-up nonsense I was originally trying to avoid before I got dickmatized. I pinch the bridge of my nose and squint my eyes attempting to stave off the impending stress headache I know I'm going to have.

"Please, don't make me say it again," I groan.

She throws her long blonde braid over her shoulder and grabs the bottom half of my blanket to cover her feet. There are at least three other blankets on the back of this couch, but of course she insists on sharing the one I'm using.

She lays her arm on the back of the couch and rests her head on it, her gray eyes narrowing in on my brown ones while trying and failing to conceal her smirk. "I'm just having a hard time understanding how you couldn't stand him a week ago, and somehow you ended up liking him enough to fuck him. But then again, I've read this book before. And so have you."

I groan and throw the blanket over my head, "Ugh, I know."

She gently pulls the cover off my face and her voice is quiet, failing to mask her concern "Jos, you don't think he's going to change, do you?"

I shrug, "I don't expect him to. It's just sex. Casual sex." I'm not going to mention the brief moment in time where I thought I was getting feelings for him because it doesn't matter. I'm not allowing myself to have feelings for him now, so it's like it never happened anyway.

"You've never once had casual sex in your life," she replies while raising an eyebrow.

"Because I'd been with Trevor for most of my adult life," I

scoff. Not necessarily denying that I'm more of a relationship person.

She grabs my hand and squeezes it, "Hey, I didn't mean anything by that. I'm all for sexually liberated Jos, I just don't want to see you hurt. I don't want you to realize you have feelings for him and then when he moves on to the next person you're heartbroken."

I squeeze hers back, "I'm a big girl, El. I'm more than capable of being able to separate emotions from sex."

Maybe if I say it enough, I'll have myself fully convinced too.

She grabs her braid and fiddles with the ends of it. "It's not just the sex, Jos. It's the pretending to be together that worries me. When pretending you're his girlfriend isn't convenient anymore, he'll move on to the next girl like he always does, but you can't because you've been pretending for so long that it becomes too real."

"I can handle it," I say curtly.

"Okay, if you're sure..." she hedges.

The truth is, I'm not sure at all, but this isn't the first time I've refused to feel my feelings and it won't be the last.

After all, I'm an expert.

CHAPTER 19

MAX

"Max get in here!" I hear Shawna yell from the office across from my desk in the common area. It should be noted that having a desk within shouting distance of your boss is for the birds. I swear she watches me like a hawk.

The first day back after a long week on assignment, especially one that totally fucks up your sleep schedule, is always exhausting. When I finally managed to roll out of bed and make it to the office, I spent the first thirty minutes zoning out and staring at my cubicle mates' cat of the month poster while thinking about how Josie's lips taste.

In case you are wondering, July is a Scottish fold. I didn't even know there were really a ton of different types of cats. I just always thought, 'oh that's a cat,' but apparently, I've been doing it all wrong. I get up from my desk before I start looking at pet adoption websites so I can find one and name it Foldemort. This is how I know I'm really spiraling: call a girl *gattina* and start getting all emotionally confused and before you know it you're getting a cat.

I rub my eyes and make the short trip dragging my feet to her office. When I cross the doorway, I see Shawna on that same giant exercise ball bouncing around like that'll shake the kid out of her faster. Her belly got even bigger in the last week while I was gone.

Not like I'd ever say that to her, I value my life. And my balls.

She looks up over her laptop and waves me in, smiling wide. Honestly, I don't know if I should be worried or not. Her smile could be the equivalent of the Joker on the verge of blowing up Gotham City for all I know. I wonder if she's noticed that I haven't been able to get a single piece of work done the entire day. Honestly, I wouldn't be shocked. The woman has a sixth sense dedicated specifically to knowing when one of her employees is fucking up.

In all fairness, I have a lot on my mind, and it's not just about this damn project or potential cat purchases. No, what I have on my mind is big brown eyes, wild curls, and curves I want to trace with my tongue.

Is this fake anymore? I don't know. Shit, I've handled this whole situation like a total ass. I needled Josie into telling me how she felt, only to say absolutely nothing back. The truth is, I have feelings for Josie, and I just have no idea what to do with that information.

Do I tell her? What good would that even do? I'm incapable of commitment. Telling her how I feel would do nothing but make everything worse, so I chose to deflect instead. Very mature of me. I probably royally fucked everything between us. She didn't say anything about it on the plane ride, but maybe she just didn't want to make an already hellishly long flight even more terrible.

She gestures for me to come around the desk and look at her laptop screen. "Max everything you collected is absolutely perfect. I had my doubts, don't get me wrong, but this is your best work to date. I mean look at this footage, the client is going to love it. Everyone wants to be you two."

As she scrolls, I see pictures of Josie and I, covered in mud, wrapped in eucalyptus leaves, jumping off the cave wall, when we kissed under the waterfall... That day was utter perfection. If I would've known just how good Josie tasted, I would've had her way sooner.

As Shawna scrolls, my heart grows heavy in my chest. It's a weird mixture between feeling guilty for straight up lying to my boss and also wishing Josie and I were still in our perfect little Fiji bubble. Before I potentially ruined everything. With facing the outside world and the threat of meeting each other's families looming over our heads plus our inevitable break up, I'm dying to go back and just enjoy each other without having to think about any of that.

I grip the back of my neck, "Thanks Shawna." I reply with more enthusiasm than I feel. What is wrong with me? A few weeks ago, I was dying for this assignment. Now when my boss is telling me it's my best work to date, I can't seem to summon up any type of excitement.

As if I don't feel guilty enough, she keeps going. "We posted a few preview photos to our socials, and everyone absolutely loves Josie. Don't fuck things up with that one, she's a gem," she says with a wink.

"Yeah, she's great," I reply awkwardly. Great? Jesus, she's more than great. Never in a million years could I have ever anticipated the summer storm that is Josie Jones currently wreaking havoc on my life. She has me thinking things that I know can never happen.

On the plane when I mentioned that it didn't really matter if my mom liked her or not, it made my chest hurt. The week that we spent together was probably the best week of my life. I'm not ready to let her go yet, but I know after I'm done meeting Mr. And Mrs. Polo-Stick-Stuck-Up-Their-Ass it'll all be over.

Shit, Josie is the kind of woman that makes me think I could change, which is toxic as fuck for me. If I said it once, I've said it a thousand times, I don't do permanent. I'd think that I could change and then end up breaking Josie's heart, and that's something that I could never let myself live with.

Breaking Josie would break me.

Hence the constant turmoil my brain is in.

"Well, I want to see more of you guys together. Next big assignment when I get back from maternity leave is yours, and thank God because Josie is way more fun than Mrs. Multi-Level Marketing Scheme," Shawna chuckles. "Now go work on editing me more footage."

"Sounds good," I respond with a tight smile. I can't help but feel guilty, because I know that by the time Shawna gets back, Josie and I will be long "broken up" by then. Nothing about that last sentence made me feel good.

I wave to Shawna before heading back to my cubicle. Talking about Josie just makes me want to see her even more. Going from seeing each other every hour of every day for a week to going days without seeing one another has made me miss her. Jesus, I even miss her rolling her eyes at me.

I wanted to see her before we go to my parents anyways, so that way she felt more prepared for what she's getting herself into. I pull my phone out of my pocket and text Josie.

Me: Hey gattina, come over tonight? I need to prepare you for dinner with the mentally unbalanced Rossi family. I'll make you gnocchi.

Gattina: Oh, Donkey Kong, you really do miss me... Yeah, I'll be there. I don't turn down free food.

Me: Yeah, just free all-inclusive vacations to Fiji.

Gattina: I went didn't I?

Gattina: Plus, that was before when I couldn't stand you.

Gattina: Now I find you mildly tolerable.

Me: Jesus don't break your hand stroking my ego so much.

Gattina: *rolling eyes emoji* *middle finger emoji*

Me: Fuck you? If that's all you wanted baby, all you had to do was ask. *winky face emoji*

Gattina: *red face angry emoji*

I smirk to myself before pocketing my phone. I wonder when getting a rise out of her will get old? It's bound to happen at some point.

Now with the promise of seeing Josie tonight, I feel motivated enough to do something in my cubicle other than contemplate the different species of cats I've been missing out on, and all the ways I've made a total mess of this entire situation. I open my laptop and start at the very beginning of the trip, editing the footage of our mud fight into a short thirty second clip, thinking about how I can't wait to see her tonight.

———

I dish up the gnocchi and ladle out the vodka sauce on top before setting the plate in front of her while she sits on the bar stool at the countertop. I don't have a table, for the simple reason that I live alone, and even when I invite women back to my place it's not like we're really eating at a table together or anything.

Having Josie in my space isn't as weird as I thought it would be. In fact, it's comforting in a way I've never experienced before. Normally my guard is up, too distracted by having a woman I barely know in my space. Who would've thought it'd be different when you actually know the girl you bring home?

Wild.

I settle in the stool next to Josie, watching her stick a forkful of gnocchi in her mouth and moan when the taste hits her tongue. *God, I love that sound.*

She has her wild curls bundled up in an orange scrunchie on top of her head wearing joggers and a giant oversized Michigan University hoodie. It'll never cease to amaze me how Josie can look just as beautiful in a giant sweatshirt as she does in that tight orange dress that haunts me to this very day.

"Okay, so don't freak out," I say before taking a bite of gnocchi.

She smirks at me and pulls a leg up to rest against her chest, "A totally chill way to start a conversation and not make me freak out," she responds sarcastically.

I chuckle, "Fair, but my whole family is going to be there Sunday."

"Yeah okay, sure, no pressure," she snorts. "Give me the cliff notes version. You'd be surprised how much I can accomplish with almost no information."

I clear my throat, "Okay, so there's my oldest sister Eleanor. We all call her Ellie. She's married to Paul, and they have my three nieces: Evie, Emma, and Erianna. In that order."

"We like E names I see," she smiles.

"Yeah, it's a whole thing," I laugh.

"Maybe I should make flashcards."

"Honestly? Maybe," I smirk.

"Oh God," she groans before resting her forehead on the knee pressed to her chest.

"Then there's Vivian. She's a shit show, but a fun one." Josie giggles and I can't help but smile at the crazy train that is Vivi. Josie's going to love her. Her lack of a filter reminds me of the out of pocket shit that Ella says but times ten.

"My mom and dad's names are Victoriana and Angelo. Don't call them Mr. or Mrs. Rossi. They hate that formal shit. Bickering is their love language." I'm sure that's where I got my love of pushing Josie's buttons from. Pop loves riling my mom up and seeing her flustered. The Rossi men have a thing for women who can put them in their place apparently.

Josie looks at her plate awkwardly, "It should be noted by the way that my parents will expect the formal shit."

"I figured as much," I shrug.

"Now, if my mom asks you to help cook, say yes. That's your in, but like I said, I'm sure at this point she'd be happy if I brought home a murderer."

"Got it," she says with a mock salute.

The gesture makes me laugh, "My dad is retired Army, but not strict like I knew most of the Army brats' dad's I grew up with were. He likes the weather channel and complaining about the economy and how cheap gas used to be."

That idea makes Josie snort, "Easy enough."

"They're loud, and over the top, and will ask questions that are way too personal, but they're mine." The thought makes me smile. My family is everything to me. Growing up, we moved so much that we usually only had each other to lean on. Hell, Liam is the first real friendship I've had outside of my family. I guess being forced to share the same tiny ass dorm room will do that.

"Is it weird that you saying that actually makes me want to meet them more?" she says with a shy smile so beautiful I can't help but smile right back. She genuinely wants to meet my family.

Who even am I right now?

Oh god, absolutely fucking not.

I can't catch feelings. I can't.

Hurry up and say something quick.

"What about you? Anything else I should know about your family besides the fact that they have terrible taste in men?" I say before stuffing my mouth with gnocchi.

"Well, basically, they're the opposite of your family," she says with a dry laugh. Something tells me she's not a big fan of that fact.

I prompt her with my fork to keep going, and she continues with a sigh. "My dad is big on table manners and punctuality. My mom likes yoga and lip injections. They're all about the grind. Work is their life, and someone with a strong work ethic is big to them. Maybe don't tell them you go on vacation for a living," she says with a wink.

She fiddles with the frayed sleeves of her sweatshirt before continuing, "My sister just graduated with her master's from Notre Dame and is studying for the bar right now. Me? I'm the family disappointment." She laughs, but there's no humor in it.

I grab her hand and give it a squeeze, "I'm sure that's not true."

"Oh, it is. Makenzie is everything my parents wanted me to be. I'm the oldest. I'm supposed to be the one to take over the family business when my parents retire. Although, I doubt they ever will," she says in a tone that makes me think it bothers her more than she's leading on.

She picks at the thread on her sleeve again and sniffles, her voice shaking. I see it then, the pain. Her eyes go watery, and I grab her hand again to reassure her. After a few moments pass, her eyes dry up and her voice steadies. She clears her throat to remove any lingering emotions left behind.

I've never seen this side of her, and seeing Josie hurt causes a visceral reaction in my chest. I realize it then, that I would do just about anything to make her pain go away. I think seeing her hurt is worse than feeling the pain myself.

"I think that's why they wanted things to work out with Trevor so badly," she remarks while stabbing gnocchi onto her fork. "They thought maybe it'd convince me to follow in their footsteps after all. They had this whole grand scheme where his family and mine would merge firms when it was our turn to take over, but I had to go and ruin it by being a guidance counselor instead. To this day my mother still maintains that working at the school is a hobby for me until I 'find myself.' I'm not brave enough to argue with her otherwise." she lifts her shoulder a little in a small half shrug.

"You make it sound like an arranged marriage and you were merging empires..." I trail off.

She shrugs again, "I mean it kind of felt like that. My parents didn't force us together necessarily, but they wanted us to work out so badly that I overlooked a lot of red flags with him. They really wanted me to forgive him after he cheated but that's where I drew the line. Ever since, I started to feel like all I do is disappoint them. The more I think about it the more I wonder if I ever really loved him at all. or if I just loved having my parent's approval again."

I can't imagine growing up in a family that doesn't just want you to just be who you are. I've never had that expectation. I knew a lot of people who came from a military family, and they already knew that once they graduated they were enlisting. I don't think my dad even pushed the subject once. He and my mom always just wanted us to be happy in whatever career we chose.

The only pressure I've ever felt was from my mom wanting me to settle down, but even then I've never felt like a disappointment, like her love was contingent on the decisions I made with my life. Your parents aren't supposed to be your harshest critics.

I hop off the stool and stand between Josie's legs, trying to comfort her the only way I know how. I lightly brush my lips with hers as she wraps her arms around my neck.

I kiss along her jaw, breathing in the scent of her hair before my lips graze the shell of her ear. "Don't worry, baby. After I meet them, I'll make sure they never say the name Trevor again."

I know how much she likes when I whisper in her ear, and I'm rewarded with a small shiver that echoes throughout her entire body. Just the sight of it makes my dick instantly hard.

I smile and lower my voice to a whisper, "Now let me take you to bed and lick that pretty pussy until you feel better."

Her breath hitches and she wraps her legs around my waist, then thin material of her joggers covering her center and settling against my rock-hard dick. The effect this woman has on me...

I'm like a fucking virgin all over again. The smallest touch or the smell of her is enough to make me ache for her.

This is becoming a problem I have no idea how to solve.

She giggles as I walk us down the hallway towards my room, "You know I think I'm feeling better already."

CHAPTER 20

JOSIE

The warm air from the balmy summer day coats my skin as we pull up the gravel driveway on Max's death-trap of a vehicle. The warmth is a shock to the system after the wind from the ride over. It was bordering on cold, and I had to wrap my body fully around Max's to stave off the chill. Now that we've stopped the air is so thick and humid it feels like I'm breathing through a wet washcloth. My skin is already slick and my thighs threaten to stick to the leather of the seat.

For the love of all that is holy and unholy I hope we're eating inside.

As I hop out of my seat and take off my helmet, channeling my inner Charlie's Angel thank you very much, I watch as Max nudges the kickstand up and unmounts the motorcycle.

He looks like fuck on a stick.

Don't ask me what that is, because I don't really know, but those are the only words that come to mind when a tattooed Roman archetype in jeans slung low on his hips and a thin white cotton t-shirt removes his motorcycle helmet from his somehow still perfectly styled hair right in front of you.

I want to lick every inch of him.

Shut up, Josie, now is not the time to lick someone! You're meeting his parents for crying out loud...

"Keep looking at me like that, *gattina*, and I'm going to say fuck dinner and go home to put you on your knees and make you eat me instead," he says with a cocky glint in his eye.

Damn it, I've been made.

"I can't imagine that your parents would find that to be a reasonable reason to skip dinner," I say with a chuckle, trying to ignore the heat in between my thighs at the thought of Max's cock down my throat.

He hasn't let me yet, but I've been dying to. I think it has something to do with the fact that I told him Trevor wasn't into giving, only receiving, oral. Anytime I try he pushes me on my back and licks and fucks me with his tongue until I come. Not that I'm complaining or anything, but I think he wants to convince me that he enjoys giving me head and it turns him on.

Believe me, I've been convinced.

He smiles as his eyes trail lazily from the tips of my toes to my eyes. "They can see how hot you look in that dress. I'm sure I'd be forgiven," he says with a wink.

"They haven't even seen me yet."

"If you don't think that they're all peeking behind the curtains right now watching us, you're even more distracted by me than I thought," he chuckles.

As he grabs my hand and leads me up to an all-brick ranch-style house with a screened in front porch, I watch the curtains in the front window sway back and forth with a small little face disappearing behind it. Max is right. They aren't exactly subtle.

My soon to be ex-fake boyfriend opens the squeaky metal door and we walk past two wooden rocking chairs and a plastic dinosaur car without a floorboard for a kid to stick their feet through and "drive" around. There are barbies piled on a wooden dollhouse in the corner, and an iron sign hanging above that says "Nonna's place the only rule is there are no rules."

It's obvious the Rossi's love their grandkids. I can't help but smile at how welcoming the house is and we haven't even gone in yet. Max opens the front door and we're immediately hit with the aroma of bread and garlic. I think this is what heaven smells like.

"Uncle Ax!" I hear a squeal from the other side of the door as a little girl with big brown curls and brown eyes comes barreling through the doorway before we even make it over the threshold.

He catches her in his arms and scoops her up as she jumps towards him. "Hey, Super Eri!" He grins while supporting her stomach and making her fly around the room like Superman. She cackles wildly as two other girls bound into the room shortly after to hug his legs.

A little girl, clearly the oldest so I'm guessing that's Evie, looks around Max's legs and spots me. "Uncle Max is that the poor, desperate, lady that you tricked into dating you?" she asks innocently while messing with the gap left behind from missing front baby teeth that haven't been replaced yet.

I snort laugh and feel my cheeks heat as Max sets Erianna back on her feet to glare at me. She has no idea just how accurate her word choice is and it's taking all of my inner strength to not bust out laughing.

Before either one of us can respond, a woman with long dark curls and the same hazel eyes as Max walks into the entryway from the kitchen. "Evie, hush! We don't say mean things like that!"

She flashes a straight white smile at me and walks towards me, arms extended while a man in a studded red affliction shirt and gelled hair follows close behind. "Hi! I'm Eleanor," she says while giving me a hug.

Oh, his family are huggers...

That's different.

I return the hug anyway because, maybe, it doesn't feel as weird as I thought it would. I've heard so much about her at this point it's kind of like I know her anyway.

"But call me Ellie! This is my husband Paul and our girls Evie, Emma, and Erianna," she says as she points at each one.

"But mommy you're the one that said..." Evie says in exasperation.

Ellie spins around and looks her daughter in the eye, "Evie, what did mommy and daddy tell you about being a snitch?"

"That unless it gets me a plea deal, I keep it to myself," she says as she rolls her eyes. She can't be more than seven and she knows about plea deals and how to effectively roll her eyes, a girl after my own heart.

"Hi, I'm Josie," I chuckle.

"Oh, we know who you are," a woman not much older than Max and me walks in with dark glossy curls and green eyes, smiling while making a beeline for me to wrap me up in a hug.

"Don't worry, *Zia* Vivi, I didn't tell her to run like you said she should," the little girl with a giant sparkly pink bow on her head says proudly. That must be Emma.

"Jesus, how much shit did you guys talk about me before I got here?" Max laughs while picking up Emma and tossing her in the air, making her squeal with delight.

"The normal amount." Vivi replies with a shrug before narrowing her eyes at Ellie. "Your kids are narcs."

"Viviana, don't speak about *nonna's* angels that way! They're my *nipotinas perfettas*," an older woman in her fifties with dark curls pinned up in a clip gushes at the three girls. She's followed by a man with salt and pepper hair and a thick mustache.

"Absolutely, Vic, never have there been three more perfect girls!" Angelo remarks.

"Pop, you literally have two daughters," Vivi scoffs.

"I said what I said," he chuckles.

"Oh my God, I never thought this day would come! I've prayed to St. Jude and I thought it was a lost cause, but here you are!" Victoriana exclaims wildly and squeezes me tightly in a hug.

"I told you you'd make her year," Max retorts.

"It's nice to meet you, Victoriana," I say as she threatens to squeeze the air from my lungs. I know Max warned me, but I had no idea. There's no way to predict this kind of welcome. As we all stand in the small entryway between a big dining room table and a china cabinet, I don't know if I've ever felt this much love in one sitting.

It's both beautiful and unnerving at the same time.

"You know, ma, now that I'm off the market you can focus all your attention on Vivi, she's still single you know," he smirks while pointing a thumb behind him at his sister as we walk into the kitchen.

Vivi takes that opportunity to loudly smack Max on the arm. "Ow, what the hell, Vivi," he scoffs.

"It's the least of what you deserve for throwing her under the bus like that," I say while narrowing my eyes at him.

"Ooh I like her already, *scemo*," Vivi retorts before flashing a smile at me.

Victoriana, who clearly hasn't heard anything we've just said, calls over her shoulder as she stirs a giant pot of red sauce on the stove making the scent of basil and garlic stronger.

"Oh, *ometto*, I already know I'm going to be praying to St. Jude for that one too" she says solemnly.

"The patron saint of lost causes?" Ellie cackles as she sits on a stool pulled against the kitchen island. Vivi tears off a hunk of bread so crisp that it crunches as she breaks it off and throws it at Ellie's head, making her laugh harder.

"For Christ's sake, I'm not even thirty yet!" Vivi yells.

"And at this rate I'll be dead by the time I see you settled down!" Victoriana fires back.

"Ma, you honestly think I won't find someone in the next thirty years?" Vivi questions, her mouth hanging open in offense.

"You don't know if I have that long! I could drop dead tomorrow and only two of my three children have settled down. I was talking to Marguerite next door, and she said that her friend Phyllis' cousin Cheryl got hit by a bus. None of her kids got married and she only had five people at her funeral! Is that what you want for me?" Victoriana yells before lifting a wooden spoon to her mouth and tasting the sauce. She must've decided it needed more of something because she grabbed a couple spice jars on the other side of her and started sprinkling the contents into the pot before stirring again.

"Vic, we all know that didn't happen," Angelo yells from the lazy boy in the next room, the weather channel blaring in the background.

"And who are you to know it didn't? You don't even talk to the neighbors!" Victoriana yells while wielding her wooden spoon like a weapon, shaking it in his general direction.

"Does that spoon double as a weapon?" I ask in a whisper as I lean towards Max.

"Only if you stand within a foot of the spoon's radius," he whispers back.

The yelling is temporarily ceased as the girls all run through the kitchen, chasing one another and grabbing off chunks of bread before running towards the living room where Angelo is sitting.

"*Nonno*, is it gonna wain?" Eri asks him before jumping onto his lap.

"See that line right there, Eri, you watch it. If that line touches where it says Indianapolis that means it will rain." he says adoringly.

"*Nonno*... I can't wead," Eri says sadly.

"Here, let me help," I say while walking through the kitchen towards the tv in the living room.

I motion for Eri to come next to me as I get close to the screen and she follows suit, sitting next to me. "See that big black dot?" I ask her.

"Yes," she says as she nods her head so hard that her curls shake.

"So right next to that is the letter I. That's the first letter in the word Indianapolis, so that's how you find it. Now that line has to hit that dot with an I and that means it's going to rain." I respond with a smile.

"Ohhh..." Eri says while smiling wide before running back towards her *nonno's* lap, making him laugh.

As I get up to walk back towards Max, I see him already staring directly at me, a look on his face that I can't read. *Maybe I overstepped?*

"Alright, dinner is ready!" Victoriana yells from the stove.

The entire Rossi family grabs plates and utensils before lining up to fill up on the vast variety of food in front of us. Salad, crisp bread with oil, three different types of meat to choose from, and a massive amount of noodles and sauce. With the amount of food there is, you'd think there were fifty of us.

We fill our plates and then make our way back to the front room where the large dining table takes up the majority of the space. I'm about to sit down next to Max when a small voice calls to me from across the table. "Yo-sie, sit by me!"

I see Eri waving her hand wildly and grinning ear to ear. *Well, who could say no to that?*

"So, you're not going to sit by me?" Max asks with a smile.

"I got a better offer," I shrug before plopping in the seat next to Erianna.

"She is significantly cuter than I am," he says, conceding.

"It's important to be self-aware," I retort with a half shrug, making everyone around the table chuckle.

I stick my fork into a pile of noodles and twirl to get a fork full before finishing the bite off with a sliver of meatball and shoving it in my mouth. I instantly groan because this is the best pasta I've ever had in my life.

"Victoriana, this is the best sauce I've ever had," I say while shoveling another bite in my mouth.

"Oh please, call me Vic, or mom works too," she says with a wink. At that exact moment I hear a choking sound from across the table and look to see Max trying very hard to swallow his food while his face looks like he might have a panic attack.

Ah, I see. The mom comment made him uncomfortable, perfect, mom it is.

"Okay, mom," I say towards Max, grinning wildly. He doesn't think it's nearly as funny as I do though.

Oh well.

Max finally manages to swallow his bite and hurriedly changes the subject. "I was thinking we should play fishbowl after dinner."

The girls next to me shriek with excitement. Whatever fishbowl is, we're apparently very excited about it.

"What's fishbowl?" I ask.

"Only the bestest game ever!" Emma yells happily before lifting up her knife to cut some of her pasta.

"Emma, I know you aren't cutting that pasta." Angelo says with a gruff smile.

"But *nonno* it's too long," Emma groans.

"Then put less on the fork. You choke on a noodle before you cut it, *nipotina*." The entire time he says this he's chuckling, making Emma laugh as well before she shakes some of the noodles off her fork.

"So besides it being the bestest game ever, what is it?" I ask again.

"It's like if charades did a line of coke in the bathroom of a nightclub and chased it with a Redbull," Paul says around a bite of bread.

"Ew, why would someone drink coke in a bathroom? That's disgusting." Evie says with her face pinched.

"Paul," Ellie says through gritted teeth, eyes growing wide as she tilts her head towards the girls.

"What Ellie? What'd I say?" he asks completely oblivious.

"Maybe don't talk about doing drugs in a club bathroom while our kids are at the table?" she gestures wildly, hands flailing everywhere.

"Girls, drugs are bad or whatever. Don't do them. Especially in a club bathroom, that's how you get hepatitis." Paul says before taking a bite of pasta. "There, problem solved." He smirks at Ellie, and she replies with a groan, clearly exhausted by this entire interaction.

"What's a hepatitis?" Evie asks.

"A sickness you get from doing bad things in the bathroom," Paul says, pointing his fork as he talks towards Evie.

"Ahhhh!" Erianna shrieks like she's been attacked and throws her fork down.

Ellie jumps up immediately, "What, Eri, what is it? Are you hurt?"

Giant pools of tears appear in Eri's big brown eyes and fall down her face in droves, "This morning I put a whole bottle of soap in the toilet so I could see if it made bubbles when I flushed. Do I have a hep-tits?"

I snort, all the adults around the table trying to suppress their laughter, "No, my sweet girl, you do not have hepatitis." Ellie says, suppressing a chuckle and sitting back down.

"Don't you mean hep-tits?" Max asks, his chest shaking with contained laughter.

"The crazy thing is, I'm still no closer to knowing what fish-bowl is," I say with a chuckle.

"Ok *gattina*, it's basically charades but with levels. You put a bunch of words into a hat, and you split everyone into two teams. Round one, you're allowed to talk to your team as much as you want to describe the word but just can't say the word. Each team gets a minute every time to get as many as they can before all the words are done. Round two you use the same words but act it out with charades instead of talking. Round three you can only say one word that describes what your word is, and your team has to guess it. Whatever team has the most after all the rounds wins."

"Oh my god, you call her kitten? That's so nauseatingly cute I might throw up" Vivi teases.

"It's easier to just learn as you go," Ellie replies with a wink, ignoring her sister's teasing remarks.

The girls seem to eat a lot quicker now that the promise of a game after dinner is on the table, and we all finish eating relatively quickly. I'm only slightly sad that the best dinner I've ever had is already over, and that I'll never get to eat this food or see his family ever again.

Okay, I'm a lot sad. And not even because of that pasta sauce, but because in the very short time I've been here I've already grown attached to all of them. They're the loud, outspoken, and loving family I've always dreamed of having.

Can you miss people you've only met once? Because it may sound crazy, but I'm going to miss them. I hope the real/fake breakup doesn't hit them too hard, especially Victoriana and the girls.

We gather in the living room with the sound of the weather channel on for background noise. I have a feeling that no matter the time of day, the weather channel is always on in the background, whether someone is watching it or not.

We all are instructed to write our word or phrase on a piece of paper and fold it up into a Colts hat that Angelo grabbed off the bookshelf behind his plaid lazy boy chair. Once we all had written something, or in Eri's case someone wrote it for her, we all split off into teams.

Max and I are put on opposite sides, which I love, and some slightly feral part of me that is unnecessarily competitive wants to win with his family teamed up against him.

Eri and Emma insisted on being on the same team that I was on. And there's no way I could say no. Poor Max looked so annoyed that his own nieces betrayed him.

"Don't worry, Uncle Max, I want to be on your team," Evie says while nudging his shoulder.

"Thanks, Ev. I'm glad at least one of my nieces is loyal," he laughs. Eri responds with sticking out her tongue in his general direction. As if she couldn't get any cuter.

As soon as the game starts, it's utter chaos. Hilarious, utter chaos. Almost every time it's one of the girl's turns we'd have to explain what the word was so they could give us the clues.

Once my phrase came up, I got lucky enough to be the one to explain my own clue. The only problem was that I made mine unnecessarily complicated. It stalled out the entire round when my team couldn't guess what the phrase was.

We went two more rounds before anyone could guess it, throwing it back into the hat in defeat. Finally, we got to the point where someone on my team was trying to describe it without saying any of the words and I shouted out, "Grippy sock vacation!"

Everyone laughed hysterically once they figured out exactly what that phrase was, and for round two it became memorable enough that it was guessed on the first try. All Emma had to do was point at the socks on her feet and everyone got it.

Going into the final round we had become well acquainted with the words in the hat, some just to name a few: noodle, fart, Jessica Alba, NSYNC, and of course, grippy sock vacation. We were doing really well considering two of our teammates were under the age of six, but we were trailing behind by four.

Victoriana and Vivi were the other adults on the team, and we huddled up before the last round to get the girls pumped up to make a classic underdog comeback.

Eri took her little fist and shook it with all her might, "Let's kick their butts!" she says with a fierce look.

"To butt kicking!" Vivi shouted back.

We were neck and neck at first, until fate smiled in our favor. They got stuck so badly on a word that no one could seem to remember, and with it being the last round, no skips were allowed. Their time was up at two, where we had finished last round with two as well.

I was responsible for the last round of words to carry our team to victory. I squared up, and prepared to say the one word that would clue them in on the right answer. Max started the timer, and I immediately began, hoping my team remembered that Jessica Alba, Darth Vader, noodle, and The Sandlot were already out from our last round and when Max's team went.

There were six left. We could do this!

Have I mentioned I'm extremely competitive?

"Butt?" I ask.

"Fart!" Emma shrieks in response.

"Band?"

"NSYNC!" Vivi yells.

"Undersea?"

"Spongebob!" Victoriana yells.

"Crazy?"

Time is running out, and my team looks at each other confused. Dang it, I thought that was the perfect word for this one.

With five seconds left a lightbulb goes off on Victoriana's face. "Grippy sock vacation!" She screams.

"Yes!" I cheer as the buzzer on the phone timer goes off. We all yell with excitement. We know that we got enough that there's no way the team could win with the amount that was left.

"Turning my own family against me, a new low." Max laughs.

"Josie, do you mind helping me with the cream puffs?" Victoriana asks while pointing with her thumb towards the kitchen.

I feel my eyes widen and immediately meet Max's gaze as he nods his head for me to follow her. This is it. My in.

She actually likes me, and I can't help the excitement that bubbles in my stomach. I don't know why I care so much about someone I'll never see again liking me, but I really care what Victoriana thinks. Even though this is the last time I'll ever be helping her cook.

I look around the cozy kitchen. The walls are lined with different copper cake pans with all kinds of animals and designs along with knick knacks lined up on floating shelves. The one I'm looking at right now has toy replicas of The California Raisins that are most definitely older than me on full display. When I look up at the gap between the kitchen cabinets and the ceiling there are different kitschy cookie jars including but not limited to: a cookie monster that opens at the mouth and a replica of Cinderella's castle from Disney World lining them.

"Come here, Josie, I'll have you help me stuff the cream puff." Victoriana says, interrupting my revelry.

I go to the sink and wash my hands while Victoriana grabs the filling and stuffs it in a piping bag. I've never stuffed a cream puff before, but I can't imagine it would be too difficult. She demonstrates one and then hands me the bag so I can finish the rest while she goes to clean off dishes soaking in the sink.

"My son, he's a good man." Victoriana says plainly while rinsing off a pan covered in red sauce.

"He is," I respond, not sure if that was supposed to be rhetorical or not. I shock myself when I realize that I'm not even lying when I say it. As I've gotten to know Max, I've learned that he truly is a good person underneath all the swagger and inflated ego.

"He's never been interested in settling down. He's always been a rolling stone that one, but I knew he just needed the right woman to wake him up. We moved around so much when Max was growing up, I think we messed him up a bit without really meaning to." she says solemnly.

"He did mention not living in one place for very long."

"He acts like he doesn't need someone, but I know he does deep down. He says he likes the freedom, but I can see right through him. Before you came around, he only had us and Liam, and we're great, but he needs more. Whether he believes it or not," she says before moving on to scrub the next dish.

I don't really know how to respond, so I just nod so she knows I'm listening. Thankfully she keeps going so I don't have to try and figure out what to say.

"I guess what I'm trying to say is, thank you. I can see how much he loves you. I didn't think he would stop being stubborn long enough to find someone as perfect for him as you are," she turns toward me then, her eyes glassy.

Well fuck, my heart hurts.

I feel so guilty because it's not like I can tell her that what she's seeing isn't love at all, but just top-notch acting abilities performed by her son.

If I can make it out of this house without the guilt eating me alive, I'll be happy.

"Oh, I don't know about all of that..." I trail off as I finish stuffing the last cream puff.

Victoriana waves a hand in my direction, "Oh, yes, it's probably too early to be talking about love and all those things, but I know what I see. He's absolutely infatuated with you."

Why does the idea of that make my stupid heart flutter in my chest?

Probably because no matter how much I try to deny it, my feelings towards Max are anything but fake. Much to my dismay they are very, very, real.

"What are my two favorite girls talking about?" Max smiles while sauntering into the kitchen and planting a kiss on my head.

Don't swoon, Josie. Don't you do it.

My two favorite girls...

"Talking about you," I say with a sigh as his lips leave my forehead. *Damn it. Stupid, stupid heart...*

"I knew it," he says with a smirk.

I take that moment to pick up a cream puff and shove it in his mouth, covering his face in cream filling. His tongue peaks out to lick some of the remnants from the corner of his lips, and suddenly I wish I was cream filling.

God, that's so cheesy.

"Delicious," he says with a devilish smirk. If his mother wasn't literally standing two feet away from us, I think I'd lick every bit of it off his face. The mere thought of it makes me shiver.

"Want some? Come give me a kiss, *gattina*," he mocks while leaning closer, threatening to transfer the leftovers to my face.

"Donkey Kong, I see your hand reaching behind you to grab a cream puff. You aren't as slick as you think you are," I say while slowly backing away as he begins to crowd me, following me with every step I take backward.

"Donkey Kong?" His mom questions with a mutter. I don't

even have time to explain because the hand currently holding the cream puff is slowly raising more and more by the second.

I turn backward to run towards the living room, booking it so he can't catch me. I realize very quickly that once I hit wood-paneled walls I have nowhere else to run. I'm boxed in.

"Hmm... girls do you think Josie needs a cream puff?" he asks with a purely evil grin.

"Yes!" All three of them cheer in unison while giggling uncontrollably at the display.

"No! I've been betrayed!" I yell dramatically, making the girls giggle even more.

"The jury has spoken," he says with a smirk before smashing the cream puff against my mouth, spreading the filling all over my lips, and sending three, little, adorable traitors into a fit of laughter so hard they fall to the floor.

Of course, because Victoriana made it, it tastes absolutely delicious. I moan the instant the light vanilla flavor hits my tongue.

"You wear it well," he says low enough for only me to hear, giving me a wink. I narrow my eyes at him even though his tone gives me hot chills down my spine.

"I think it's time to leave," I say breathlessly, giving my full intention away.

"Took the words right out of my mouth," he groans.

Max takes my hand and curls his fingers in mine, making his voice loud enough for everyone in the living room and adjoining kitchen to hear him. "We're about to leave!"

The girls whine and Evie groans, "But we were having fun!"

"Sorry girls, don't worry though we'll see you soon," he says while giving them a big group hug and lifting them all up at once causing yet another giggle fit.

We'll. We'll See you soon.

My heart flutters at the idea that maybe he doesn't want this to be the last time either.

Of course, there's always the chance that he just misspoke and has no qualms about me never seeing his family again. Or that he's just straight up lying to them.

God, they really need to make a manual on how to navigate your feelings towards your fake boyfriend that used to drive you insane. But now he's the best dick you've ever had in your life and makes you see other dimensions when you orgasm. But has never been emotionally available to another woman before and may or may not reciprocate your feelings. But somehow he's always so sweet and kind and thoughtful in ways I've never felt.

On second thought, maybe that's more of a niche thing specific to me.

As we say our goodbyes it takes us another fifteen minutes to actually leave, otherwise known as a Midwest goodbye, before we're walking towards Max's motorcycle.

I grab my helmet and fasten it on my head without a second thought and hop on the back, wrapping my arms around Max's waist.

"I'm going to suck your dick so good tonight," I whisper low in his ear, my chin resting against the cool leather of his jacket.

A low growl rumbles in his throat before he starts the motorcycle and we take off towards his place, the comfy brick home growing smaller behind us.

Chapter 21

Max:

I am in serious fucking trouble. I wish I could say that I'm not slowly unraveling at the seams, but I'm long past lying to myself. Exactly four hours past lying to myself to be precise.

I could lie to myself when I first kissed her and say that she was just hot, and that I liked the pouty way her lips pursed in annoyance any time I spoke.

I could lie to myself and Shawna when I needed to come up with a fake girlfriend on the fly, saying she was just randomly the first person to pop into my head.

I could lie to myself when I asked her to keep this stunt going for longer than just a week, saying it was to help convince Trevor that she was over him.

I could lie to myself when I tasted her on the rocks behind the waterfall, telling myself I was just proving I could make her orgasm.

I could lie to myself, and say I fucked her because I'm a horny asshole and she wanted to add getting dicked down to our arrangement. That I kept it going because her pussy is unreal, and I'd willingly drown myself in it.

But I can't lie to myself anymore. Seeing her with my family made it all different. She fucking fit right in, just like I knew she would. Even now as we walk upstairs to my apartment our family group chat is blowing up about how much they love Josie, and that if I fuck this up they'll disown me and adopt her in my place.

They aren't wrong though because if I fuck this up, I'll disown myself.

The truth? I'm fucking falling for Josie Jones, and it's not a gentle fall. It's a no-parachute, skydiving from thousands of feet, splattering on concrete kind of fall.

She haunts me. All I can think about when I'm not with her is how I can make up some dumb excuse so that I can be with her.

She's consuming me, and I have no goddamn idea what I'm doing. I've literally never felt like this before, and there truly is a 98% chance that I will fuck this up in some capacity.

I can't tell her how I'm feeling. Not until I know that I can do it without ruining everything. Damn it, I worked so hard to never let this happen. And yet here I am. Falling for my fake girlfriend.

"Um, hello? Donkey Kong? You going to open the door big guy?" Josie says while her hand skates down my back. A hot summer wind blows through and carries the coconut smell of her up to my nose, and it takes a Herculean effort to keep myself focused enough to unlock the door and not fuck her right here against the wall.

She leans in against my back and moves her hands to my front, lowering them until she's cupping the already prominent bulge in my pants. I can't even be embarrassed about how easily she gets me hard anymore. It's just a way of life. If Josie is near me, my dick is at full attention in a silent prayer that it'll get to be inside that tight cunt I love so much.

I groan as I push the door open and pull her through the doorway before quickly shutting and locking it behind me. In an instant I have her pinned to the door, hand gripping her throat before my lips crash into hers. Fuck, I love making her wear my tattoo like a necklace. No one has ever worn it better.

No one ever will.

She mewls a soft sound and I can feel the vibration in her

throat beneath my hand as she parts her lips so she can coax my tongue into playing with hers. My blood heats at the taste of her, instantly craving more. I want to feel every single part of her. To taste and claim her until there isn't an inch of her body I haven't tasted.

The terrifying realization that I need her more than I've ever needed anything before comes to the forefront of my brain and I want to tell her. Right here, right now, that I never want this to end. I want to pour every part of myself into her and let her drag me down to the depths, but I know I can't.

At least not yet.

Not until I've come up with a plan to show Josie that I'm not just some fuckboy, and that we can be more than just fun. We could be epic.

"On your knees," I command while fisting my hand in her curls and guiding her to the floor in front of me. We didn't even make it past the doorway. I haven't stopped thinking about her mouth on my dick since she teased me on my bike. Now all I can think about is smearing her red lipstick all over my cock and her face while I make her gag as she takes me to the back of her throat.

She hasn't given me head yet, but that was more purposeful on my part. That asshole she was with before was into receiving and never giving. I needed to show Josie that I'm not like that, or a lot of guys aren't anyway. Honestly, I'd rather give head than receive it any day of the week. I fucking love having the taste of her on my tongue.

But I'm not a saint by any means, if a woman is on my bike and whispers in my ear that she wants my dick in her mouth, she's going on her knees the second we're alone.

Her big brown eyes are full of need as she looks up at me from the floor. Josie immediately begins to claw at my belt while I massage her head where I grip her hair. She moans desperately once she has me unbuckled and tugs my pants and boxer briefs down to my ankles in one fell swoop, causing my dick to bob directly at mouth level.

She licks her red-painted lips slowly, and it's all I can do to keep myself from coming right then and there as she gently flicks her tongue out, and licks the precum leaking from my tip.

"Mmm..." she moans as she revels in the taste of me before flattening her tongue and licking me all the way from the base of my cock to the head.

"Fuck," I grit out as she continues to lightly lick around my leaking head but never letting me sink into her mouth.

"*Gattina*, quit teasing me, baby, please," I groan desperately as she gently licks my balls, making my spine tingle. Usually, I'm the one taking charge, but fuck if I don't want to let her have this moment. She may be the one on her knees, but I'm the one at her mercy. I want to sink into her hot mouth and make her gag on my dick more than I want air in my lungs.

She smirks up at me, "Should I put you out of your misery, Maximiliano?"

I inhale sharply at the use of my name. I've never had a woman call me by my full name while we fucked, not until Josie anyway. It does something to me. Something intimate and powerful that makes me want to do just about anything to hear my name on her lips over and over again.

She knows full well what it does to me, and she can't help but smile cockily, enjoying the effect she has on me. The pure mixture of bliss and torture that is Josie Jones on her knees for me and calling me by my full government name.

My hand is still fisting her curls, and I use the leverage to bring her lips back to my tip as she groans. My girl likes a little pain with her pleasure and I fucking love it. She may look like the girl next door, but she fucks like a whore.

Incredible.

Her lips wrap around my head, sucking lightly at first as her tongue plays with my slit, making me feel like my soul may just leave my body. The only warning I get is her eyes full of mischief and a smile around my cock before she sinks all the way down, making me bottom out down her throat.

She stays there, letting her tongue play at my base, licking up and around.

She feels like heaven.

"That's my girl," I moan as she lets drool fall from her mouth. Coating me. She takes her fingers and gently plays with my balls, now slick with her saliva before rubbing gentle circles with her thumb.

This is easily the best head I've ever gotten in my life. I don't know if that's just a testament to Josie's skills or if it's because I'm actually developing feelings for her, but either way I don't want this to ever end.

She takes her hand and wraps it around the base of my cock, pumping me while she pops her mouth off of me.

An audible groan is pulled from my throat at the loss of the heat from her mouth, and my hips have a mind of their own as they rut against the firm hold she has around my dick.

I watch as she takes one look at me, opening her mouth so I can see the saliva pooling there, and then gently alternates between licking my balls and sucking them in her mouth while continuing to run her hand up and down my length.

"That may have been the single hottest thing I've ever fucking seen," I moan as she massages my balls with her hand and takes me back into her mouth. Her head is bobbing up and down on my dick; her hot tongue teases with each and every thrust.

She grins with her mouth full before taking the fingers massaging circles on my balls and pressing at the sensitive spot behind them.

I moan loudly as the combination from the pressure on my perineum and my balls mixed with the ungodly things her tongue is doing to my shaft makes my legs shake uncontrollably.

"The couch. Now." I command while pulling her to her feet by her hair before kicking off the clothes pooling around my ankles.

"I wanted you to come," she pouts as we walk towards the black sectional in the middle of my living room. I pull her back towards my front and grip her thighs, pushing the hem of her dress upwards until my hands grip her hips, pushing her ass against my rock-hard cock. Her drenched, thin, pink thong takes nothing for me to hook my fingers into and pull down. My girl is soaked for me, and I need to feel her wet and hot and clenching around me desperately.

I unzip the back of her dress and yank it to the floor, leaving her bare and completely naked in my living room. Even my dreams could never be as good as the vision in front of me.

"Believe me if we kept going, I was going to. Now face the couch and put your knees on the floor," I command before discarding my shirt and watching as a naked Josie gets to her knees once more and leans over the couch.

I settle behind her, the warm skin of her back pressed against my chest. "Spread your legs for me pretty girl," I moan into her ear, making her shiver as she widens her stance.

My hands skate down her thighs to her center while my lips graze at the sensitive skin of her neck. She whimpers when my fingers find her wet and begging to be filled. Her hips buck against my hand as I circle her clit, causing her to grind her ass against me.

"Fuck, *gattina* you're so wet there's going to be a puddle on my floor," I groan as my fingers pick up their pace.

"If you keep. That up. I'm going. To. Come." She whimpers.

She rocks her hips against my length while I use my thumb to continue circling and I plunge two fingers inside her. She cries out and fucks my fingers as I feel her clench around them tightly. Josie rides out her release, grinding down her hips as much as she can and leaning her head back against my chest.

Her breathing is erratic as she comes down, and when I pull my fingers from her, they're sticky with her release.

I'm desperate for a taste.

She watches as I bring the middle and ring finger coated with her to my mouth and suck desperately. The tang of her hits my tongue and I audibly groan at how good she tastes.

"You taste so good, baby," I moan, her gaze never leaving my lips. "Why don't you see for yourself?" I urge, gripping her chin and forcing her lips against mine. I part them for a kiss and let my tongue glide against hers.

"Oh, fuck," she gasps, and I know she's still turned all the way on.

I can't take it anymore, I grab her hands and clasp them together, stretching her arms against the couch and locking them in place. The angle elongates her back, displaying her beautifully.

I notch my rock-hard cock against her entrance, and I'm desperate to fill her. Desperate to claim her. Desperate to say with my body what I can't say with my mouth. That I want, no need, her to be mine.

"Max, baby, please I need you to fill me. *Please*," she whines while wriggling her hips.

"You know I can't say no when you beg me so sweetly," I tease before slamming her down to the hilt in one thrust.

"Oh my God," she screams as I fill her.

"You take that dick so good," I praise as I begin to thrust in and up. From this angle I can see my cock disappear in and out of her from the back, her perfect ass jiggling with every thrust.

I smack it, making her cry out as her wet pussy all but strangles me. The slick heat of her makes me dizzy with need.

"You like when I smack that perfect ass, pretty girl?"

"Yes, oh my god, yes," she whimpers as I deliver another slap to her other cheek, never stopping my punishing rhythm.

"Say my name," I grit.

"Max," she pants.

"Not like that. You know what I want." I say with another smack.

I can practically feel her grin, "Pound me, Maximiliano, please. God, I'm so full."

My free hand snakes to her front and teases at her nipple, forcing a whimper from her throat. "Such a *good girl*," I praise once more as my spine begins to tighten, my hips getting more and more erratic with each thrust.

"I'm going to make you wear that pretty necklace you love so much."

"Please," she whimpers.

I release her hands and use the one tattooed with the rosary to hold her neck, using it as leverage to fuck her harder while applying a little bit of pressure. She babbles incoherently, and I can feel her gushing with how turned on she is.

I need her to come. If I'm honest, I don't even know how I made it this long. Must be from sheer willpower alone. I know exactly what she needs to get her there once more, my body so in tune with hers it knows what she needs without a second thought.

My fingers stop teasing her nipples and slide down her stomach to her clit, swollen and begging for an orgasm once more. I pick up my circles once again, causing unintelligible moans and words to fall from her lips.

Her walls begin to clamp down on my cock in a vice grip, making my balls tighten as my release begins to build.

"Come for me, Josie," I moan into her ear. That's all it takes to send her over the edge once more, her wet hot pussy clenching and spasming around me.

She screams, crying out in pleasure, and the sound sends me right over the edge with her. My vision blackens around the edges, guttural sounds coming from my throat as I bottom out inside her.

It feels too good, sending shockwaves through every vein in my body until I'm coming down, all tension in my body channeling through my dick as I empty myself inside her.

We're panting and sweating, sinking into one another as our souls come back to our bodies. She leans against my chest, and I drink in the coconut and sex smell flooding my nostrils.

"Stay the night," I find myself asking.

She turns around, raising an eyebrow at me. "Now that doesn't sound very fake boyfriend like," she retorts.

"Humor me," I reply while nuzzling her neck.

"Fine, but I have free reign to steal whatever t-shirt I want to sleep in and then take it home, never to be seen again." She says teasingly.

"Deal," I grin.

———

The next morning I wake up next to Josie dressed in my old worn out Beastie Boys t-shirt and nothing else. The sight of her tangled up in my sheets sound asleep is too beautiful for words, and I reach near creep levels as I watch her sleep.

Fuck. I've got it so bad. My heart beats erratically in my chest just looking at her. I'm fighting an internal war on whether I should bury myself beneath the sheets and wake her up licking her to orgasm or let her sleep.

As I have my internal debate, she turns on her side and stretches, facing me and looking at me sleepily with her big brown eyes.

"Good morning, Donkey Kong," she smiles.

"Good morning, *gattina*," I smile back before giving her a light kiss on the nose.

Nose kisses.

Have I been body snatched?

"You're a pretty good snuggler there, sir," she says with a wry grin.

"Well, you know, I am a man of many talents," I reply while wiggling my eyebrows suggestively.

She sighs and flings herself to her back, using her arm to cover her eyes. "Ugh, just add it to the never-ending list of things you're good at I guess."

I lean over, bridging the little space between us so I'm pressed against her side. "Sorry to disappoint," I chuckle before trailing kisses down her neck.

"Ughhh, I should probably leave soon. It's wash day." She groans.

"Wash day?"

"Yes, the day of the week I wash and deep condition my hair. These curls don't maintain themselves you know," she states matter-of-factly.

I push her shirt upward until she peals it over her head, and then continue trailing kisses down her chest before stopping at her nipple, gently teasing it with my teeth before sucking it between my lips, causing Josie to inhale sharply.

"You do have the most beautiful hair I've ever seen," I say before trailing kisses towards her other nipple and teasing it.

"You're just saying that because my tit is in your mouth," she snorts.

I look up at her then, "No. I'm not. I'd think that even if you weren't about to let me lick your clit," I smirk before trailing kisses down her belly.

"I don't remember saying anything about that—" she stops with a gasp as my tongue gently slides between her folds.

I quickly stop, lifting my head to look at her once more. "Oh, sorry, should I stop then? I know you have big plans today." I tease.

"Nope," she says breathily before shoving my head back down under the sheets to finish what I started.

———

"So, have you figured out you're in love with her yet?" Liam asks jokingly before tossing the basketball at my head.

Liam and I frequently play basketball after our workout. Well, I play. He loses. About 98% of the time. He's on a weird streak today that is starting to concern me though.

He's only beaten me twice. Once when I was hungover and the other time when I let him win after his ex, Blair, broke up with him and he needed the morale boost. Not that he knows that though.

"Don't throw the ball at my head you little dick," I retort before catching the ball right in front of my nose.

"Believe me, there's nothing little about it," he smirks, wiggling his eyebrows at me before crouching down to block me.

"Yes, yes, your girlfriend tells you that you have a massive hammer dick or whatever," I say in exasperation.

"*Mjolnir.* Jesus, know your superhero weapons," he scoffs.

I dribble the ball and try to cut to the right, but to my complete shock he meets me step for step and knocks the ball out of my hand.

"Quit deflecting and answer the question," he orders while dribbling the ball down the court.

"Yeah... About that..." I trail off before swiping at the ball and missing again.

God, what is with me today?

Liam stops in his tracks and signals for a time out. I don't know why. It's just the two of us. "I fucking knew it!" He shouts happily before adjusting his glasses. Ever since Ella told him almost a year ago that his glasses were cute, he hasn't gone back to his contacts.

"Woah, woah, woah, don't get so excited or anything. It's not like I'm marrying her."

"...but you, Maximiliano Rossi, actually have feelings for someone? *Romantic* ones? I-want-to-cuddle-up-in-a-hospital-bed-and-die-at-the-same-time-when-we're-old feelings." He's enjoying this far too much.

"Seems oddly specific," I deadpan.

He shrugs, "Ella made me watch *The Notebook* last week. Shit's romantic as fuck. I'm a bird, you're a bird and all that made me tear up."

"Well, the problem is that I have no actual idea how to date someone. If I hypothetically did want to date them. But after seeing her with my family... That's it. I don't know how to do this, but I'm willing to learn. For her. Because... well..."

"Because she makes you want to build her dream house with a wrap-around porch and blue shutters by hand as a physical manifestation of your love for her?" He supplies.

"Again. Very specific."

"I may have watched it three more times since she showed it to me," he shrugs again.

I snort, "Yeah, I guess. More like a shed. I don't know if I'm ready for a whole house right now. Let's start with a shed."

He rolls the basketball from one hand to the other, "Hmmm... yeah. What says, 'love shed?'"

"You know, Josie and Ella are a lot alike. I've known Josie for a long time and her parents may be Daddy Warbucks rich, but she isn't impressed by fancy stuff. Ella said one of Josie's biggest pet peeves about Trevor is that any time they had a problem he would throw money at it. Shit's disingenuous. All she wanted was for him to spend time with her and care about what she likes."

"So, something cheap and romantic. That says I don't need to buy your feelings...?" I hedge.

"Exactly!" Liam answers.

"Like a picnic?" That's something I know Josie would like. She's a foodie, and if I go to Trader Joes and get some cheese and wine and then set up a nice little spread for us at Holliday Park. I know she'd like it.

"Dude, perfect. Woo her with a picnic." He says excitedly before using his IU Robotics t-shirt as a towel to mop up the sweat on his forehead.

"Woo her with a picnic. I don't know if anyone has ever uttered those words in a sentence together before," I chuckle.

"Hey, if you think I won't trademark that phrase in commemoration of the first time Max actually came to me for relationship advice, you're dead wrong." He smiles cockily.

"I don't like what this is doing to you. Between stealing the ball from me, talking about your hammer dick, and giving me relationship advice, you're becoming drunk with power." In a flash I steal the ball from his hands and score a basket with a lay-up. I throw a shit-eating grin Liam's way, and do a little dance in celebration of his defeat.

"Don't worry the moment is ruined," he says, narrowing his eyes at me with fake dejection.

———

I have everything set up perfectly, and it's romantic as hell if I do say so myself. I grabbed my blue quilted blanket my mom made me for Christmas a few years ago and made a Trader Joe's run. Fifty dollars later I have champagne, three different types of cheese, crackers, grapes, water, and strawberries.

Yes. The champagne was five dollars. Nothing wrong with a little bottle of Andre' once you spruce it up with some strawberry juice. *The idea is to woo her with the picnic, not how much I spent on the picnic... right?*

I made Josie meet me here so I could have everything set up when she found me. Something I probably should've thought about before trying to put everything in my small hatch attached to my bike. Ever try driving a motorcycle while trying to balance a massive brown paper Trader Joe's bag?

Don't.

Since Shawna gave me the go ahead to work from home today and Josie is on summer break, a picnic in the middle of the week at Holliday Park is great because it's not very crowded right now. We have the ruins to ourselves. They recently reopened them after decades of them being closed, and the stone archways help shade from the nagging July sun beating downward.

I walk up the stone steps and head inward towards the middle of the structure before deciding on a decently shaded area to lay down the blanket. As I pull everything out of the bag, I start to realize that I didn't grab cups... or a knife... or anything to eat with.

Well, I guess I'm really leaning into the cheap wooing concept. "Jesus," I mutter to myself before grabbing a bottle of water and rinsing the grapes and strawberries so they're edible. I also take out the cheese, and use the plastic wrap around it as a makeshift plate.

The first attempt at a picnic woo is not going how I wanted it to, but hopefully Josie takes pity on me and lets me down gently when she breaks off our arrangement the moment she sees cheese being served to her on plastic wrap and is forced to drink straight from the bottle of Andre'.

"Donkey Kong, what's all this?" I hear from over my shoulder. I turn around to see Josie in a yellow dress with white flower print and her curls wild in the way that drives me crazy, with her lips a pinkish orange color that gives me the urge to mess it up.

She's so beautiful it makes my heart rate spike and that must be why the phrase, "A picnic woo," is my response.

Her brown eyes are full of repressed laughter, "A picnic... what?"

"Hah, nothing. Come sit?" I ask patting the spot on the blanket next to me.

A small smile plays on her lips, as she sits at my side. I grab the bottle of champagne and I'm grateful that's what I chose when I realize I don't have a wine opener on me anyways. I quickly pop off the cork and take a swig, letting the bubbles burn down my throat and praying that they calm my nerves.

What is it about this woman that makes me so nervous? I'm desperate for her to see a new side of me. One that doesn't say "I don't know anything about being a boyfriend and have the romantic attention span of a fly on its last hour of life."

I hand the bottle to Josie, and she quickly wraps her black painted nails around the neck of the bottle before bringing it to her lips. I watch her throat work as she takes a few gulps, removing the bottle on a giggle.

"Ahhh, good old Andre'."

I grab a strawberry and bring it to her lips so she can take a bite to balance out the champagne, and some of the juice drips down as she laughs. I desperately fight the urge to lick it off her chin.

"I didn't realize picnics were part of the fake-boyfriend bundle." She smirks before taking another sip from the bottle.

"Call this an added benefit," I smile before grazing my thumb beneath her lip, catching the excess juice.

"We sure have added a lot of benefits to the original agreement," she remarks before nipping my thumb with her teeth.

The feel of her biting my thumb before lightly sucking it sends all of the blood in my body straight to my cock. "*Gattina...* if you keep doing that I'm going to say, 'fuck this picnic' and fuck you against that wall until you come."

Her lips release my thumb with a pop. "What if that's what I want?" she says coyly.

"Then fuck this picnic," I laugh before grabbing the back of her neck and pulling her lips towards mine.

The taste of her lips mixed with the strawberry and champagne; it sends me reeling as my tongue licks against her lips to tangle with her own. I've barely had any alcohol and I feel drunk. The urge to claim her right here, right now, is so strong I can't take it.

I wanted this to be different. I didn't want this to be just about sex with us, but as her teeth lightly tug at my bottom lip I'm starting to wonder why anything else in the world other than tasting Josie ever mattered.

She hastily grabs at my belt while my hand grips her thigh, inching its way upward. I quickly pull away to look at our surroundings, making sure we aren't facing a public indecency charge, before grabbing Josie's hand in mine and pulling her up against the stone pillar, our mouths never leaving each other.

A loud moan escapes her throat when I brace her against the wall and wrap her legs around my waist, forcing me to use the hand not gripping her hip to cover her mouth.

"Quiet, *gattina*, those moans are only for me," I grunt before pressing kisses down her neck.

Her fingers deftly work against my button, undoing it and

pulling my cock free from the hole in my boxer briefs, before giving it a rough stroke that makes my blood boil.

"You have two minutes to come baby, I can't risk anyone seeing my pussy." I grit before moving her lacy white thong to the side and notching my cock to her entrance.

"Oh, fuck," she whimpers behind my hand before I slide myself in all the way to the hilt. I use the leverage of the grip on her hips to drive her down against me, fucking her hard while she drenches my dick. She feels like a wet dream.

"You moan so sweet for me," I say while biting down on her neck, picking up my pace and moving my hand from her mouth to circle her clit with my hand.

Her eyes begin to water with the strain of her repressed screams and the sight nearly has me coming right then and there. I quicken the speed of my circles until she begins to shatter around me.

Her pussy clamps down on my cock with a vice grip as she convulses around me. The sensation sends me right over the edge along with her as I bury my face in the crook of her neck to keep from yelling.

Her lashes flutter as she comes down, tracing light kisses across my jaw until our breathing evens out. I could stay like this forever, buried inside her. And even though this isn't how I intended for our afternoon to go, it just reaffirms it, Josie Jones is the one for me.

CHAPTER 22

JOSIE:

My feelings are just one giant jumbled mess. I'm like a walking Usher album right now and I don't know what the hell to do. Never in a million years would I think that I'd be caught up and fawning over freaking Maximiliano Rossi.

No one tell Ella. She'll never let me live this down. It'll be "I told you so's" until we're in the retirement home playing Mah-Jong and eating a Salisbury steak dinner at 4:30pm together.

He packed a fucking picnic and took me to my favorite park; I mean how could I not physically melt at the sheer idea of that? Max has only really known me less than a month and knew what I would like more than a man I was with for literal years.

He just gets me in a way no man ever has before. We have fun, conversation is easy, and he does unholy things to my body. Things that even if he didn't have everything else already going for him, I would be inclined to never leave solely based on that.

The man can dick me good. That's for sure.

The question isn't just does he like fucking me, but does he actually have feelings for me? I mean the man planned a whole date, and sometimes when he looks at me I feel like there's a whole lot more there than lust, but what do I know? He could just be really committed to our agreement.

The fact of the matter is I can't expect that I'm going to be the unicorn of a woman that's going to convince Max to commit. Me. I'm the same person who couldn't even get a man to commit to her after he bought a literal fucking ring and put it on my finger and promised to marry and love me forever.

The irony of it all truly is astounding.

I grab my orange scrunchie off the coffee table and throw up my hair in a bun on top of my head before curling up on my beanbag chair. Ugh, I was probably just getting my own feelings for Max confused for how he feels about me.

To make matters worse, I angered a God somewhere and in the midst of my emotional turmoil I also started my damn period with the cramps sent from Beelzebub himself. All in all, I'm content to shut myself up in my apartment and weather this storm until it's over. However, as good as I am at gaslighting myself, I don't know if I'll be able to do it when it comes to Max.

I think I need to tell him how I feel.

I feel my phone vibrate in my pocket and pull it out to find a text from the man in question.

Donkey Kong: Can I come over?

Me: Sorry just started my period. The cave of wonders is currently under remodel and isn't accepting visitors.

Donkey Kong: As if that would stop me...

Donkey Kong: Just saying that doesn't bother me. If you want me in the cave of wonders I'm in there like Aladdin searching for a magic lamp.

Donkey Kong: In case you're wondering, your clit is the genie lamp in this scenario.

I can't help but laugh at the imagery that produces. I've never even attempted that before. I know I've more than established the fact that Trevor and Max are completely different, but whenever this time of the month came around Trevor called it "blow job week."

Lord, I do really want to see him, no matter how potentially dangerous it is to my heart.

Me: Rumor has it if you rub it, I'll grant you three wishes.

Me: Interesting offer, but I'm in a shit ton of pain, so that's probably not going to happen.

Donkey Kong: Jos, we don't have to have sex to spend time together.

Is it possible for your heart to explode from a text? Because it truly feels like it's going to. Be still my bleeding vagina, he's so sweet. This is not helping with the confusion I'm feeling though that's for sure.

Me: I guess I don't really understand the parameters of this fake relationship anymore...

Donkey Kong: Come on Josie, you know we blurred the lines of fake a long time ago.

Donkey Kong: Let me come over and take care of you gattina.

It feels like my heart is in my throat. That really seems like he's trying to tell me I'm not crazy. That his feelings for me are about as fake as the ones I have for him

Me: Okay Donkey Kong, come over.

An hour later I'm answering my door to a beaming Max, his hands carrying target bags through the doorway before I follow him towards my kitchenette. He sets the bags on the countertop and I look over the spread before me.

"What is all of this?" I ask while pulling a bottle of Oliver soft red from the bag. *My favorite wine?*

"Period supplies!" He says excitedly before pulling out a box of Midol and handing it to me.

"How do you…?" I trail off.

"I have a mom and two sisters. It'd be embarrassing not to know. Plus, I may have texted your best friend to see what some of your favorites were," he says proudly.

Ella's in on this? She was literally the one telling me she didn't want me to get hurt and now she's giving my fake-boyfriend pointers. What changed in the last couple of weeks?

"What a little sneak," I smirk.

Max rifles through the bags, pulling items out as he goes. "We've got peanut butter M&Ms, popcorn, Ben and Jerrys, and dark chocolate almonds." I can't help but smile because he's so proud of himself he keeps beaming at me.

This feels very boyfriend-y.

"Max, this is so sweet, really, thank you." I say before tilting up and pressing a kiss to his cheek.

"She also mentioned that I needed to suggest that we watch a movie that is at least fifteen years old, but to act like it was my idea." He opens up the freezer to put my ice cream in and I grab the bag of popcorn off the countertop and walk over to my loveseat.

"Wow she even added Millennial Movie Marathon into the mix. My best friend, the puppet master," I say coyly.

Again though, I ask, what changed? She clearly knows something I don't.

"Where's your heating pad?" Max asks, interrupting my thoughts. I point to the closet next to my kitchenette and he goes to grab it.

"Go sit down, baby," he says before pulling my heating pad out of the closet and plugging it in behind me, settling the fabric behind my back. He grabs a blanket and drapes it over me as the heat from the pad immediately starts to soothe the pain in my back.

Max ques up the movie *John Tucker Must Die*, and the nostalgia alone almost kills me dead right there. "Oh my God, I love this movie!" I say excitedly.

He gives me a smirk, "I can't take all the credit. My fairy godmother helped me out."

Really Ella? John Tucker Must Die? A little on the nose don't you think. I can't tell if she did that on purpose or it's a sign from the skinny scarf and low-rise jean gods that I really have a chance at reforming my player.

He settles onto the couch next to me and wraps his arms around the back, drawing small circles with his thumb on my shoulder as we watch the movie. This is far too comfortable, and my heart is 100% not going to be able to take much more of this. Max was easy to blow off when he was the cocky player always hitting on me, but sweet Max that watches cheesy movies with me and steals my popcorn when he thinks I'm not paying attention is far too much to handle.

As I watch Kate convince John Tucker to wear a red thong and scale the hotel building, I rest my head against his muscular arm and look up at his beautiful hazel eyes full of laughter.

"You know, I used to think you were a John Tucker." I tell him before a big smile spreads across his face at my comment.

"Used to?" he presses.

I hook my fingers with his and bring his hand to my lips, planting a small kiss there before setting it back down. "Yeah... Used to. Let's just say you've surprised me."

He leans his head down to give me a soft kiss on the lips, so gentle and so full of emotion that I can't help but read more into it. That comment means more to him than anything else I ever could have said, and I'm starting to realize that he truly wants to change. I think that maybe I really am the unicorn of a woman that's going to change his mind.

CHAPTER 23

MAX

Realistically, I knew Josie's family had money. She never hid it by any means. It wasn't a secret. But as I walk up the stone pathway of an obscenely long cobblestone driveway leading up to literal mansion of a house, I didn't realize it was fuck you money.

That's the only phrase I can think of to describe the massive white colonial in front of me. Seeing my motorcycle in the expansive driveway, I don't think I've felt poorer in my entire life. Don't get me wrong, it's not like I live in an empty refrigerator box on the side of the highway, but compared to this... I might as well.

I feel Josie nudge my arm, making my rampant thoughts disappear like smoke. She's a pro at getting off my bike now, and she does a dramatic gymnastics style "stick the landing" gesture before taking off her helmet and shaking out her curls.

We could've taken my actual car, and believe me I offered, but she insisted this would have the more desired effect. She also apparently didn't even know I had a car, but living in Indiana isn't exactly a year-round option for a motorcycle. I guess it's not like I've exactly shown it to her yet since it's only been summer since this whole thing began.

Two months. That's how long it's been since Josie and I

drunkenly kissed, forever altering the course of our lives. I was nothing but a man-whore she couldn't stand being around for longer than a minute then, but now I've come to realize that this whole time we've been nothing short of inevitable.

I'm supposed to be meeting her parents as her fake boyfriend, but since my epiphany a couple weeks ago I haven't been able to bring myself to once again alter the terms of our agreement. I don't want fake anymore, I want real.

I just need to show Josie that's something I'm capable of, and in order to do that, I need to actually make a good impression on her family. Suddenly this dinner that was no big deal when we first planned it now holds the fate of my first ever relationship in the balance.

I feel absolutely no pressure right now. None.

"Hey, where'd you go just now?" she asks.

I lightly clear my throat and flash a smile. I hope it looks genuine and not at all like it's a mask for how I feel on the inside. "Nothing, *gattina*, just thinking about how your face will look when they offer me your dowry and ask if I want cows or sheep."

She snorts, "No suitor of mine would accept anything less than both. I've grown accustomed to a certain lifestyle after all."

I chuckle and intertwine my fingers with hers before we walk up the stone steps to ring the doorbell. If Josie is nervous, she's hiding it well. Meanwhile, my stomach feels like it's going to fall out of my dick.

A man with deep set wrinkles and a receding hairline answers the door. "Welcome Ms. Jones, your parents and sister just moved to the table for dinner. You and your *friend* can meet them there." Why am I not a fan of the way he emphasized the word friend so much in that sentence?

Josie flashes Sir Butler Snootington III a winning smile, "Thank you, James. I can show him the way."

Personally, I think my name suits him better.

Josie tugs me by the hand through an entryway that looks like something out of a robber baron's wet dream. All polished white marble and echoing footsteps as we go down the long hallway to what I'm assuming is the dining room slash conservatory slash fine china display room. Maybe I should've done what SpongeBob did and forget everything that wasn't fine dining and breathing before coming here, because this is a lot.

I suddenly feel underdressed in my gray chinos and black button up, like maybe I should've worn a tuxedo before they even let me through the door. Josie on the other hand looks like this is just any other day and pastes a maroon-painted smile across her face that I only now know is a mask.

She's nervous.

That makes two of us.

"Hey, you say the word and we turn back around." I say in a whisper barely loud enough for her to hear. She grips my fingers tighter, giving them a squeeze before we reach the dining room. I feel her back straighten immediately.

The room is large, with a dark oak table long enough that twelve people could sit comfortably in the black chairs that line the outside. Say what you will about her parents, but they do have good taste. In another life where I wasn't here as Josie's peasant boyfriend brought to make a point, I might even tell them that.

Her father sits at the head of the table, with her mother and sister sitting to the left of him, three place settings sit across from them for what I assume is for Josie, me, and the queen in case she happens to stop by. I try and school my features, unsure of how to proceed.

Do I like kiss his rings and bow or...?

Thankfully, her dad stands up from his seat and the rest of the family follows suit. His dark umber skin crinkles around his eyes as he smiles towards his daughter, revealing bleached white teeth.

"Jojo Bean, so glad you made it," he says before placing a kiss on top of her head. He all but towers over her. The man is a mountain, even taller than Liam.

"You're late," he chastises. "Am I to assume that's because the car you drove in on lost two wheels and four doors on the way here?"

Okay. So not off to a great start. Cool.

"Daddy," she says, steeling her voice. "This is my boyfriend, Maximiliano Rossi." She gestures towards me.

"You can call me Max." I say while trying to flash him the most winning smile I can muster. "Pleasure to meet you sir."

"Cecil. You can call me Mr. Jones." He responds with a firm handshake and a grunt.

Alrighty then...

"Hello Max, I'm Laura, Mrs. Jones," Josie's mom says while extending her perfectly manicured hand in my direction. She's all poise and gives me a brief smile before Makenzie extends her hand to shake mine as well.

So formal. Are all families like this? Mine all but tackled Josie the moment she walked through the door of my parents' house. Not for the first time I'm reminded just how different our two worlds are. My family is so loud that when you leave you almost have a ringing in your ears from the volume. In here you could hear the echo of a pin dropping on the marble flooring on the opposite end of the house for how quiet it is.

We take our seats around the table and a woman in all black brings us salads. I stare at Josie until I see what fork she picks up, so I know which one to grab. She notices my confusion and she gives me a small smile before squeezing my thigh, reassuring me.

"So, Max. What is it you do for work?" Cecil asks me before taking a sip of the red wine in front of him.

I take a bite of my salad quickly, buying myself time on how to phrase it so it doesn't "sound like I go on vacation for a living" as Josie puts it.

I swallow the bite along with the lump in my throat, "I write for a travel company."

"Oh? How interesting. You must travel a lot." Laura remarks before taking a rather large gulp of her Chardonnay.

"I do. That's actually how Josie and I went to Fiji."

"Max is an incredible writer. The Fiji project was his biggest assignment yet, and if it does well his boss says that he'll be offered many more when she gets back from maternity leave." Josie says with a proud smile, giving my thigh another squeeze.

"And that pays well? Good benefits?" Laura hedges.

"I admit most of the benefit is the travel and flexible schedule, assuming I meet my deadlines, and writing has always been a passion of mine. I do okay considering all of that." I respond politely.

That, apparently, was the wrong answer. I see Makenzie's eyes dart back and forth before folding her lips in on themselves and paying entirely too much attention to the salad in front of her.

"And you and my daughter, you'll be able to live comfortably on 'doing okay?'" Cecil asks bluntly. "She's a guidance counselor for God's sake, she's barely able to take care of herself financially, let alone you."

I see Josie clench her fork in a death grip from the corner of my eye. "I do just fine, Daddy. You guys really don't have to interrogate him so thoroughly before we've all even finished our salad." She says pointedly.

"Well, someone certainly has to. Do you even know this man?" Cecil asks gruffly.

The grip on her fork has become white knuckled, and I feel bad for the silverware in question as it seems to be taking all of Josie's wrath. "Of course, I do. He's my boyfriend," she says between clenched teeth.

Why does that phrase coming from her lips make me feel all fuzzy on the inside? Josie's boyfriend. If only I could actually be so lucky.

I'll convince her, I will, but we've got to get through this dinner as unscathed as humanly possible before I do all of that. I could listen to her call me her boyfriend again and again and never be tired of it though, something that would've sent me running all but two months ago.

Laura scoffs loudly, flinging her newly bleached platinum

blonde hair behind her shoulders. "Oh, please! We've never even heard of this man until a little over a month ago. One second, we're at Ella's house and you two aren't dating. Then suddenly we have to find out from your sister that you're posting pictures with him in another country!"

Josie narrows her gaze diagonally across the table at her sister, "Yeah, thanks for that by the way Kenz." Her sarcastic tone is about as subtle as a moose in an antique shop.

Makenzie finally lifts her gaze towards her sister, the same doe brown eyes as Josie's. You can tell they're related, except Makenzie's hair is stick straight, burned into submission from a flat iron. and her voice is softer. In general, her presence seems... smaller than Josie's' somehow.

"I wasn't trying to be a snitch or anything," she says, her voice trembling.

Before Josie can respond back, Cecil interrupts her. "Don't blame your sister. Hell, if anything you could stand to learn a thing or two from her."

I feel bad for the woman that has to clear our salad plates and replace them with the main course. Her eyes widen, but she keeps her head down, focused on setting the plate of roasted chicken, potatoes, and asparagus in front of us. I whisper a thank you to her before she all but flees the room.

Josie scoffs loudly before piercing a piece of asparagus on her fork. "Of course! I should be just like Makenzie. So perfect, doing exactly what mommy and daddy expect her to. God, you should just clone her and get rid of me all together! Have a little army of Makenzie minions at your disposal so you don't have to have a daughter that thinks for herself!"

The entire room goes impossibly still at her words. Clearly this is something Josie has thought about before, and she blanches at realizing the words actually flew out of her mouth in her rage.

"Shit, Kenz I'm so sorry," Josie says in a flurry of words. I can hear the guilt in them instantly. From what Josie has told me, the relationship she has with her sister is a complex one. I think because of the way their parents constantly compare them, there wasn't much time for them to do anything other than resent each other.

Makenzie's voice is barely louder than a whisper as she stares down at her plate. "It's... fine. I just... need a second." She says before scooting her chair back loudly and leaving the room.

"Now look what you've done." Cecil grits before taking a long gulp of his wine.

Before Josie can say anything the doorbell rings, echoing around the marble floors and bouncing up to the high ceilings.

"I'll get that!" Laura says before jumping up and running to the front door. *That's weird. I thought they didn't answer their own doors.*

My answer comes minutes later, when a smarmy looking blonde guy in a dark suit that looks straight off the cover of the *GQ Boats and Polo* issue comes strolling in, a shit-eating grin spread along his very punch-able face. I know who he is before he even says a word.

"Hey, baby, miss me?" He says cockily.

"Trevor," Josie hisses.

Well... Fuck.

CHAPTER 24

JOSIE

I thought I knew rage.

I really did.

I thought I had hit the limit when I caught him cheating on me over a year ago, but apparently that was just scratching the surface. Because how I'm feeling right now, this is a new record.

This is the Hulk getting ready to smash everything around him to bits and needing to be told "the sun's getting real low" before he levels an entire city, kind of rage.

"What the hell are you doing here?" I say through clenched teeth. I feel Max lift to get up out of his seat, but I grip his thigh as a silent plea for him not to move.

"I was invited, baby," he says with a smirk while adjusting his cufflinks. I can't believe there was a time in my life where I thought I was going to marry this man. The word baby coming out of his mouth feels like someone injected venom into my veins. He is basically a snake. Well, if snakes liked gelling back their hair and voting against women's reproductive rights while kicking puppies in the shin.

On second thought, snakes are far better than this man. At least with a snake you can see it unhinging its jaw first before it bites you and fills you with venom. A luxury I wasn't afforded with Trevor.

"I seriously doubt that," I hear Max all but growl from the seat next to me. I apply more pressure to the hand on his thigh, but I don't think that's going to hold him off much longer.

"Don't you dare call me baby! You lost those privileges when I found you with your dick in your receptionist." I seethe.

My mother leans on the table, making the place settings clatter together with the force. "Josie Ann! That's enough. I invited him. It's time to end all of this foolishness. Stop punishing Trevor for something that happened over a year ago and take him back. We all know this isn't serious."

The literal audacity of my mother. Dear God I never in a million years would've thought she would stoop as low as to ambush me at a dinner my boyfriend is supposed to be meeting her at with my ex. Well, my fake-boyfriend, but it's not like she knows that.

"Are you out of your mind?" I yell.

She levels her sharp blue gaze at me, narrowing her eyes. "No. I actually think I'm the sanest person in this room. How could you throw away everything we've built for you because of one mistake?"

"Wait... are you guys seriously taking one-percent Ken's side over your own daughter?" I hear Max ask while looking between my mom and dad.

"With all due respect, Max, this is none of your concern." My father says, his deep timbre echoing across the table.

Before I can even respond I hear Trevor scoff. "Yeah, JoJo, this is about you and me, and I'm really sorry. Just forgive me already. I get it, cheating is bad. I learned my lesson. Now dump the minimum wage idiot and come back to a man who can actually take care of you."

Max lunges forward, "You little fucking—"

"Max don't." I say, placing a hand on his chest. "I've got this.

Trevor, what you're not going to do is talk to the man I love like that."

I don't even realize the words I said until they leave my throat, but by then it's too late, they're out and tangible as I feel Max stiffen next to me. "Love...?" he whispers questioningly. The words are so quiet that they're barely audible at all.

The word shocks even me, but I know I can't pretend that I said them as part of the ruse. Those came from the deepest part of me. Because it's true. I love Max. I think I have for a long time and pretended to hate him because I couldn't handle the attraction I had for him.

This isn't the time to dwell on this now, and I know now more than ever that I've got to tell Max how I feel, but first I need to yell at my ex. "This isn't the 1800's. I can take care of myself! But believe me, he takes care of me in ways you never could."

I knew that comment would sting. Trevor's a guy whose pride means more to him than just about anything, and I can't even find it in my heart to be embarrassed that I said this in front of my parents because the look on his face is just too priceless.

Trevor's jaw clenches, and I think I got him, that is until he opens his big dumb mouth again. "Oh yeah? And how is that? Look at him! He probably clubs you over the head before carrying you back to his cave. Is that the life you want? To be with a man you'll have to struggle with? Live in a two-bedroom ranch with ten dollars in savings and a ring with a diamond so small you need a microscope to see it? You deserve more than that and you know it."

Max is impossibly still beside me, and I can't even imagine what's going through his mind right now, although I can guess he'll never want to date me for real after all of this is over. "I am so fucking sick of everyone telling me what they think I deserve! Hot take, Trevor, you and I aren't together anymore so you don't get to have an opinion on how I choose to live my life."

I turn my ire towards my parents. I'm not nearly done letting out a year's worth of pent up anger. "And you two. How..." my voice threatens to break, and hot angry tears build up behind my eyes. But I refuse to let them see me cry. "How could you do this to me? When am I ever going to be good enough to be your daughter? Why am I only good enough when I'm pretending to be someone I'm not?"

I look up to the ceiling, begging gravity to do its work and make my tears fall backwards behind my eyes. I fucking hate being an angry crier. On the outside I feel weak, but on the inside all I feel is rage.

I look to Max then, a calm in my raging storm. "Why is Max the only person at this table that cares who I really am?"

His hazel eyes soften, and in this moment I know that I could walk away from the table and leave this life I never wanted behind me. I'm strong enough to stand up to my parents now. Not because Max changed me, but because for the first time in my life I feel safe enough to change.

I grab his hand in mine, no longer sad for what I have to do next, just angry. I am so damn angry at the years I wasted trying to be who everyone else wanted me to be. "I've had enough. Let's go."

My parents sit there in stunned silence as I take the cloth napkin off my lap and throw it angrily down on the table before scooting my chair back so rapidly that it makes a loud screeching sound. Hopefully it scratched the marble flooring beneath it.

Max follows suit and I grab his hand, all but tugging him with me. I feel more rage still bubbling to the surface. The audacity of this man, my parents, it's too much and all I can see is red.

I spin around on my heel and face the table once more. "And another thing, this is where the clit is!" I yell while pointing to the outside of my dress. "Something apparently you need a microscope to find! Did you know I can actually have an orgasm from sex? I didn't! Not until I met Max anyway. I guess I'm not 'one of those women who don't come' like you so elegantly mentioned before."

Max snorts, trying to conceal his amusement, and now he's

the one guiding me towards the door. I should probably stop talking. A saner woman would.

Unfortunately for me, my sanity and any pretense I have about what comes out of my mouth has long since left the building. "You're all cut off except Kenz!" I shout as I walk towards the front door before spinning back around to give one last parting shot.

"Oh, and in case you're wondering, his dick is definitely bigger than yours!" I call out over my shoulder before we exit down the hallway that leads to the front door. The pin-drop silence I receive back makes me confident that I made my point.

"Okay, killer, I think they got the message." Max says with a chuckle before handing me my helmet.

My nerves are shot, and the adrenaline surge is starting to make my hands shake as I get on the back of the motorcycle and wrap my arms around Max. The loud rumbling of the engine drowns out all the noises and thoughts in my head except one.

I cannot believe I just did that.

CHAPTER 25

MAX

It's the day after I basically had to extract Josie from her parent's house, and I don't think I slept longer than an hour last night. I'm sick to my stomach.

She had already been through the ringer last night, so she wasn't in the mood to talk about the little phrase she said back at her parents. I'm sure it was just part of the lie that we're together, but still, hearing it made me feel like my chest cavity had been cracked open and she grabbed ahold of my heart.

I wanted to so badly tell her that I love her too, because God help me, I do, but it didn't stop my brain from running all fucking night.

I hate myself for what I'm about to do.

As I stand on Josie's *Scooby-Doo* welcome mat with the phrase *"Relcome,"* scrolled across in orange font I can't bring myself to raise my fist to knock on the door. I've been standing here for three minutes already and each time I chicken out.

No part of me wants to do this.

The sad truth though is that Trevor is right, as much as saying that threatens to make the cereal I had this morning come back up my throat, it's true. Not the part where Josie should be with him, because he absolutely does not deserve her, but the part where Josie is too good for me.

Because she is.

Josie deserves more than a guy who's never been in a committed relationship before. More than a guy who would just disappoint her anyway. More than a little bitch who can't even tell her that he's in love with her.

Because I am. After watching her stand up for herself last night, how could I not love her? She was incredible.

When you love someone, you want what's best for them, and the reality is that I'm self-aware enough to know it's not me.

Just fucking knock on the door already, Max, Jesus. Rip it off like a band aid.

I finally knock and a few moments later Josie's answering the door, smiling brightly at me in just her panties and a Dolly Parton t-shirt.

Fuck. Me. I just want to throw her over my shoulder and lay her out on her bed.

Don't be selfish. This is for the best. Don't back down now.

"Hey, Donkey Kong," she giggles before leaning over and planting a kiss on my cheek.

"Hey, Josie," I say in the most even tone I can muster.

As I shut the door and follow her inside, she looks over her shoulder at me, giving me an assessing gaze. "Did you just call me Josie?"

Okay. Moment of truth. "I just figured since our agreement is over, we'd go back to using our government names," I say plainly.

"Our agreement...?" She turns around and folds her arms across her chest, looking me dead in the eye.

I clear the blockage forming at the back of my throat. "Yeah, we don't have to pretend we have feelings for each other anymore."

"Pretend?" She scoffs. "I'm sorry, were you not the one who told me 'We'd blurred the lines of fake a long time ago?'"

"Momentary lapse of judgment," I shrug. Lying like this hurts way more than I ever could've imagined. The acid in my throat burns like hell.

Her eyes grow watery and full of indignation. I know my words sting. I hate myself for it, but not as much as I would hate myself if Josie ended up settling for me. "So, this entire time... This has been fake for you? I'm just another tally mark in your little black book?"

No. "Yes."

"Say it," she says, her brown eyes shining with suppressed tears and her mouth pinching in a fine line.

"Say what?"

"Say, 'Josie, this whole thing is fake. I've never had feelings for you.'"

I suck in air through my teeth, my heartbeat slowing in my chest. "Josie, this whole thing is fake. I've never had feelings for you."

"Unbelievable. My God, you are so full of shit, Max."

"You knew what this was," I say before turning towards the door.

"I can't believe I fell for this shit. I fucking knew better, and yet here I am, again, falling for a guy whose emotionally unavailable. God, I am such an idiot."

I reach for the doorknob, but I can't bear to look over my shoulder right now and see her face. "You're not an idiot, Josie. You just deserve so much more than either one of us could give you. I hope you know that."

I open the door and shut it behind me, but not before I hear her whisper, "that's not for you to decide."

CHAPTER 26

JOSIE

I wish I could just crawl in a dark hole until my going numb superpower starts working again. It's been days since Max broke off our arrangement, and according to my timeline I was supposed to be done with my allotted grieving time last night. Operation never think of Max again was supposed to commence officially this morning.

So why am I still not able to force myself to get out of my bed with the pillow that smells like his cologne and take a fucking shower?

Why am I not able to stop thinking about him for one damn second?

How safe I felt in his strong tattooed arms.

How he made me laugh even when I didn't feel like it.

How he could command my body in ways I didn't even know were possible.

How proud he was of his family.

How he defended me in front of my ex and my entire family.

How I thought I would actually be able to trust someone with my heart again, when I thought that would never be possible after what Trevor did.

How I was falling for him.

I pull my weighted blanket over my head, so it blocks out what little light is shining through the window from the dark and cloudy day. At least the temperamental Indiana weather has the decency to match how I'm feeling. Any minute now the rain will start, and I'll let the sound lull me back to sleep.

I've been sleeping a lot.

At least when I sleep my brain is thinking about something as insane as a flock of geese interrupting a surprise party I was throwing in the theater from *Phantom of the Opera* and not how Maximiliano Rossi's lips tasted.

Just as I begin to think about how those lips would whisper husky sounding words into my ear there's a loud banging coming from my front door. "Josie Ann Jones, if you don't open this goddamn door, I'm calling your landlord and performing a wellness check."

Ella.

Naturally I should've known this would happen at some point when I haven't been answering her texts for the last few days. I couldn't do it. I couldn't bear hearing "I told you so." Not that she would ever say it to me, but I would feel it every time I looked at her.

Because she was right. I've read this plot line again and again and I still fell for it. I thought I was stronger than the great fake dating trope, and I wasn't.

"Damn it, Josie! If you actually are dead in there, I'll never forgive you." I hear her yell through the door. For someone so small she sure is loud.

I roll my eyes and wrap my blanket around myself before unlocking the deadbolt and shuffling to my bean bag chair, plopping down on it.

Ella comes into my apartment in a flurry. Her strawberry blonde hair piled on top of her head in a messy bun and wearing a Gavin DeGraw shirt we got from his concert last summer.

She holds up her phone, pointing at it dramatically. "Hi. Yeah, I'd like to introduce you to this device called a cell phone. Typically, when our best friend texts us multiple times we respond. You may remember it from, oh I don't know, the thousands of times we've texted before."

"Sorry." I grumble.

She forces me to scoot over and lays her head on my shoulder. "I'm just worried about you. I know you like to go in your little hovel when you get sad, but usually you at last respond to me."

"Just go ahead and say it," I say, my voice trembling with unshed tears.

"What?" She looks up at me with genuine confusion.

"Just tell me you were right. You warned me and I didn't listen and now my heart's broken. You were right, I was wrong."

"What? Jos, no, I would never! It's not like I wanted this to happen. I was really hoping you two would work out." She says while laying her head back on my shoulder.

"I thought you said we were a bad idea," I reply, choking back a sob.

"Well... I did... but that was before... well..." she bites her lip hesitantly, conflicted on whether she wants to say what she's thinking or not.

"Before what?"

She sighs, "Before he told Liam that he wanted to date you. Like for real date you."

"What? What changed?" I ask, my eyes barely restraining the tears behind them.

"I'm not sure, Jos," she says, her face solemn. "But I really thought he had changed this time."

"Me too," I whimper, feeling a traitorous tear escape from my eye and fall down my cheek.

"Oh, Jos..."

And that's about when the dam breaks. Tons of ugly cry tears falling down all at once from being held back for days. "I... love... him..." I choke out between sobs.

"Shhh... I know, Jos..." she whispers soothingly.

"What's wrong with me? What is it about me that's just never enough for anyone?" I croak.

"Josie Ann! You are more than enough. Don't ever say that again. Anyone that says any differently is a dumb idiot." She chastises while using her shirt sleeve to dry up my tears.

"Now, you already know what time it is. Go shower and I'll get out the wine and snacks. How are we feeling about early 2000's Amanda Bynes? I'm thinking we start with *She's the Man*."

I wince, the memory of having dinner with Max's boss and talking about the tampon trick is still too raw for me to want to think about. If this man ruined *She's the Man* for me, I will truly never forgive him.

"Umm... can we just watch *What a Girl Wants* instead?" I hedge.

Her eyes go wide, "Oh shit, yeah, the tampon thing. Damn it. I'm so sorry." She groans.

"I'll get it all queued up, go shower." She says while shooing me away.

"I get it, I smell bad." I yell over my shoulder while walking towards my bathroom.

"Not bad necessarily, just like Cheetos and self-deprecation," she shouts back.

After sufficient scrubbing, a fresh t-shirt, and M^3 with my best friend, I almost feel human again. I almost feel like I don't have a giant fucking crater in my chest. I almost feel like I may not fracture into a thousand pieces any time I think of him.

Almost.

CHAPTER 27

MAX

"Get up and answer the door dumbass, or I'm using my key." I hear Liam yell through the door after knocking loudly. I just know Mr. Lee is going to give me shit for it the next time he accosts me by the mailboxes.

I drag my sorry ass off my couch and shuffle to the door, opening it with a glare before marching right back to the spot that might as well have a dent the size of my butt for all I've managed to get up from it. I've watched the entirety of *Parks and Recreation* since I left Josie's place, calling into work and not even bothering to go to the gym. I've been in a shit mood, and the only thing that I can pretend makes me feel better are the antics of the Pawnee Parks Department. Oh, and Lord Foldemort.

A small mewl comes from the aforementioned gray fuzzball as he walks up to Liam and rubs his head against his shin. "What the fuck is that?"

"That's Lord Foldemort," I say blandly before flopping back on my couch.

"Lord what?"

"Foldemort. He's a Scottish Fold."

"Uh... that's a cat dude. You got a cat, and you didn't even tell me?" he asks as if he's affronted before shutting the door behind him.

"I realized that the only pussy I need in my life is one that shits in a box. Plus, his eyes remind me of Josie's. All big and brown. I saw his picture online, looking all sad and lonely just like me. We're kindred spirits, he and I."

Liam looks around my disheveled mess of an apartment and shakes his head, "Honestly, who raises a cat in this environment? I refuse to let my god-cat live like this."

"Your god-cat?" I ask while pinching the bridge of my nose in frustration.

"Well obviously in the event that you contract some rare shut-in disease caused by a vitamin-D deficiency, I'll take Lord Foldemort. I've already become attached."

"You've known him for two-minutes," I deadpan.

He bends down to give Lord Foldemort chin scratches, "And I already like him more than you."

"Who wouldn't?" I groan.

"Jesus Christ, you look like shit," Liam says while finally looking at my face. "You look like a badly taxidermied racoon."

"Thank you...?" I ask sarcastically.

He narrows his eyes at me and crosses his arms over his chest, "It's not a compliment. Care to tell me how you went from wanting to make things legit with Josie to gaslighting and breaking things off with her. She thinks you played her."

"I did." I shrug, trying to feign more nonchalance than I feel. "I don't do serious. Everyone knows that."

"That's bullshit and you know it," he grumbles.

"Is it? Because Josie is too good of a person to be the one I experiment that theory with. She deserves the fucking best of the best. She deserves someone who knows how to love her the way she's always wanted to be, and we all know that." I want my voice to sound like it's full of conviction, but I know it just sounds more defeated than anything.

He scoffs, "Again, I call bullshit. It's an excuse and you know it. You're scared you'll fuck it up, so you think if you end it now no one gets hurt, but it's a little late for that don't you think? You're both miserable and no one is better off for it."

"She's better off in the long run. Years from now she'll be happy I broke it off." I supply evenly.

"And what about you? Will you be happy years from now that you ruined your chance at an actual relationship because you spent so much time with your head up your own ass that you didn't realize how good you had it?" He paces my living room floor, more annoyed with me than I think he's ever been.

"I know how good I had it. Believe me, it's all I can fucking think about," I grit. "But it doesn't matter what's best for me. Josie and her happiness are what's important. I don't give a shit about me."

"Oh, and I guess that's for you to choose? You decide for her that she deserves better and don't even bother talking to her about it. You think you know better than she does?"

Damn it... why is he making sense right now.

"Even still—"

"Do you love her?" Liam interrupts.

"It doesn't matter..." I trail off.

"Do. You. Love. Her?" He enunciates each word. "Yes, or no?"

Am I in love with Josie? That depends. Is love when you feel like you can finally breathe after holding your breath for an eternity, the second that person is nearby? Is love when you feel like you would rather carve your heart out with a rusty butter knife than to see her cry? Is love when you feel like you'd change everything you thought you knew about yourself, just to be someone worthy of her?

The answer is painfully obvious. "Yes, I love her, so fucking much," I groan painfully as I rub my chest at the phantom pain there.

"Yeah, obviously!" He yells while waving his hands around. "So then stop making both of yourselves miserable and go tell her that. Let her decide for herself what she deserves. If you don't then you're no better than her parents or Trevor or anyone else that tried to control her life and make decisions for her."

Damn it... how did I not see that before?

"Oh, fuck. I fucked up." I pinch the bridge of my nose at my sheer stupidity. Here I was, knowing how much Josie had struggled her entire life with everyone telling her what she wanted, and I did the same damn thing.

"Shit, but the last of my project is due by end of day today. Shawna leaves for maternity leave in two days and she said that if I didn't have my last article done by then she would feed me my balls through a straw after she wired my mouth shut." This fucking project, the one that started all of this. The place that made me fall in love with her.

Wait a minute...

"Shit, okay, I think I have an idea. Can you get Ella to take Josie to the coffee shop she likes tomorrow at 2pm? That's when my article goes live." I'm floundering now, checking my phone for the time and scrounging around for my laptop so I can redo my entire project in a matter of hours and somehow convince my very pregnant and hormonal boss not to murder me all before 5pm.

"Wait... are we grand gesturing?" Liam asks, his voice going up an octave and not even remotely containing his excitement.

I laugh for the first time in days, "Yeah, man, we're grand gesturing. Now are you going to help me or not?"

"You know for damn sure I'm going to help you win back the woman you love. You know how I live for that shit. I'm romantic as fuck, and this is you building her dream house with blue shutters and a wraparound porch."

I roll my eyes and chuckle, "Is this another *Notebook* reference?"

"I think you know it is buddy," he replies while clapping me on the shoulder. "Now, let's go get your girl."

———

"So let me make sure I'm understanding all of this... you lied to me just so you could get this assignment, and then convinced this poor girl to actually go along with it?" Shawna's now very angrily bouncing on her exercise ball, a sign that she's probably five seconds from throwing her stapler at my head.

"Yes..." I hedge while trying not to let her smell the fear on me.

"And then, in a twist that literally anyone could've seen coming, you fell for her. Hard. Now you want to use the biggest account we've ever gotten as a grand gesture to get her back?" Her voice is all thinly veiled rage.

"Yes, and as you say it, I'm realizing that it's a selfish request—"

"I should fire you," she interrupts before her angry bouncing stops. She gets up from her desk and walks towards me.

Oh fuck. I don't know what it means when the frantic exercise ball bouncing stops, but I have a feeling it's going to end with me going through the window behind Shawna's desk.

This was a terrible idea.

I should've just gotten Josie flowers like a normal person.

I clear my throat, "Honestly? Probably." The reality of my employment situation is becoming more and more grim by the second. No matter what happens though I have no regrets, especially since everything up to this moment has led me to the woman I love.

Love...

Wow. Me from three months ago would never believe this shit.

I see the barest twitch of a smile break through her scowl. "Fortunately for you, this is the best piece you've ever written, and we're on a deadline. There's no time to fix it, but even if there was, the new angle is inspired."

"Wait... what?" I'm barely capable of forming words at this stage.

She sighs heavily, "I'm saying, it's brilliant, Max. I don't know if the client will go for it given it's not exactly what they were asking for, but I'm willing to back it."

"Seriously?" I know my voice just went up an octave and I don't even care because holy fuck she's going for it.

"Now go home and prep for tomorrow. It's a big day." She smiles.

I breathe a sigh of relief. "Thank you, Shawna, thank you. You won't regret this!"

I walk towards the door to her office before I hear her voice and it stops me, causing me to look over my shoulder. "Oh, and, Max? If you lie to me again, I really will fire your ass." She says with narrowed dark brown eyes.

"It won't happen again, Shawna, I swear," I say while making the boy scout symbol with my hand.

"It better not," she says matter-of-factly before I leave her office and head out for the day.

It won't and I know it. I'm not ruining shit for myself anymore. I fixed things with my boss, and now all I have to do is pray to whatever saint is in charge of business that the clients like the new angle we're going with, and that the article is good enough to convince Josie that I've changed.

A lot is riding on this article going live tomorrow, and not just my career.

CHAPTER 28

———

JOSIE

"Ugh... why are you making me do this?" I groan as Ella all but drags me towards my favorite coffee shop, Gold Leaf.

"Because if I didn't do something soon you were going to fuse to that bean bag chair like the pirates on the Flying Dutchman." She said pithily while her short little legs work more forcefully than I think I've ever seen them.

"Yeah, well part of the ship, part of the crew I always say." I deadpan.

"Yeah, well when your ship is a bean bag chair and the barnacles attached to you are leftover Cheeto crumbs I have a right to grow concerned," she fires back.

"Fine."

It's been days since I've seen Max, and at no point in the entire time I've known him would I have ever thought I'd actually miss him. Looking back at it now, I don't know how I was ever able to refuse his advances for as long as I did.

Maybe if I would've taken him up on one of his many attempts at hitting on me, we could've started dating for real first. Instead, I didn't even realize my feelings for him until well into our fake-relationship.

No wonder he doesn't think he's capable of dating me for longer than three seconds. I didn't even want to be with him until we had an expiration date. *How can you know whether or not you can find permanence with someone if you start your entire relationship on a lie?*

The truth is this is the real world. Not one of my smutty romance novels. Book boyfriends aren't real, and I can't make someone be something they're not. Just because I know Max is capable of being who I need him to be, doesn't mean he'll see it. I can have all of the confidence in the world that he could commit to me, but it doesn't mean he'll hold himself in the same regard.

Well, I guess at least I'm getting coffee for my efforts. There has to be some benefit to leaving the bean bag hovel I've created for myself.

Ella flings open the door to the coffee shop, and I feel a pang in my chest as I look at the corner table that Max and I sat at all those weeks ago when he proposed his inane scheme to me.

Shit, I must be even more pathetic than I think because I swear the vision has come to life and he's sitting in that same damn booth.

Wait...

Not a vision. He's very real, and very much sitting in the exact same booth as before, two coffees in front of him. "Max...?" my voice comes out shakier than I would've liked, barely above a whisper.

"I think you should go talk to him. Just hear him out," she gestures towards the booth. "I'll be right over here if you need me."

I eye her warily, "Look at you becoming president of the Max and Josie fan club."

She shrugs, a small smile playing on her lips. "Well technically Liam and I are co-chairs, but let's just say he's convinced me, and I want my best friend to be happy." She squeezes my hand before we part our separate ways and I walk over to the booth where my no longer fake boyfriend is sitting.

He smiles warily, "I got you your favorite, iced americano with almond milk and three pumps of classic syrup."

I sit in the booth across from him, willing my heart not to crack any more than it already has. "So, you rope my best friend into tricking me and meeting you at my favorite coffee shop and then bribe me with my favorite coffee. Feels like a trap."

He shifts awkwardly in his seat, placing his tattooed hands on the table in front of him, instantly my traitorous brain remembers how it felt to have that hand braced against my throat sending shivers down my spine. "I figured if I was the one who asked you to meet me, you wouldn't have come."

I lean against the back of the booth, crossing my arms like it's a shield that could prevent him from seeing the emotional sinkhole happening in my body. "Yeah, that's a pretty good assumption."

"My article came out today. You know, the one that started all of this. I wanted to read it to you." I can see the pleading in his eyes and hear it in his voice, but I can also feel the fracturing in my chest.

"Why are you doing this?" My voice cracking, tears threatening to pool in my eyes.

"Please? I promise it'll make sense after I read it." The man in front of me is almost unrecognizable. He's not the cocky player that I first met, but instead a man desperate to be heard.

After everything we've been through, I guess I can give him this. "Okay, sure."

He pulls out his phone, his hands almost imperceptibly shaking. He steadies his voice and starts to read. "Falling in love in Fiji: how the beauty of this country taught me how to do something I never thought I was capable of."

I suck in a sharp breath, about to say something before he interrupts me. "Just let me read the whole thing, ok?"

I give him a small nod, urging him to continue.

"I spent my entire life thinking love was something I would never have. I grew up an Army brat, my family moving every couple of years like clockwork, and I guess I never really liked the idea of being anywhere or with anyone for too long. I'd been burned too many times.

That is, until I met Josie. Suddenly, everything I ever thought I knew about myself was turned upside down," and then he was telling our story. How we started out pretending to date so he could get this assignment and I could force my ex to move on. How we flung mud at each other, took a shibari class, swam in caves, and jumped from balconies, all while he was falling more and more in love with me.

As I listen to everything he has to say, I feel the fractured pieces of myself start to mold back together, and the tears from earlier are coming down in full force now.

Once he finishes reading, he looks up from his phone, "*Gattina,*baby, don't cry," he says with barely concealed emotion, collecting my tears with his thumb.

"Did you really mean what you said? You love me?" I say through uneven breaths.

"I do. I meant every word of it. I love you. If I haven't completely fucked up everything, I want to know if you'll give me a chance. To date you for real. I'm so damn sorry I decided I wasn't good enough for you before even talking to you about it. I thought I was doing the right thing, but I wasn't." His voice is shaking, the adrenaline from baring himself to me causing it to come out in deep timbre.

"Do you have any idea how much you hurt me?" I say brokenly. I need to know if he realizes the gravity of this, and that he won't hurt me like this again.

His eyes lower, "Yes, baby, and I'm so sorry. I'm no better than your parents or Trevor or anyone else, never consulting you before making decisions for you, and I swear to you that if you give me another chance, I'll never do that again."

I can see how serious he is, and a feeling of complete and utter relief washes over me, because that's all I needed to know, that he wouldn't make unilateral decisions about our relationship without consulting me.

Slowly I move out of the booth and walk to the other side of the table, pressing myself against Max's side as I watch his eyes grow wide. I trace my fingers along his chin before gripping it and forcing his beautiful hazel eyes to look directly into mine. "I love you too, Donkey Kong."

Before he has a chance to say another word, I pull him down so his lips fuse to mine. Whatever tension is left in my body immediately releases in his arms as he deepens the kiss and puts the last pieces of me back together, and I know now that against all the odds, sometimes the smutty romance books get it right.

EPILOGUE

JOSIE - 6 MONTHS LATER

As we walk up the gravel drive to Crenshaw's, the frigid winter night broken up by the neon signs illuminating the dark parking lot, I watch Ella fidget and adjust her dress for the thousandth time.

"Will you stop fidgeting? You look hot as fuck. For crying out loud it's just Crenshaw's." I say before tucking my frozen fingers into my coat pocket.

"Yes. Crenshaw's after you just took me to get my nails done." She says while eyeing me suspiciously.

Shit... just play it off Josie, play it off.

"Yeah, so?" *Smooth, Josie. Real smooth.*

Her eyes narrow even more as she folds her arms in front of her chest. "After I woke up to a text from my mom this morning that was the length of *The Odyssey* saying how much she loves me and how great Liam is?"

God damn it, Shoshanna!

"You know your mom, she was probably just high off her morning sun salutation endorphins and palo santo," I say dismissively.

"Don't gaslight me, Josie Ann!" She yells. "I'm not an idiot. You don't think I would find the fact that Nikki texted us earlier and said 'You know what'd be super fun? If we just randomly dressed cute for Crenshaw's.' even a little bit suspicious?"

Our twosome has recently become a threesome (not like that you little whore) after Ella and I became fast friends with the new art teacher, Nikki Phaser, and share our affinity for cartoons, early 2000's movies, junk food, and sweatpants.

"I don't see your point," I say nonchalantly.

"You're being purposely obtuse!" She shouts.

"The audacity! Seriously, Ella, you're starting to sound insane. Should I fashion you a tin foil hat so the aliens can't hear your thoughts?" One thing about being a person who spent almost her entire life being gaslighted, you're going to be good at doing it to other people.

She huffs out in frustration, "And Liam, the love of my life, decided to go golfing tonight. Should I point out that A. He's never golfed once in his life and B. It's December and both freezing and pitch black out by 6pm."

Jesus, Liam, you couldn't think of literally anything else to tell her?

"Maybe he's at Top Golf...?" I really have a lot riding on the assumption my best friend will believe the flimsy lies I've told her. Thankfully, in about thirty seconds this will no longer be my problem to skirt around.

As we approach the door Ella stops and faces me. "It's happening, isn't it? When I open this door, what will I find?"

I can't help but grin widely, ecstatic that my best friend has found a man that loves her this much. "I guess you'll just have to open it and find out," I say with a shrug.

Ella takes a deep breath and pushes open the creaking front door over the green carpeting of Crenshaw's. Her eyes grow wide as she sees all our friends, both her and Liam's parents gathered near the other side of the bar.

Lola comes into view, grabbing Ella's hand and leading her towards the front. "We have a special seat up front for the guest of honor," she says with a smile.

Ella sits down on the stool in front of the karaoke machine and begins to laugh along with everyone else as Liam emerges in a giant fluffy pink *Sixteen Candles* dress. I never thought Liam could pull off the whole pink ruffle vibe, but even I have to admit he looks adorable.

"El, eight months ago you made an absolute fool of yourself just to profess your love for me. Now I want to do the same, to show you just how being loved by you feels. Like pure happiness, tons of laughter, and yes, sometimes like a complete fool."

Liam then breaks out into what has to somehow be an even worse rendition of 'Don't You Forget About Me' by The Pretenders than the one Ella sang all those months ago, causing her to double over with laughter.

When the song ends, Liam walks towards the stool Ella is sitting on and gets down on one knee. "Ella, will you continue to be the source of my pure happiness, laughter, and foolishness for the rest of our lives and be my wife?"

"Yes!" She shrieks as he puts the ring on her finger before she launches herself off the stool to wrap her arms around his neck, planting a giant kiss on his lips.

Everyone starts cheering and clapping as one voice yells from the back of the room where Stella is standing on top of a chair, one of her famous shawls wrapped around her shoulders. "Let's get fucked up!"

Laughter rings out from around the room before Makenzie, yes, my sister Makenzie, Lola's newest hire, starts dishing out shots. How she got here is a long story, one that'll be saved for another time.

All of a sudden, a commotion at the front of the bar catches my attention as I watch Nikki take the drink that's in her hand and throw it in Sergio's face before storming off, leaving him soaked in what I can only assume is Nikki's Moscow mule.

I stifle a laugh as Max comes up to my side and wraps his arm around my waist planting a kiss on my head. "Why is Sergio all wet?"

I snort, "He pissed off Nikki. Again."

"Those two just need to fuck and get it over with," he chuckles.

I eye him mockingly, "You know people said the same thing about us."

"Yeah, and they were right! I should've listened. I would've been with the love of my life that much sooner." He says before tilting my head up towards his and kissing me softly on the lips.

"Who, me, or Lord Foldemort?" I ask wryly. I've always been a cat person, so when Max told me he was so distraught that he got a cat because it reminded him of me, I was ecstatic.

He pretends to mull it over, "Hmm... a little bit of column A, a little bit of column B."

I chuckle before kissing him unabashedly, like we're the only two people in the bar. "I love you too, Donkey Kong," I smile up at him.

As improbable as it may seem, it looks like the books I love were right. Somewhere my real-life book boyfriend was out there, and he's more incredible than I ever could've imagined. Once again, we've proven that no matter how determined you are, the fake dating trope always wins.

The End

www.ingramcontent.com/pod-product-compliance
Lightning Source LLC
Chambersburg PA
CBHW020321180726
47991CB00018B/168